Temptation

Temptation

By K.M. Golland
Book 1 in The Temptation Series

HARLEQUIN®MIRA®

First Published 2012
First Australian Paperback Edition 2014

ISBN 978 1 74356 801 9

TEMPTATION
© 2012 by K. M. Golland

Published by Harlequin Mira
An imprint of Harlequin Enterprises (Aust) Pty Ltd.
Level 13, 201 Elizabeth Street
SYDNEY, NSW 2000
AUSTRALIA

Printed and bound in Australia by McPherson's Printing Group

MIX
Paper | Supporting
responsible forestry
FSC www.fsc.org FSC® C001695

ABOUT THE AUTHOR

"I am an author. I am married. I am a mother of two adorable little people. I'm a bookworm, craftworm, movieworm, and sportsworm. I'm also a self-confessed shop-aholic, tea-aholic, car-aholic, and choc-aholic."

Born and raised in Melbourne, Australia, K.M. Golland studied law and worked as a conveyancer before putting her career on hold to raise her children. She then traded her legal work for her love of writing and found her dream career.

For my husband and children.
Two separate loves; one no greater than the other.

PROLOGUE

'Uh-oh' and 'I didn't mean it' are two sentences a mother hates hearing materialise from the mouth of her five-year-old child. 'Fuck' and 'Mum, I'm stuck' are another two ... but we'll talk about that another day.

Those dreaded words 'uh-oh' were only spoken moments ago by my daughter, Charlotte. And as per usual, they were spoken while I was in the middle of something I did not want to interrupt, such as what I was currently immersed in — washing.

'Uh-oh what?' I shouted, while trying to balance the washing basket on my hip, inevitably freeing my other hand to shut the lid of the machine.

'Nothing, Mum,' Charlotte replied, her voice slightly hesitant. 'Nothing' was another word a mother was not fond of hearing when clearly 'nothing' always meant 'something'.

'That did not sound like nothing, Charli,' I grumbled. 'Where are you?'

An intuitive dread started to bubble inside my stomach at the thought of what my daughter was obviously trying to hide, so in order to find out I made my way down the hallway toward my bedroom, where I could hear Charlotte making noises.

As I was about to enter the threshold of my room, the phone rang. 'Ah, crap!' I swivelled around, careful not to squash myself between the wall and the washing basket, which was still balanced on my hip, and walked briskly to where my phone sat in its cradle on the kitchen bench.

'Hello,' I answered with little enthusiasm.

'Alexis, darling. Have I caught you at a bad time?' my mother asked.

'Umm ... no, well ... kind of, yes,' I replied, holding the phone to my ear with my shoulder. Like most women, I was quite good at securing objects with body parts other than my hands. This was a skill us stay-at-home mums excelled at, because, let's face it, our hands were always full.

As I stood there in my awkward phone shoulder-hold position, I noticed the Bolognese sauce bubbling at more than a gentle simmer. I retrieved the wooden spoon which was sitting on a dish by the stove and quickly stirred the pot. 'I'm just in the middle of cooking tea and doing the washing, Mum,' I explained.

'Oh, okay. Never mind,' she replied dismissively.

Burnt remnants of sauce started to make their way to the surface as I stirred, so I turned the stovetop burner down. *Shit! Crap! Balls!*

'Mum, you obviously called for a reason,' I responded, a little too grumpily, stirring the burnt bits back into the sauce.

What my husband and kids don't know won't hurt them. Besides, a little charcoal adds to the flavour, right? That, or I'll just tell them it's spaghetti with a smoked beef Bolognese sauce — the newest craze.

Feeling a little guilty for snapping at my mother, I softened my frazzled demeanour and apologised. After all, my multi-tasking failure wasn't her fault. 'Sorry, Mum. I just have a lot to do today and nothing is going as planned.'

'Anything I can help you with?'

'No, not really ... unless you can do my washing, clean the bathroom and toilet, and sew Nate's school pants for me?'

'Sorry, sweetheart. If I lived closer to you, you know that I would.'

I sighed and turned the stove burner to the lowest possible setting then hoisted the washing basket on the bench, giving my hip instant relief. 'I know, Mum. So what did you call for?'

'Well ... just quickly. When you have a second, can you please send me some Bejeweled Blitz coins?'

Mum's request instantly had me rolling my eyes with a smile. I slapped my hand to my forehead and rested my elbow on the benchtop. Unfortunately, this action resulted in me accidentally clipping the tip of the wooden spoon, catapulting it forward and sending a spray of Bolognese sauce across my face.

'Ah, shit!' I moaned.

'What?'

'Nothing.'

'That wasn't a "nothing", Alexis,' she replied, knowingly.

Instantaneously, a feeling of déjà vu hit me at my mother's words and, whether I liked to admit it or not, I was more like her than I realised at times.

'It's fine, Mum. I just spilled some sauce.'

'Spills are easily cleaned, darling. Now, speaking of messes and things that need cleaning, where is that granddaughter of mine?'

Mum's mention of Charlotte triggered my earlier unease, reminding me that before I answered the phone I was on my way to find out what she was up to. I realised I needed to end the current conversation to go find her. 'Mum, I've got to go. Talk to you later, okay?' I hung up before she could object and quickly swiped my face with the tea towel.

'Charlotte?' I called out.

'Yeah?'

'Don't "yeah" me, you cheeky ratbag. Come here.'

'Um ... okay. I'm coming.'

As I turned around with the intention to hunt her down if need be, my incredibly inquisitive — and it would appear, artistic — daughter rounded the corner with tentative steps and a proud smile.

I couldn't help but take in her appearance and wasn't sure whether to laugh or cry at what I saw. 'Charli! What have you done?'

'Mummy, I'm Kiera from *Barbie: The Princess & the Pop-star*,' she answered, smiling and turning in a circle while holding out her skirt.

I watched in horror — and what seemed like slow motion — as Charli twirled, her blonde hair streaked with purple texta marker, her eyelids densely covered in my pink eye shadow, and her lips and parts of her cheeks smeared with fire-engine red lipstick.

Slowly, I became aware that my mouth was agape and my breathing hitched. So I closed my eyes and reined in the pending outburst of laughter, tears or anger — or God knows what else — and took some deep breaths.

Just as I was able to compose myself, a knock sounded at the front door.

'Urgh! Wait here, Charli,' I huffed, annoyed at whoever was interrupting our Barbie makeover crisis.

Pivoting, I quickly made my way to the front door and, before I had even a chance to open it completely, I was greeted by a young man.

'Hello, ma'am. My name is Anil, and I am from Energy Australia. How are you today?'

Oh, for the love of fuck. My eyes uncontrollably rolled back in annoyance and irritation. The timing of these utility company representatives was bloody impeccable.

The young man's expression instantly morphed from over-exaggerated enthusiasm to curiosity when he looked up to meet my frustrated scowl.

'Honestly, Anil, I'm really not in the mood for whatever it is you wish to try and sell me. I'm kind of busy.' I took a step back.

'Ma'am, you —'

Raising my hand to indicate he stop, I interrupted. 'Look, I don't want to be rude. I know you are only trying to do your job, but I don't want to switch electricity companies. Okay?'

'But, ma'am, you have —'

'What I have, Anil, is a good electricity rate already. I'm happy with my current situation.'

'No. You have a —'

'I'm sorry. What I don't have is time for this. Have a nice day,' I said quickly before closing the door. *Seriously, fuck off.*

As I turned back to face my clown-like daughter, I caught sight of my reflection in the mirror on the entryway wall.

'Oh, great! Could this day get any worse?' I cursed to myself, taking in the spaghetti sauce smeared across my nose, cheek and forehead.

'Mum,' Charli said tentatively, 'I have to tell you something.'

Squinting with a scrutinising glare, I took in the way she was nervously playing with her fingers.

'I promise, I didn't mean it,' she squeaked.

'Didn't. Mean. What?'

'It got stuck. It wasn't my fault.'

'What got stuck?'

'The toilet roll. It accidentally fell into the toilet and got stuck.'

I laughed a little too sarcastically. *Yes, Alexis, of course your day can get worse.*

Allowing my head to fall quite heavily onto the wall beside me, I closed my eyes for a brief moment in order to get a grip on the control I was very close to losing.

Slumped against the entryway wall in my house, it was in that short-lived moment of time-out when I decided that after Christmas I was going back to work. I was going to rediscover the Alexis Summers I had been before motherhood had taken over my life.

I was going to find my life's balance.

CHAPTER

1

Many of us have been faced with moments when our reflection in the mirror stared back and resembled someone we did not recognise. That was the case today as I fastened the last bobby pin into my hair. Having recently lost twenty kilograms as a result of a mad affair with my local gym, I now fitted into a size 12 which I was more than happy with.

As I stood there and took myself in, it wasn't my size or shape that had me screwing up my nose. It was the fact that I honestly did not know how to look the corporate part any more. In the mirror before me was a thirty-five-year-old woman with just a touch of make-up on. My blonde hair was neatly twirled into a bun, and I was wearing a black pinstriped skirt-suit, a pale pink blouse, and black peep-toe heels. *Your feet are going to hate you tonight, Alexis. Surely you realise this?*

I looked down at my feet with sympathy, knowing these shoes were sure to punish me. Unfortunately, my fluffy slippers were not an option for today, nor would they complement my skirt. Gone were the days of comfortable clothing.

For the past nine years, I had been shrugging on a pair of jeggings and t-shirt, or gym pants and a singlet, as those years had been spent getting the kids ready for school and kindergarten. I guess that was the reason why make-up and corporate attire were the last things on my mind. If anything, my daily self-appraisal had been a quick glance in the mirror on my way out of the house, checking that I had no food stuck to my face or teeth.

Today was an entirely different day, though. Because today was the day I started my first full-time job since having my two children, and I was beyond nervous.

Sighing at my lame attempt to look professional, I smoothed down my skirt. *Ugh! This will have to do.* 'Okay, ratbags, are you ready?' I shouted from the bathroom. 'We need to leave or Mummy will be late for her first day at work.'

I took one last look at my reflection before making my way into the living room where both my adorable children were waiting by the garage door. I couldn't help but lovingly smile at them. 'Charli-Bear, your shoes are on the wrong feet. Nate, can you please help her fix them?'

Nate rolled his eyes, then bent down and fixed his little sister's shoes. Like most siblings, they were both each other's best friends when not being worst enemies. Charlotte was six years old and in her first year of primary school, and Nate was three years her senior and living in his own land of sovereignty.

'Mum, do I have to go to before-school care? I really don't want to. It's for babies.'

'Nate, it's not for babies. And yes, you do have to go. Please don't make this difficult. I'm really excited about my new job, and anyway, you'll get the chance to sit quietly and draw your pictures.' I raised my eyebrows encouragingly and tilted my head.

Nate dropped his head in disappointment and turned for the car, momentarily filling me with guilt. My nine-year-old son, despite being extremely independent, was still very much a mummy's boy and not very happy about my decision to go back to work.

'What time will you be home, Mum?' he sulked.

I reached forward and snagged his arm, pulling him in for a cuddle. 'I'm not sure, sweetheart. Hopefully before dinner. Dad will pick you both up at the gate after school. And ... I have your favourite meal cooking in the slow cooker, so it's all sorted.' I kissed his golden head and gently pushed him toward the car where his sister was already seated and buckled in.

* * *

Not even an hour later, I drove onto the entry ramp of the Tullamarine Freeway and headed toward the city. *Oh, my God! Alexis, you are actually doing this, you are going back to work.*

Apprehension, excitement and a little bit of dread started to stir in the pit of my stomach. Of course, I had known that this day would eventually come, but being a stay-at-home mum for the past nine years was what I had grown accustomed to; it was routine ... comfortable. Then again, to say that it was comfortable is not an entirely accurate statement, because my life wasn't comfortable. In fact, it was far from it at times and certainly not easy.

I don't deny that by staying home and raising my children, I've had the perk of not having to deal with clients, customers or an overbearing boss on a daily basis. And, admittedly,

I could wear my slippers most days and throw my hair into a ponytail without even brushing it. So yes, that part was comfortable. But being a stay-at-home mum for nearly a third of my life was also draining, and lonely, and not very exciting. And because of this, I could honestly say that I was more than ready to welcome a change.

Speaking of change, driving into the city at 7.30 in the morning was definitely something I was not used to. The traffic was horrendous: stop, start, stop, start. How my husband did this day in and day out, I would never know. It was crazy!

Prior to stopping work and having children, I had been a secretary to a suburban solicitor close to home, thereby never actually having dealt with bumper to bumper traffic before. So this mayhem called 'peak hour' was new to me and absolutely absurd.

Needing a distraction from the traffic around me, I pressed play on my CD player and let the sounds of Kings of Leon filter through my car. As I did this, an impatient arsehole in a silver BMW, tried to sneak into the space — or lack thereof — in front of me. *Don't honk your horn at me, you idiot, I was in this lane first.*

Clearly, I was out of my comfort zone, not only amongst crazy city commuters, but also in the sense that the job I was about to embark on was a complete career change for me. That prospect alone was beyond terrifying.

My new role was as one of the Concierge Attendants at City Towers, which was part of the biggest entertainment complex in Victoria. City Towers was a luxury five-star hotel with forty-three floors, four hundred and eighty-one rooms, thirty villas, and the penthouse residence. I had always loved City Towers

and I'd had the privilege to stay in a suite with my fiancé —
now husband, Rick — a year after we got engaged. And at that
time, and for us, that in itself was quite an exclusive event.

* * *

As I pulled into the city complex staff car park, I noticed I was
running short on time. I hated being in a rush. Really hated
it. You'd think that after nine years of raising my babies I'd be
used to it, but I wasn't. And, of all the days I could be late,
today was *not* going to be one of them.

Finding the closest parking spot, I rushed out of my car and
beelined straight for the entry door, knowing exactly where I
had to be by 9 a.m.

Despite my crazy, busy lifestyle with sports, pick-ups,
drop-offs, running errands and shopping, etc, I was brilliant
at organisation and multitasking, having already visited the
complex three times in the past fortnight to become familiar
with where I was going to be starting my new career. Thankfully, due to this obsessive preparation, I had made up some
time by taking a few shortcuts, thus allowing me a minute to
pop into Gloria Jean's for my favourite drink — hot white-
chocolate with a marshmallow.

As I waited at the counter, it was obvious that the young,
bright and bubbly attendant enjoyed her job, happily going
about her task of preparing my drink. But it wasn't until
after she proudly handed me the paper cup that I noticed her
cheeks flush and her entire demeanour change.

'Thank ... you,' I said with confusion, due to her sudden
shift of personality.

Dubiously, I turned around and that's when I slammed
straight into the person in line behind me, spilling my entire

white-chocolate down the front of the both of us. 'Oh, shit! Shit! Jesus, that is hot! Oh, I am so sorry!'

I apologetically looked up, expecting to see an extremely livid gentleman. After all, I had stupidly and clumsily doused him in my milky drink.

Staring down at me, however, could only be described as the most delectable specimen of a man I had ever seen, and he was smirking at me. Yes ... smirking. Not livid or furious as I had expected, but arrogantly smirking. Well, more of a knowing grin, that charmed rather than offended.

I blushed ever so slightly with embarrassment for the simple reason that I had spilled my drink over somebody. But to top it off, I just happened to have spilled it on an extremely sexy man, and that was ... well ... that was just beyond horrifying.

'I am so sorry. I didn't even stop to think that someone was behind me. I'll get you a towel, hang on a second,' I babbled apologetically as I looked around in desperation for something to wipe us both with.

Mr Sexy Handsome Gentleman gently brushed himself down. 'Never mind that, Alexis, it's fine.'

'Mr Clark, I'll get you a wet cloth,' the bubbly attendant offered, her friendly persona toward me from moments ago now appearing quite volatile. She glared in my direction, giving me the sense that she was about ready to pounce over the counter and scratch my eyes out.

'No, Stacey, that's quite all right. Alexis and I will have to change.'

With that, the sexy beast of a man, gently — yet with complete command and control — grabbed me by the arm and directed me out of the café.

It was mere moments later that I snapped out of my stunned state and became aware I was being led to some place, by some person I knew absolutely nothing about. And regardless of how gorgeous this particular person was, or how unusually wonderful his hand felt against the skin of my arm, every fibre in me told me stop.

I gently shrugged out of his grasp and halted my steps. 'I'm sorry, who are you and how do you know my name?'

He appeared somewhat amused at my perfectly reasonable question and this time placed his hand on the small of my back, his touch sending excited currents right up and down my spine. The sensation shocked me but, unexpectedly, not in a bad way.

'Ms Summers, your name is on that ID tag which is pinned to that soaking blouse of yours. And I am Bryce Clark, your employer.'

Oh, shit! Crap! Balls! What have I done?

What I had done was spill my drink over my boss before I had even started my first shift. *Great start to the rest of your life, Alexis. You fucking idiot.*

Mr Clark leaned in closer and spoke directly into my ear. 'I don't know about you, Ms Summers,' he said, lowering his voice, his tone sexually intoxicating, 'but I don't like to wear hot chocolate to work.'

'No,' I stuttered, feeling highly mortified yet a little turned on. 'I don't blame you.'

Suddenly realising my predicament, my mind started to race. *Crap! I don't have any spare clothes, and I certainly don't have a spare pair of trousers or shirt for Bryce ... I mean, Mr Clark.*

Before panic could set in any further, he applied a gentle pressure to my back and ushered me forward. 'Come with me.'

* * *

Moments later, we were in front of Versace, one of the high-end fashion stores in the City Towers precinct. The entire situation had me feeling utterly ridiculous. So much so that during the short time it took us to get there, I hadn't really said anything to him. My muteness was probably a result of shock due to the fact I had spilled my drink on someone and that it had been my boss. I was not normally so clumsy.

'After you, Ms Summers,' he directed with his sexy voice, guiding me into the glamorous store.

Upon entering, I felt even more overwhelmed and out of place. I had never been into such a prestigious shop and it made me feel very uncomfortable — not to mention the minor issue of my attire being covered in hot chocolate.

Bryce approached the lady behind the counter. The woman — possibly a little younger than me — had an aura of sophistication and was a naturally beautiful brunette with flawless skin.

'Clarissa,' he said warmly, 'Ms Summers and I had a bit of an accident with a hot chocolate. I'll need a suit and she will need something suitable for the hotel's front office.'

'Certainly, Mr Clark,' Clarissa replied sweetly. 'Follow me.'

Having no choice but to follow like a little lost puppy, I did just that as she led us both into the change area. I still felt like a complete idiot.

As I stepped into the new room, I glanced around, unable to stop myself appreciating the overly large room. The decor was elegant with rich brown carpets, gold trimmings and fixtures, and seats covered in deep blue velvet. What was also unusually captivating was that the change cubicles circled the outside of the room, giving you the sense of standing in the middle of a clock face.

'If you'd like to go in here, Ms Summers,' Clarissa smiled, directing me to the cubicle at the three o'clock position. 'I will be back in just a minute with a beautiful day dress for you. And, Mr Clark, if you'd like to go in here,' she said, pointing him to the one at the two o'clock position, 'I will be back with your replacement.'

Intrigued and basically continuing with my new-found ability to just do as I was told, I stepped into the cubicle as Clarissa left the room. 'Mr Clark, I really don't think I need a new dress,' I called out, pleadingly. 'My blouse isn't too bad. I can just wear my blazer over the top.'

I assessed my blouse in the mirror with the realisation of having just lied: the stain was bad, really bad, and because of this, anxiety settled over me as I stood there focussing on my reflection. It was in that moment — and for only a second or two — that I debated whether or not I had made the right decision to go back to work. Maybe I just wasn't ready. Maybe I had been premature with the notion of needing to establish myself in the workforce again. Maybe this just wasn't me any more.

The curtain behind moved ever so slightly, startling me from my inner turmoil. I quickly gathered my bearings only to find Bryce standing there holding a lovely black wrap-dress, the dress in question draped over a hanger and dangling from his middle finger. It looked very smart and definitely something I would wear if I could ever afford it. The man standing before me also looked very smart, not to mention suave, and incredibly sexy.

He handed me the dress and raised his eyebrows in a seductive glare that twisted my stomach. 'Alexis, please put on the dress. You are not wearing a blouse soaked in hot chocolate around my hotel.'

Realising I had no choice but to accept, I gave him a sheepish grin. 'Of course not, thank you.'

He nodded and stepped backward, closing the curtain behind him. And it was then that the past hour and a half's events hit me like a Mack truck.

Oh my God! What am I doing here in Versace, holding a ... shit! ... a $2,000 dress? And holy crap, my boss is so fucking hot. I fanned my face with my hand and nearly stumbled into the wall. *He is the most glorious-looking man I have ever seen. And that hair — that clean-cut, dark-blond hair which falls to just above his ears. I just want to touch it. Not to mention those chiselled cheekbones and jawline, and let's not forget those eyes. They are probably the most alluring blue eyes imaginable.*

I groaned to myself. Well, at least I hope I groaned to myself. I couldn't be one hundred percent sure that I hadn't just opened my mouth and let that groan come out. What also had me in a state of perplexity was the sense that perhaps he was flirting with me. *Surely not, why would he be flirting with me? Alexis Summers, thirty-five-year-old mother of two, and married. Yes ... happily married to Rick Summers, my childhood sweetheart.* I shook my head. *No, I'm imagining it.*

Stripping off my damp blouse and skirt, I put on the dress and stood there looking in the mirror. I barely recognised myself, it not being too long ago that I was a size 16 and very plump in all the wrong places, always having struggled with my weight. And after giving birth twice, I'd stacked on a horrible twenty kilograms. But after finding out, in recent times, that I had fructose malabsorption, I was finally put on a diet that didn't make me horribly ill. That, together with a lot of exercise, had allowed me to reach a weight and body shape I was happy with. I was no skinny supermodel, but I had curves and was toned, so I could not complain.

The Versace dress I was now adorned with suited me. It felt wonderful and I could honestly say I loved it, except I couldn't get the damn zipper up.

'Clarissa, would you mind giving me a hand?' I called out from my cubicle while desperately trying to reach the zip at the centre of my back.

'Is everything all right, Alexis?' Bryce answered instead.

'Um ... yes, Mr Clark,' I replied, my attempts to secure the dress failing. 'I just need a little help with the zip. Is Clarissa there?'

He moved the curtain aside and answered. 'No, but I'll help you.'

Shocked by his brazenness, I stood still and just stared. Bryce did the same, eyeing me from top to toe, neither of us saying a word for what seemed like several minutes. The silence between us had me quivering with anticipation. I felt my face flush, and had no doubt it resembled a beetroot.

Realising he was not about to leave and was there to zip me up as he had said he would, I turned, baring my back to him and accepting his offer of assistance.

Waiting for the feel of his fingers to caress the sensitive skin between my shoulder blades, the oxygen in the cubicle appeared to suddenly evaporate, a result of my anxious deep inhalation of air. For some reason, I couldn't for the life of me let out the breath I had just taken in — the anticipation of his touch, the knowledge that it was coming, causing my frozen state. *Oh shit. Oh shit. Oh shit.*

The wait was torturous, his touch not instantaneous, and I couldn't help but feel as if he were deliberately dragging it out. Finally feeling the soft graze of his fingers against the surface of my skin, I buzzed with expectation as he gently grasped the zip. He placed his other hand just above my bra strap and began to pull the zip up, slowly … very slowly. *Oh, holy crap! I shouldn't be feeling this, I'm a married woman.*

I couldn't help but flinch at his touch, and I think he noticed.

'Are my hands cold?' he asked, almost defensively, letting go and rubbing them together.

If anything, his touch burned me. 'No, not at all.' I giggled with nervousness. 'They are fine.' *Giggled? They are fine? Really, Alexis, get a grip.*

He resumed zipping the dress up, placed both his hands on my shoulders and spun me around, seeming quite pleased. 'There, now you look very much the part of Concierge Attendant.'

Bryce's obvious satisfaction projected upon me, helping me feel a little more comfortable. Not to mention that I was now fully dressed. 'Let me ask you something, Mr Clark. Do you give this much attention to all of your staff?'

'No, Ms Summers, only the ones who share their drinks with me,' he said with a wink as he walked back out of my cubicle and into his own. I had to admit, his playfulness was not lost on me and left me feeling somewhat naughty.

Smiling, I picked up my soiled clothes and stepped out after him, stopping momentarily when I noticed his curtain partly open. And being a woman who appreciates the sight of a very nice-looking man, I couldn't help myself, squinting just enough so that I could get a glimpse. *Oh, fuck! He is magnificent.*

I could only see his back but it was enough to make me blush and fumble with my clothes. *What am I doing? Stop it, Alexis, you dirty little perve.* Ashamed of my pervy self, I once again picked up my clothes and then sat patiently on the sofa in the middle of the change area.

Clarissa returned moments later just as Bryce stepped out from his cubicle. 'Mr Clark, I suspect you are happy with the fit?'

'As always, Clarissa, thank you. If you don't mind, could you possibly arrange for the hotel's housekeeping to collect our clothes, have them dry-cleaned and then delivered to my room later today?'

'Certainly.' She smiled and collected our damp clothes then headed out of the room.

Bryce nodded toward the door. 'After you, Ms Summers,' and we exited the store.

* * *

I looked at my watch as we made our way toward the hotel, noticing it read 10.30 a.m. *Oh crap! I was an hour and a half late.*

'Come along, Ms Summers. I will need to explain your tardiness.' *Tardiness? What? Are we back at school? He really is quite cute.*

'Aren't you my boss?' I asked, slightly confused as to why he would have to explain.

'Yes, but you are supposed to be in a briefing, are you not?'

'Yes, with Ms Maroney.'

'Exactly, so I will need to explain to her. Unless you would like to do it yourself?' he suggested, lifting that sexy eyebrow again. *Is he challenging me?*

'Oh ... I don't mind explaining. I really shouldn't take up any more of your time. I can only imagine how incredibly busy you are.' I felt terrible occupying him for as long as I already had.

He smirked again — *stop doing that* — and ushered me along until we stopped at the City Towers front office where an immaculate-looking young man was standing behind the desk.

'Good morning, Mr Clark. How may I assist you today, sir?'

'Good morning, Liam. Where is Abigail?'

'Just a moment, sir, I'll track her down for you.' Liam flittered along the large desk to his computer and started typing away. 'She's in Conference Room Three, sir. Is there anything else I can help you with?' he asked with a raised eyebrow while giving me a kind but curious look.

'No, that will be all thank you. Oh, by the way, Liam, have you met Alexis Summers? She will be training as Concierge Attendant.'

Liam's smile grew wide. 'Alexis, it's a pleasure. I look forward to working with you,' he stated, seeming quite genuine.

His pleasant demeanour had me feeling that the two of us would get along very well. 'Nice to meet you, too, Liam. Hopefully we'll have time later to get better acquainted.'

'Yes, I hope we do. Mr Clark, would you like me to escort Alexis to Conference Room Three for you?'

'No, Liam, I will take her there myself.'

Blushing bright red yet again — which before this day I had not done very often — and feeling like a schoolgirl being escorted to the principal's office, Bryce returned his hand to the small of my back and gestured me forward with a sexy smile. Liam nodded, and in turning to answer the phone, curiously smiled at me once more. Honestly, I felt as if I were in the middle of *The Twilight Zone*.

Moments later we were standing in front of the elevators and waiting, awkwardly glancing sideways at each other with polite smiles. Thankfully, the elevators were those rare ones: the types you are not standing around and waiting for all day. The doors opened and guests disembarked before Bryce politely gestured for me to enter before him. We both stepped in and he pushed the button to take us to level five.

'Thank you, Mr Clark. I am terribly sorry for this,' I said, apologetically.

He glanced at me again, displaying his smirk, the smirk that made me feel like a naughty child. 'I remember my first day, Ms Summers. It wasn't as action-packed as yours, but it was nerve-racking nonetheless.'

I found it hard to imagine this handsome, perfectly dressed and extremely assertive man ever being nervous about anything. He oozed confidence and self-possession.

I smiled back at him, amused at his obvious attempt to rid me of any embarrassment I held — it really was quite sweet of him. In all honesty, he could've been the complete opposite: furious, angry, and understandably rude. He could have fired me on the spot, but he hadn't.

* * *

We reached the fifth floor and he led me along a corridor to Conference Room Three, then gently knocked on the door.

A short middle-aged lady opened it and greeted us both with uncertainty. 'Mr Clark. Is everything all right?'

'Yes, Abigail. Sorry to interrupt, but I believe you are missing a Ms Summers from your Concierge Attendants' briefing this morning?'

'Yes, sir. I am.'

'Well, I bumped into Ms Summers this morning and, unfortunately for her, spilled my coffee down the both of us. So of course I had to see she was well looked after and delivered to you.'

I subtly gasped and shot him a shocked glance.

He ignored me and continued. 'Abigail, this is Alexis Summers. Ms Summers, Abigail Maroney.'

Abigail gave me a strange look, then smiled and thanked Mr Clark. 'Come in, Alexis, and take a seat.' She turned and headed for the large oval desk in the centre of the room.

Before entering and following after her, I turned to Bryce. 'It was a pleasure meeting you today, Mr Clark.' And, in a whispered voice, I added, 'Again, I'm so sorry.'

He stepped backward and nodded while giving me that trademark smirk. 'Ah, Ms Summers, the pleasure has been all mine.'

I couldn't help but smile back at him. 'Oh, Mr Clark, by the way, it's Mrs, not Ms.'

Putting two fingers to his lips, he winked and turned. 'I know,' he called behind him, and then he was gone.

CHAPTER

2

I humbly settled into my seat and apologised to Ms Maroney and the rest of the occupants in the room. So far, my morning had been a bad dream. How could I have been such a klutz? This job required me to be on the ball, organised, and completely professional. Unfortunately, I'd displayed none of those traits thus far.

'I am so sorry for disrupting your briefing, Ms Maroney,' I offered, smiling apologetically at Abigail and the five other Concierge Attendant trainees sitting around the table.

'Never mind, dear, Mr Clark seemed to have your situation under control and, please, call me Abigail. Now, Alexis, just to get you up to speed. Yourself, along with Jessica, Samantha, Jonathan, Marcus and Lorell,' she explained, gesturing to the others as she mentioned their names, 'are training as Concierge Attendants. You will each assist the Head Concierge from all three of City Towers' hotels.

'Alexis, you will join Samantha and will concierge here in City Towers. Jonathan and Jessica will concierge in City Metropol, and Lorell and Marcus at City Promenade.

'If you open your brief, you will see a manual with everything you need to know about City Towers and the entire City Towers complex, including the casino and shopping precinct. Your mobile phone and keycard are your life. Please keep them on you at all times.

'Your keycard will give you access to every room in the hotel, with the exception of Mr Clark's penthouse residence, of course. Special instructions regarding his requests are also in your brief. Your iPhone is also pre-programmed with all the relevant contacts.'

Turning away from me, Abigail then addressed the others. 'Jonathan and Jessica, City Metropol's Head Concierge is expecting you both in the Metropol Lobby. Lorell and Marcus, your Head Concierge will meet you at the Concierge Desk in the Promenade building. Enjoy your day and don't hesitate to contact me if needed.'

Jonathan, Jessica, Lorell and Marcus stood up and made their way out of the room, although not before thanking Abigail.

'Now, Alexis and Samantha, as you are both aware, I'm the Head Concierge here at City Towers, and our office is in the Lobby. For today, I want you to familiarise yourself with the hotel; after all, you will need to know this building inside and out. You both have a timetable to follow for the week which enables you to get a good feel for how the hotel runs on a day-to-day basis. Any questions?'

Both of us shook our heads and smiled with confidence.

'Very well. Enjoy your day, ladies. I will check in on you both as the day progresses.'

We thanked Abigail, gathered our briefs, and made our way to the hotel kitchen where Samantha and I introduced ourselves to each other properly.

She was twenty-three years of age and fresh from a Bachelor degree in Travel, Tourism and Hospitality from Deakin University, similar to the Bachelor degree I had completed online while raising my children. Samantha was single and living with her parents in Doncaster. She was approximately five foot seven, and I guessed she was probably a size 10.

Obviously taking considerable pride in her appearance, Samantha's make-up was impeccable and her strawberry blonde hair was pretty much styled to perfection. She also wore heels higher than the Eureka Tower. I was impressed — walking in those was quite a talent.

I decided early on that I liked Samantha — there were not many people I didn't like — but I could tell she was highly competitive because of minor things, like entering each room just ahead of me, always walking a couple of steps in front of me. She also had a knack of asking questions over the top of mine, which became apparent during our tour of the kitchen and laundry; it was as though Samantha had to have the last word every time. She kind of reminded me of my best friend, Carls.

The City Towers kitchen had an area dedicated to staff. So after our tour we were able to get ourselves some fruit and, before leaving, Samantha also grabbed a tomato juice, and I, a cup of tea.

We decided — or more so, Samantha decided — to eat our morning tea on the hotel's sun deck, which worked out to be perfect as it was simply beautiful. I was glad Samantha had made the decision to take our break there, in the end, as summer in Melbourne was my favourite time of the year. I just loved thirty degree days and, this particular morning, the sun — with its glorious vitamin D — was just lovely.

Peeling my banana and opening my brief, I took note of the entire section devoted to Mr Clark and his penthouse.

Mr Clark is the owner of City Towers Entertainment Complex and resides in the penthouse of City Towers. As CA (Concierge Attendant) you are required to assist Mr Clark as a matter of priority. Any request he has must be attended to as soon as possible. His meals (when requested) are to be delivered to the penthouse at the following times: Breakfast at 6 a.m., morning tea at 10 a.m., lunch at 1 p.m., afternoon tea at 3.30 p.m., dinner at 7 p.m., and supper at 9.30 p.m. You are required to collect his daily brief from his personal assistant each morning at 9.15 a.m., which will contain instructions on the following day's menu, as well as specific housecleaning requests. Mr Clark's mail is to be delivered to him as soon as it is received by the hotel's Reception.

His office also forms part of the penthouse and all clientele, by appointment, are to be personally escorted to the penthouse foyer where his personal assistant will meet them.

'Mr Clark is so hot in his company picture. Was he as drop-dead gorgeous in the flesh? I couldn't see when you came in,' Samantha asked, while goggling at me like a schoolgirl.

'Oh ... yes, he is very handsome and very understanding,' I answered, awkwardly.

'Understanding and apparently accident-prone. Lucky you! He can spill his drink on me any day.' Samantha continued to read her timetable as I closed my brief. 'We have a housekeeping demonstration next. Then, we are scheduled to go up to the penthouse to meet Mr Clark's PA.' *What? The penthouse?*

Already, I had a sense of butterflies fluttering within my stomach and I realised I desperately wanted to see him again. Remembering the way he had spoken to me and had looked at me had me squirming in my seat. I couldn't help but revert back to this morning, perving at him through his cubicle curtain, his naked back exquisite. I wanted to run my hands up and down it.

A loud slurping noise snapped me out of my reverie as I refocussed on Samantha, the horrid noise a result of her over-enthusiastic sucking of the last bit of tomato juice through her straw. Sensing that my cheeks were red, I also realised I had been licking my lips and I quickly wiped them with my finger. *How embarrassing. What am I doing? I'm happily married and have a very healthy sex life with Rick.*

Rick was my childhood sweetheart and I had only ever been with him. We were like two peas in a pod. In twelve years of marriage, we had rarely fought and had spent less than a week apart. He really did make me happy, my Rick. So these feelings — if I could call them that — were foreign territory for me.

Once again dismissing my incoherent thoughts toward my new employer, I stood up and threw my banana peel in the bin. 'Housekeeping demo! It's not glamorous but essential to witness nonetheless.'

Samantha rolled her eyes, but agreed. 'Then to the penthouse,' she said with a sly grin. 'Now that ought to be glamorous.'

I nodded. 'Yes, I hope so.'

As we walked back inside — Samantha one step ahead of me — I began to wonder what Mr Clark's personal assistant would look like. Probably drop-dead gorgeous and straight from a Victoria's Secret catalogue. *Hopefully with more clothing on.*

* * *

Housekeeping was as expected. I'd observed the most perfect hospital corner and, strangely enough, was keen to give it a go on my own bed when I got home. Samantha had not been the slightest bit interested in sheet folding, instead having been annoyingly fidgety and impatiently jittery knowing that our tour of the penthouse was soon to follow.

The City Towers penthouse was on level forty-three, comprising Mr Clark's private office and his private residence and, as I stood in the elevator on our way up to see it, I also started to fidget. I was pretty sure it had nothing to do with excitement as it was in Samantha's case. For me, it was more nerves and agitation. I couldn't quite fathom why I had these feelings; they were more than strange to me. Yes, I found Mr Clark extremely attractive ... of course I did. I would be very surprised if there was a woman alive who didn't. And it's not as though I had never found another man other than Rick attractive before, because I had. It was just, this seemed different, and I couldn't quite put my finger on it.

Trying desperately to push the unfamiliar and quite annoying thoughts and feelings out of my head, I took in a deep breath as the elevator doors opened. I boldly stepped out into the penthouse foyer, which was when I became quite certain the breath I had just taken in had been instantly knocked right out of me — knocked out by the sight before my eyes. I was aware of the fact the air had left my lungs, because I found myself standing there, trying to suck it back in again. *Oh. My. God!*

The foyer was beyond beautiful. There were gold fixtures and fittings. Cream-coloured floor tiles with golden edging.

Floor-to-ceiling windows with a view of the city skyline line that had to be seen to be believed, and the curtains dressing those windows were simply superb. I love curtains — they are a secret obsession of mine. A window is not a window if it is not dressed properly. These curtains were stunning: golden silk fabric, with gold seams and tassels from which the light bounced, illuminating them. *Oh, they are to die for.*

Openly gaping at the window furnishings of my dreams, I stumbled forward and continued to walk into the foyer — Samantha now two steps in front.

Directly ahead of us was a solid mahogany desk and sitting behind that desk was a very pretty young woman. She rose to her feet and waddled toward us. And when I say waddled, I mean it. She was approximately seven to eight months pregnant.

'Hello, you must be Alexis Summers and Samantha Taylor. I'm Lucinda Clark, Mr Clark's personal assistant. Welcome to City Towers.'

Gracefully extending her hand to each of us, she was radiantly beautiful, and I couldn't help but feel very intimidated by this brunette goddess. She was probably the most beautiful mother-to-be I had ever come across.

Almost instantly, my chest pained. *Wait a minute ... did she just say Lucinda Clark? Yes, she did. Oh, shit! She is Mr Clark's wife, his very beautiful, pregnant, wife.* A feeling of devastation and hurt washed over me. But it was stupid and, more to the point, ridiculous of me to feel that way. I had absolutely no right.

Just as I swallowed heavily and pushed away my unreasonable reaction to Lucinda, the elevator doors opened. All three of us turned our heads to see Mr Clark enter the foyer, heading straight to Lucinda's side.

He gave her a kiss on the cheek. 'Good morning, Lucy.'

I watched with envy-filled eyes as they exchanged a quick loving embrace. *Envy? Surely not.*

'Morning, Bryce. Alexis Summers and Samantha Taylor are the hotel's new Concierge Attendants. They are here for the tour of the penthouse offices,' she informed him after they pulled apart.

Mr Clark looked at Samantha and spoke to her first. 'Miss Taylor, if you wouldn't mind following me, please. I'd like to get better acquainted. And Lucy, if you wouldn't mind showing Ms Summers around, I will see her next.' He directed Samantha to one of the mahogany wooden-panelled doors to the right of Lucinda's desk then looked back at me, displaying the same smirk I had seen earlier.

How dare he? The arrogance of this man. How dare he look at me like that in front of his wife and child-to-be? I was mortified beyond belief, and more so when Lucinda turned and looked directly into my eyes, raising her eyebrow, displaying a similar smirk to Bryce's. *Oh, holy shit, she's on to me.*

'Very well. Ms Summers, if you'd like to come with me,' she requested, almost looking amused.

I was horrified. Somehow, I felt that she knew I'd been daydreaming of her husband on and off since meeting him. Of course, she'd have to be telepathic or some kind of magic mind-reader to be privy to that information. But, regardless, her new facial expression had me feeling all sorts of uncomfortable shit.

Trying to mentally settle my nerves, I followed her into a large conference room which was to the left of her desk.

'As you would be aware, Ms Summers, Mr Clark is the CEO of Clark Incorporated and owner of City Towers Entertainment Complex. He resides here in the penthouse which also houses his personal office. The rest of Clark Incorporated's offices are situated on levels seven and eight. Most of his personal meetings are conducted here. However, the direct running of Clark Incorporated takes place on levels seven and eight.'

We walked through the conference room to another door and into another foyer. Lucinda pointed to yet another door which was to my right. 'Mr Clark's personal office is through there.'

Eyeballing the wooden obstruction, I realised that if ever there was a time in my life where I wanted X-ray vision, it would have been then. I thought to myself that maybe, just maybe, if I squinted hard enough, I could quite possibly see what was going on in there, more than likely spying him obnoxiously flirting with Samantha like he had with me.

My blood started to boil, so I looked away.

'Just through here is a kitchenette, and off to your left is a bathroom,' Lucinda continued to advise.

So far, the penthouse floor really was impressive, and I'd only borne witness to the offices. It made me wonder what Mr Clark's personal residence was like ... what his bedroom was like. *Stop it, Alexis. Enough of perverse imaginings that are completely irrelevant to what you are doing here.*

'Alexis, are you finished with scrutinising the kitchenette?' Lucinda asked, standing impatiently in the doorway and waiting for me to leave the room.

'Yes, sorry,' I stuttered, and quickly rushed out, back to the foyer.

Straightaway, I spotted a table which was the centrepiece of the room, and on it was a large vase of beautiful lemon-coloured roses. They were fabulous and smelled divine, their floral perfume penetrating my senses and hypnotising me like a drug-induced high. I loved roses ... loved them. I had many rose bushes in my garden at home and loved the array of colours my garden displayed in the spring.

'Through there is Mr Clark's private residence,' Lucinda instructed, breaking me from my rose-high and pointing directly ahead to a large door which was locked by security card.

To say I was in awe of my surroundings was an understatement and my expression seemed to give away my inner feelings.

'It's pretty impressive, isn't it? All of this, I mean,' Lucinda affirmed with a knowing smile while watching me admire the room.

'Oh, yes, this is an exquisite complex. I'm thrilled and fortunate to be working here.'

She smiled. 'Yes, Clark Incorporated is a wonderful company to be a part of, and Mr Clark is a brilliant employer.'

I couldn't help but find it quite strange how she kept referring to her husband as 'Mr Clark' and 'employer': it was very formal. My guess would be that they both liked to maintain a professional manner in the presence of staff. Well, it would appear Lucinda did, anyway.

'Here, take a seat. I'm sure they won't be too much longer,' she politely offered, while gesturing me to sit next to her on an elegant day lounge which was situated next to the door to Mr Clark's office.

I smiled and took my seat then opened my mouth without thinking. 'I hope I'm not being intrusive, Lucinda, but when are you due?' I asked, sheepishly, hoping she did not see my question as brazen, rude or simply none of my business. I was genuinely interested in her answer.

Thankfully, she smiled, then naturally caressed her very full belly. 'I'm thirty-four weeks along.'

'That's wonderful. You and Mr Clark must be very excited. Is this your first child?' *Oh my God! I can't believe I just said that.* And by the strange look on Lucinda's face, I was sure I had just overstepped the mark. 'Oh, never mind, I'm terribly sorry. I'm being intrusive.'

I looked down at my feet in horror.

'Oh, no, that's quite all right. Yes, this is my first child and yes, Mr Clark is thrilled, thrilled that in the coming weeks he will be an uncle.' *What? Uncle? Yes, she did just say uncle. Oh ... uncle ... of course.*

To say I was unreservedly relieved would be an understatement. But how could I have been so wrong? I'd doubted this wonderful man who hadn't fired me for covering him in a hot, white-chocolate drink, and who had come across as being kind and caring despite being utterly rich. I felt like a complete idiot.

'You thought we were married, didn't you?' Lucinda said, knowingly.

I put my hand to my head and peeked through my open fingers, finding her smiling mischievously at me. 'Yes, I did. You can't really blame me though. You both share the same surname and obviously share a special bond.'

'We do.' A look of admiration was plastered over her face. It was very sweet, but I felt I was intruding into their special relationship, so I changed the subject.

'You know, speaking from experience, you are about to embark on a crazy, wonderful roller-coaster that is motherhood.'

'Do you have children?'

'Yes, two. Nate is nine and Charlotte is six. They are ador-able, but I guess I'm biased. I love them to pieces, but gone are the days of solely using my brain to decide what we will eat three times a day, and whether to dust, mop, vacuum or all of the above.' I began to rant, something I tended to do when discussing my children. They had pretty much been my life in its entirety for the past nine years.

'That sounds lovely. I'm looking forward to using my brain to decide what brand of nappies to use, and to breastfeed or not to breastfeed.'

We both laughed. I really liked Lucinda, especially now that she was no longer Mrs Clark.

The door to Bryce's office opened, and Samantha appeared with a not-so-impressed look on her face.

'Alexis, Mr Clark will speak to you now,' she announced unpretentiously.

I stood up and brushed my hands down the stunning dress I was wearing. *I think I might sleep in it tonight. Surely there's nothing wrong with that!*

Turning to Lucinda, I offered her a hand. 'It was a plea-sure meeting you, Miss Clark, and good luck in the coming weeks.'

She gracefully accepted my hand and thanked me. I then nervously entered Mr Clark's office, closing the door behind me. As I turned to face him, chills of excitement were already prickling my spine.

CHAPTER
3

Mr Clark had his back to me as I walked into his office. He was behind his desk looking out of the floor-to-ceiling window at the view of Port Phillip Bay. He appeared to be lost in thought, with one hand in his pocket and the other on his chin. My eyes instantly found his arse which looked particularly nice in his Versace suit. It was obvious he worked out, or was blessed with not only wealth but good genes. I'd take a guess and say he was maybe six foot five, and his hair was distractingly luscious.

My husband, Rick, was tall, dark and very handsome. Admittedly, though, I was partial to blond men, there being something about them that often had me clenching my thighs together. This particular dark-blond man had me clenching like never before.

He turned around, his expression worrying me. 'Alexis, take a seat,' he said, gesturing to the cream-coloured, leather lounge suite in the middle of his office.

On the table was what looked like a strong black coffee and a hot, white-chocolate, topped with a marshmallow.

'You never got to drink the one you bought this morning, so I took it upon myself to get you a replacement,' he continued, his tone very stern.

I smiled nervously and made my way to the sofa. *No, I didn't get to drink it this morning, Bryce. But I would have been more than happy to lick it off you. Alexis, you devil, get a grip.*

'No, I didn't. Instead, I spilled it and got myself a new dress, but let me tell you that was not my intention.'

He analysed my little black Versace number. 'Hmm,' he groaned, his groan almost primal.

The sexy sound made me shift in my seat. Clearing my throat, I continued: 'In all seriousness, Mr Clark, thank you for the dress. And thank you for replacing my drink. It was very thoughtful of you. Technically, I should be getting you a replacement for the one you never got to order.'

'I wasn't going to have a drink, Alexis,' he advised nonchalantly, as he took a seat opposite me.

I screwed up my face in confusion. 'Oh, perhaps you are a muffin type of man then?' I asked as I took a sip of my drink.

'No, I'm not a muffin man. I wasn't there for anything that morning. In fact, I noticed you briskly walking through the casino and out to Gloria Jean's, so I thought I'd introduce myself. You see, Ms Summers, I make it a priority to know every single tiny detail there is to know about my staff.'

And there it was again, that smirk.

I went to clear my throat again, but thought better of it, the sound of my incessant oesophagus-unclogging even annoying to my own ears. 'Every single tiny detail, really? Well, I'm not sure if that is impressive or creepy.'

He laughed, and I felt his initial rigidness wear away. 'So, Alexis, how has your morning been so far?' he asked, as he picked up his coffee and took a sip.

His full lips caught my attention instantaneously, the way they pressed firmly over the rim of his cup. It had my thighs involuntarily clenching tighter at the thought of him putting those lips on me. *Seriously, Alexis? You've been out of the house one day. One day, and you have pretty much undressed this man in your head, and now you want to do naughty things with him.*

'I'm sorry ...' *Shit! I forgot what he asked.*

'Your day,' he smiled. 'How has it been so far?'

'Oh ...' I blushed. 'Well, apart from spilling my drink on my boss, it's been great. I've really enjoyed seeing this beautiful hotel from behind the scenes. I've always loved City Towers. I stayed here once before with my husband, although he wasn't my husband at the time.'

Mr Clark raised his eyebrows and took another sip. 'So, how was it?'

'The tour has been great, the staff are lovely, and —'

'No, not the tour. The time you stayed with Rick.'

I was about to answer when realisation dawned on me, stunning me into silence. *He said 'Rick'. He knows my husband's name. Then again, he did say he made it a priority to know 'every tiny detail'.* I decided this time it was impressive investigatory skills rather than creepy, so I smirked back, and this seemed to amuse him. He really was quite cheeky. I liked that about him. He was a man with immense power and authority, and there he was being playful and cheeky with me. I couldn't help but play along with him. Why not? It was just harmless fun.

'So,' I drawled, 'you have done some creepy research.'

Never would I have dreamed of talking to any of my previous employers like this, nor flirted my arse off as I was doing it. Honestly though, I couldn't help myself. It was as though he was drawing the naughty little minx version of Alexis out of me.

Despite a tiny feeling that I was about to enter dangerous territory, I opted to continue. 'It was wonderful. The room was sophisticated and the view, breathtaking. However, we didn't really leave the room all that much.' *Shit! I cannot believe I just said that.* I was on a roll, but could I keep it up? *Quickly, Alexis, say something else suggestive or give him a flirtatious smile, or something.* No matter how hard I tried, I couldn't do it. Instead, blushing bright red, I looked down. *Oh my God, I am so out of my league.*

This sexy masculine man had me in knots and I could not keep up.

'I'm glad it served its purpose, Alexis. I built this hotel with beauty and romance in mind. I want it to be enjoyed, whether it is down on the casino floor or within a suite's walls.'

I was still looking down at the cup in my hands and feeling embarrassed by my offer of too much information, when there was a knock at the door.

'Come in,' Bryce announced.

I looked up to find Lucinda entering the room, followed by a food and beverage attendant with a trolley. The interruption — as far as I was concerned — was more than welcome.

Kindly ushering the young man to the coffee table in front of Mr Clark and me, Lucinda smiled encouragingly as the food and beverage attendant very carefully placed the food cloche down and removed the lid, displaying a platter of fruit and hors d'oeuvres.

'Thank you, Sebastian,' Bryce said in a friendly tone. 'That will be all.'

Sebastian nodded to Mr Clark and promptly pushed the trolley back out of the room with Lucinda following.

'I don't know about you, Alexis, but it is lunchtime, and I like to eat my meals when they are due. As we are not done yet, would you like to join me for lunch?'

'Oh, yes, this looks wonderful. Thank you.'

It really did look wonderful. The fruit platter was divine and it seemed to only contain fruits that I was able to eat. Having fructose malabsorption definitely had its limitations, but the platter in front of us was perfectly stacked with strawberries, raspberries, blueberries and bananas. The cantaloupe and orange segments were cut into flowers; they were gorgeous.

It suddenly dawned on me that this was no coincidence. I quickly glanced up at Bryce. 'Let me guess, more creepy research?' I asked.

He leaned forward and reached for a strawberry, popping it into his mouth. 'It's what I do, Ms Summers.'

I smiled and followed suit. 'So, what other creepy research have you done?'

'Just the stock standard. You have been married to Rick Summers for twelve years. You have two children: Nate, who is nine, and Charlotte, six. You live in Attwood and have done so for ten years. You were born in Victoria to Maryann and Graeme Blaxlo, who now live on twenty-eight hectares near Shepparton. You are one of three children. You are fructose intolerant, love roses, cars, football and world landmarks. You also have a soft spot for frogs, and hate spiders. Shall I go on?'

I was literally shocked. Stunned. Fucking floored. *How the hell does he know so much about me?* Not knowing what to feel let alone say, I chose to momentarily remain silent, slowly shaking my head from side to side. At that point, I also realised my mouth was open, and I must have resembled one of those carnival clowns, the ones with the big mouths you put balls in. Suddenly, I lost my appetite and felt extremely uncomfortable.

'Alexis, you look a little pale. Listen, what you need to understand is that I am a very resourceful man who happens to take great pride and ownership of my assets. I need to protect them and, in order to do so, I need to be able to trust those who represent my company.'

I was still speechless, processing the enormity of everything that was this man, as he continued to speak.

'Now, as my CA, I will need you to represent my assets with the utmost professionalism by showing every guest the greatest courtesy and understanding. You also need to be as knowledgeable about this hotel and complex as I am of my staff. There can be no stone left unturned. Do you understand, Alexis?'

'I understand,' I stuttered, still in shock.

'Good. Now, I have changed a few job tasks between you and Miss Taylor. Miss Taylor will focus more on the hotel guests and less on my needs. I will now require you to solely handle my concierge requests. I find that one attendant performing this task is much more efficient.' He pointed to the fruit platter. 'Please, it is better to taste than to admire, I assure you.'

'Oh.' I smiled nervously, fumbling as I grabbed a strawberry, raspberry and cantaloupe flower, placing them on a small plate. I opted for the strawberry first as it seemed less messy and the safest option. Biting into it, I felt myself relax a little.

Mr Clark grabbed a couple of blueberries and popped them into his mouth all at once, displaying how comfortable and at ease he now seemed to be. He also seemed to be waiting for my response. When I didn't offer him one immediately, he got up and walked over to his desk.

Just as I was about to bite into my raspberry, he bent over. *Oh, shit!* Juice squirted out, and I felt some of it land on my chin. I jerked at the sudden splatter and, in doing so, nearly choked on what I had just put in my mouth.

Bryce looked up and noticed me gagging. He rushed back to the lounge. 'Are you all right?' he asked, and started patting me on my back.

'Yes, I'm fine,' I choked out. *What was I? One, and just learning to chew solids?*

His hand was still on my back, but he was now rubbing in a circular motion. It felt good, and if I were a dog, my leg would have started to twitch. My eyes felt heavy and began to close of their own accord. *Shit, Alexis, snap out of it!*

'I'm fine, sorry, just choked a little. Really, I'm fine,' I said dismissively, pushing the plate into the centre of the table and brushing down my dress to indicate I had finished.

Bryce took my hands in his, pulled me up to stand before him, and then handed me a folder. 'This is my personal Concierge Brief. It contains my requests for the day. You will need to come up here every morning and get it from either myself or Lucy.'

I smiled appreciatively and took the brief from him. He placed his hand on the small of my back and gently directed me to the door. Just as I reached for the handle, he put his hand up to my chin. The intimate gesture had me frozen solid. *What is he doing? This is highly inappropriate, I'm married.*

I was about to object when he gently wiped my chin. His touch was so soft and there was just something about the way he looked at me as he wiped that made me feel something I had never felt before. The problem was, I didn't know what the hell it was that I felt, only that I had never felt anything like it before. EVER.

'There you go. I can't have my CA wearing raspberry juice around my hotel.'

I automatically followed his wipe with one of my own and felt myself go crimson. 'Oh, sorry. No, you can't, that's not a good look. Thank you for lunch, Mr Clark, it was lovely.'

He leaned forward and opened the door for me to walk through. I obliged and made my way out into the foyer. Thankfully, Lucinda was not at her desk, so I hurried to the elevator and pushed the button. Standing there and waiting for the doors to open, I could sense he was still watching me. It made me feel uneasy but, surprisingly, not in a bad way.

The doors slid open and I stepped inside the car. As I turned around, our eyes met, fixed on one another in an intense stare. He lifted his hand to wave and, like a robot, I did the same. The expression on his face was one of amused, sexual playfulness, taking the form of his biggest smirk thus far, and not being able to resist that look, I couldn't help but smile back at him until the doors closed in front of me.

* * *

Stumbling back to the far wall of the elevator, I steadied myself on the handrail. *Holy shit! What the fuck was that about?* This irresistibly gorgeous, filthy rich, privacy invading, control freak was flirting with me, and me with him. I needed some air. I needed a place to settle my heart, which was racing like mad in my chest. Perhaps I needed my vibrator. *No, no, you don't. Right, no, I don't.*

I looked at my timetable and found that I was due back at the front office in fifteen minutes time, so I opted for the sun deck and pressed the button for level two. It was still a glorious day, and I really had enjoyed that particular spot earlier in the day.

Finding an empty table by the pool, I sat down and opened Mr Clark's brief. The brief was empty, with the exception of a yellow post-it note stuck at the back of the folder and, handwritten in pen, was a note from Bryce.

Ms Summers,
Today's Requests: — Try not to spill any drinks!
Mr Clark

Was that it? No 'organise housekeeping to collect my laundry'? No 'deliver tomorrow's meal requests to the kitchen'? And, no 'book a table request for tonight at Lago's for me and my extremely sexy, supermodel girlfriend who you know nothing about'?

I was officially confused.

* * *

The rest of the day went as scheduled. I knocked off at 6 p.m. and made it home just as Rick was dishing up the beef stroganoff I'd put in the slow cooker this morning. As I walked through the front door, Nate jumped up from his seat at our dining room table, ran toward me and wrapped his arms around me so tightly I couldn't move.

'Sweetheart, ease up on the grip, yeah!' I instructed as I squeezed him back. He complied with the lessening of his grip, but did not let go completely, inevitably making it quite difficult to walk to the buffet. I laughed. 'You are going to have to let go now.'

'No,' he said stubbornly, but with a hint of playfulness in his tone.

I pried his arms from around my waist and kissed him on the top of his head, then took off my jacket and put my bag down.

'Mum, you weren't wearing that dress this morning,' Charlotte stated in a matter-of-fact tone. Of course, my overly observant and fashion-conscious daughter had noticed my change of attire.

'It's a long story, Charli,' I said with a kiss before looking up at Rick to give him the I'll-tell-you-later look.

'So, how was your first day, babe?' Rick asked as he carried the plates to the table.

'Yeah, really good. The hotel is stunning from the lobby all the way up to the penthouse.'

'The penthouse? Wow! What's the penthouse?' Charlotte asked, wide-eyed and eager for an explanation.

'The penthouse is the suite at the very top of the building. It's also where Mr Clark — my boss — lives.'

'Oh, cool! Can we go and see it, Mum, can we? I want to see a penthouse.'

'Maybe, Charli. I might take you one weekend and sneak you past Lucinda, Mr Clark's assistant.'

I kissed Charlotte on the nose and helped Rick retrieve the remaining plates. We then ate our dinner, which was lovely — even more so because it had cooked itself.

* * *

Exhausted was the perfect word to describe how I felt after reading Charli a book and then putting her to bed, followed by helping Nate with his homework and kissing him good-night. I was so exhausted, I then opted to head straight to bed myself.

Rick followed shortly after, kissing my neck and cupping my breast. 'Oh, poor baby. Are you exhausted after one day?' he taunted.

'Shut up,' I teased while nestling into his arms.

'So, how did you end up with a new dress?'

'Don't ask,' I groaned. 'It was so embarrassing. I was buying a hot choccie from Gloria Jean's this morning and, as I turned around, I bumped into Mr Clark, spilling it down the both of us. To cut a long story short, he organised replacement clothing for the two of us at Versace,' I explained, trying to make the last part sound casual.

Rick was not stupid though. 'Oh, he just organised a replacement at Versace, did he? Just like he wipes his arse with $100 bills?'

I couldn't help giggling at his lame joke. 'You idiot, yeah, something like that. Now, shut up and go to sleep, I have to work tomorrow,' I mumbled through a yawn while repeating that last bit in my head. *I have to work tomorrow.*

Just the thought of it had me drifting off to sleep, dare I say, with a large smile plastered across my face.

CHAPTER

4

The next morning, I pulled into the staff car park ahead of time — the school drop-off and drive into the city having been a lot smoother than the day before. Nate had again sulked but he accepted defeat and had not put up a fight, thus assisting in my early arrival at work. That was one of the qualities I loved about my son. He knew when to stand his ground and when to graciously bow out and make the most of the situation. He was very much like his father in that sense. Charlotte, on the other hand, was as stubborn as they come. And when she had her mind set, it was almost impossible to change it. This quality — I am continuously told by my mother — had come from me.

I adored my two ratbags as much as humanly possible, and I enjoyed raising them and watching them grow from sweet little babies into confident and well-behaved children.

At first, I had struggled with the decision to go back to work full-time, as I did not want my time away to have a negative impact on Nate and Charli's lives. Having been a very hands-on mum, I was worried the separation would hurt them. But when making the decision to take the bull by the horns and head back into the workforce, I had made myself a promise that I would still be as hands-on as I possibly could.

Of course, being a parent helper at school was no longer possible, but I had every intention of continuing to bake cakes for their school lunches and for their sausage-sizzle days. I also had every intention of continuing to help them with their homework and school projects when needed.

Sighing at the thought of a mother's never-ending duties, I stepped out of my black Ford Territory and grabbed the stunning Versace dress which was hanging up in the back. I had plans to get it dry-cleaned and returned to Bryce as soon as possible. As much as I loved the dress, I didn't feel right in keeping it. Yes, he appeared to have all the money in the world, but that was no reason for me to accept such an expensive item.

I made my way to the car park elevator and observed my reflection in the mirrored walls. My blonde hair was down and sporting a light wave, reaching to just above the small of my back. I had opted for a navy princess-style dress with a matching belt and navy pumps. Seeing as my feet had, surprisingly, survived the day before, I had decided to give them the benefit of the doubt and wear heels once again.

After handing the dress to the hotel's dry-cleaning service, I had some time to kill, so chose to grab myself an English Breakfast tea and check out the shopping precinct.

* * *

City Towers offered a fantastic shopping experience, showcasing some of the world's leading designers: Versace, Burberry, Bulgari, Louis Vuitton, Prada and many more.

As I slowly drifted from storefront to storefront, sipping my tea and enjoying my extravagant window shopping, I spotted a gorgeous, nude-coloured mesh dress in Burberry that was simply stunning. What was also simply stunning was the $2,400 price tag. *Holy shit! That is pretty much my monthly mortgage repayment! Move along, Alexis. Move along.*

Continuing to window-shop, I stopped abruptly when reaching Versace. I couldn't help but think back to the day before when Bryce had touched my back and zipped my dress up. A shiver went down my spine at the memory, and I felt my cheeks blush in recognition. I'd truly never felt anything like the surge of electricity that went through my body at his touch — it was very different to what I felt at the hands of my husband.

With Rick, I felt content, loved, safe, warm and adored. But this feeling, this feeling at the hands of my boss, was exciting, exhilarating, and utterly hot.

'Alexis, fancy seeing you here,' Samantha said as she came up behind me. She was bright, bubbly and looked effervescent in her grey A-line skirt and baby-blue blouse. 'See anything you like? There's a tote bag in Bulgari I'm dying to buy. Oh well, there goes my first week's wages,' she said with a shrug of her shoulders.

'Hi, Samantha. I'm just killing some time before we start,' I answered, quickly shaking the memory of Bryce's electrifying touch from my mind. 'I'm heading to the hotel now, are you coming?'

'Yes, take me away before I blow next week's wage, too,' she groaned, holding her arms out before her and resembling a zombie.

I giggled, grabbed hold of them, and then led her away.

* * *

Liam, the hotel's receptionist, was flicking through some paperwork at his desk when we entered the hotel foyer. When he spotted our entrance, he raised his eyebrow at me, then looked toward Samantha who was now leaning across the reception counter. 'Ladies, how was your first day?'

'Can I ask you something, Liam, off the record?' Samantha enquired.

'Oooh, this sounds serious! Yes, ask me.' Liam moved closer to Samantha, and I found myself leaning in also, so that I could hear what she was now saying in a hushed tone.

'Mr Clark ... is he an arrogant prick, or is the tough big-bad-boss attitude just an act?'

At first I was a little taken aback by her accusation, until I recalled the way she had left his office the day before.

Liam also appeared to be trying to hide a smug smile. 'He is a very diligent, professional and kind man, but watch out if you piss him off. Why do you ask? What did you do?' Liam probed, looking intrigued. So did I, come to think of it.

She turned to me with a critical glare. 'Nothing, I didn't do anything. He just informed me that I would not be required to concierge for him privately and that anything he needed would be handled by Alexis.'

'What? I had nothing to do with it,' I answered in defence. 'He explained that his needs were more efficiently handled by one concierge alone. I couldn't argue with him, he's the boss.'

'That or maybe he felt guilty for spilling his drink on you,' Samantha murmured in a childish voice. She was obviously pissed off.

'I don't know. Yeah, maybe,' I flippantly replied.

If that's what Samantha wanted to think, then that was fine by me. 'Anyway, I don't know why it's bothering you, Samantha. You have less to worry about, unlike me who now has to go up there,' I said, pointing to the roof. 'To retrieve his brief,' I added, while childishly poking out my tongue which Liam found amusing.

He laughed. 'Off you go. You don't want to piss him off.'

I smiled and dramatically bit the ends of my fingernails in response, then headed for the elevator.

* * *

Lucinda was behind her desk and, as I walked in, the phone rang. She smiled and put her finger up to indicate she would not be long.

'Bryce Clark's office, Lucinda speaking, how may I help you? No, Gareth, I'm sorry, but he's out at the moment. Yes, Gareth, he's at self-defence class. He'll be finished soon. Yes, ten o'clock is fine. Okay, we'll see you shortly.' She rolled her eyes in frustration then hung up. 'I'm so glad you're here, Alexis, you're just in time. I desperately need to pee. Can you answer the phone for me while I'm gone?'

'Sure, not a problem.'

'Just take a message if it rings. I'll be right back.' She waddled off then yelled back. 'Love the dress, Alexis. Navy really suits you.'

'Oh, thanks,' I replied, but she was gone. I smiled to myself thinking back to the vivid memory of the increasing urge to pee during pregnancy. *When you've got to go, you've got to go.*

The phone chimed, bringing me back to the present. I was still standing on the opposite side of the desk, so I automatically leaned over and answered it.

'Bryce Clark's office, Alexis speaking, how may I help you?'

'Alexis, is it?'

'Yes, can I help you?'

'I just spoke to Lucinda, is she available?'

'She just stepped away from her desk. Can I take a message for you and get her to call you back?'

I started to jot down the gentleman's name: Gareth Clark. *Didn't he just call ... like two seconds ago?*

'Is Bryce in the office yet?' *No, you impatient idiot, he wasn't a minute ago and he's not now.*

'No, he's not back yet, sir.'

'Let him know that I'll be there shortly.'

'Yes, I will pass that on for you. Thank you, goodbye.' *Fuck, he was pushy.*

As I finished writing down the message, it dawned on me ... the name Gareth Clark. *Yes, he is vice-president of Clark Incorporated. I've seen it written down somewhere.* I walked around to the back of the desk and returned the phone to its cradle.

'Good morning, Ms Summers.'

'Shit!' I squeaked, practically jumping through the roof.

Placing my hand across my now pounding heart, I looked up to find Bryce, standing there in all his sweat-stained glory. *Oh, fuck!* His hair was damp, and he had on a loose tank, shorts and a towel tossed over his shoulders. His biceps were simply mouthwatering; and those legs! I could imagine having those wrapped around me in a hot, steamy bath. *Alexis, I think you just drooled on yourself.*

Barely finding the voice to reply, I opened my mouth. 'Good morning, Mr Clark. Sorry, you frightened me.'

'Like a duck to water, I see.'

He looked so incredibly delicious and, again, I found it increasingly hard to speak. 'Yes, so I am. Sorry, Lucinda desperately needed the ladies' room.'

He strutted past me and sat on Lucinda's desk. *Oh, please don't do that, I can't breathe.* His close proximity allowed me to smell the remnants of his workout — which I would normally find off-putting — but for some reason on him it smelled good.

I was obviously blushing.

'You know, Alexis,' he said, leaning toward me, 'Lucinda will go on maternity leave any day now and I will need a replacement. She is a hard act to follow, but I think you could handle it with a bit of training.' He got up and walked toward his office. 'Meet me here for lunch at noon and we'll discuss the finer points.'

Before I could object, he had shut the door behind him. *Shit, is he serious? Work as his personal assistant? What would that mean for my Concierge Attendant traineeship?*

There were too many questions floating around in my head when Lucinda waddled back in.

'Thanks, Alexis, my bladder was at the brink of bursting.' She paused for a minute and appeared to be assessing my expression. 'Are you okay? You look a bit flushed.'

'I think Mr Clark just offered me your job.'

A smile spread across her face in response. 'Well, someone has to do it. He has knocked back all the applicants I have shown him so far. So he likes you, eh? Great! No more point-less searching for applicants who were doomed before they even got here.'

Lucinda's phone buzzed, her smile broadening as she hit speaker. 'Yes, Bryce?' she answered in a singsong voice.

'Block out lunch from noon till 2 p.m. for me, please, Lucy. And schedule training for Alexis to start as of tomorrow. I'm sure she has filled you in already. Alexis, what would you like for lunch?'

'Oh, so I get a choice in regards to lunch, but the job ... that's been decided for me already, yeah?' I asked with a laugh, but still a little shell-shocked.

'On second thoughts, Lucy, order Alexis a grilled calamari salad and an English breakfast tea,' he said quickly, before dis-connecting the call.

I stared at Lucinda in amazement. She just laughed and shrugged her shoulders.

'Do I get a say in this?' I asked with a baffled expression. It was a reasonable question, I thought.

She smiled and handed me the brief. 'When it comes to my brother, Alexis, no, I don't think you do. He always gets what he wants.'

'I guess I'll see you at midday then,' I surrendered, still slightly taken aback.

She put her hands on my shoulders, turned me around, and gently pushed me toward the elevator. 'You're going to love my job, Alexis.'

As we approached the doors, they opened, and a tall man in a grey suit stepped out. He seemed agitated, but smiled and politely said 'good morning' as he held the elevator doors open for me.

'Gareth, this is Alexis. She'll be taking over for me when I have the baby.' *Oh, I am, am I?* Lucy gave me a wink.

'Ah, Alexis, it's always nice to put a face to a name,' he said with an unusual look on his face. His expression left me slightly unnerved as he watched me step into the elevator. I wasn't exactly sure why.

'Likewise, Mr Clark,' I politely responded with a smile, despite the eerie feeling about the man. Gareth Clark was not only vice-president of Clark Incorporated, but also Bryce and Lucy's cousin.

'Please, call me Gareth.'

I pressed the elevator button for hotel reception and nodded to Gareth in response as he removed his hand to allow the doors to close. As I descended to ground level and away from his presence, I was more than glad to get some distance; my skin was crawling with hundreds of little prickles. I couldn't quite put my finger on it, but for some reason Gareth gave me the creeps.

Before reaching the ground floor and still in shock over Mr Clark's proposal — or demand, I should say — I contemplated what it could mean for me. Working as his PA was a terrific opportunity and would look fabulous on my résumé, but I had studied to be a Concierge Attendant and, after only one day, had really enjoyed it. I decided to call Rick, needing someone else's perspective, so I quickly hit the level two button and dialled his number on my phone.

I stepped out of the elevator and headed for the sun deck just as Rick answered his phone.

'Melbourne Mortgages, Rick speaking.'

'Hi, babe, it's me.'

'What's up? You haven't spilled another drink, have you?' he asked with amusement.

'Ha ha, very funny. No, quite the opposite actually. I've just been given a promotion ... I think.'

'Promotion, what do you mean?'

'Mr Clark has asked me to take over from his sister, Lucinda, as his PA when she goes on maternity leave in a couple of weeks.' Silence followed. 'You still there?'

'Yeah, so what does that mean?' he asked with scepticism.

'I don't know, we will have a meeting over lunch to discuss the nitty-gritty. What do you think?'

'Is it more money?'

'Is everything about money for you? I'd assume so, but I think it would mean longer hours. Look, I will see what he says at lunch and talk to you about it tonight.'

'Okay, babe, talk to you tonight. If it's more money, go for it.'

'Great help you are. See ya.' *Well, that phone call was a waste of time.*

For Rick it was always about the money. For me, however, money was not always the deciding factor. I did not want to work longer hours. Longer hours would mean I'd see less of the kids.

Attempting to make a decision now, though, was useless. So I decided I would first hear what Mr Clark had in mind, then determine the path my career would take after that. The problem with this particular course of action was that I felt the decision had already been made for me.

* * *

For the next couple of hours, I spent most of my time reviewing a list of upcoming VIP guests and events that were planned in the hotel precinct over the next month. Midday had come around quite quickly, and I found myself rehearsing questions in my head in preparation for my meeting with Mr Clark. *Right, I'll need to start no earlier than 8.30 a.m. and finish no later than 6.00 p.m. I'll need leniency over school holidays. I'll need an entire Versace wardrobe. I'll need a keycard to your private residence. I'll need an extensive pay rise, and I'll need to watch you work-out in the mornings. As if, Alexis, as if!*

I stepped out of the elevator and into the penthouse foyer, where I found Lucinda beaming at me. 'Hi, Alexis, he's waiting for you,' she said in her singsong voice. She had a ridiculous smile on her face and nodded toward Bryce's door.

I playfully rolled my eyes and shook my head, smiling at her. 'Thank you.'

Upon entering his office, if it were at all possible to be hit by a wall of sexual tension, then that wall just well and truly smacked me in the face. My knees felt weak as I met his gaze, and I found myself questioning if I could, in fact, handle this day in and day out. I guessed there was only one way to find out, depending on his offer and answers to my questions, of course.

Bryce was already comfortably sitting at the conference table in the far corner of his rather large office and lunch had been set out in front of him. As I walked toward him, the food smelled delicious.

'Please sit, Alexis,' he offered, while pointing at a food cloche in front of a seat which I assumed was for me.

Taking my seat, I studied him intently. He really did take my breath away. His vivid blue eyes were incredibly alluring and I felt myself transfixed after only seconds of looking at him. Bryce removed the cloche and, true to his word, directly in front of me was a delectable looking calamari salad.

I picked up a fork, stabbed a piece of calamari and rocket leaf, then looked at him and shook my head.

Before I could accuse him of abusing his powers in the field of research, he laughed. 'It's what I do, Ms Summers.'

'What if I said I was allergic to seafood?' I challenged, raising my eyebrow at him.

'I know mouth-to-mouth, you'd be fine,' he sincerely declared.

Just the sheer mention of mouth-to-mouth had my pussy tingling with excitement. Crossing my legs while mentally telling my pussy to go back to sleep, I raised my eyebrows at him and slowly took a bite. His stare was equally challenging and, if I weren't mistaken, I would take a guess and say he wanted me to stop breathing just so he could prove his proficiency where mouth-to-mouth was concerned.

After I swallowed my mouthful, he removed the cloche cover from his own meal and cut a nice big slice of T-bone steak, pausing when he noticed me watching him.

'It's okay, Mr Clark. Go ahead, I know mouth-to-mouth as well.'

'Well, in that case, Ms Summers, I'll order satay next time.'

I looked at him, slightly perplexed, before deciphering what he had just said. *Hmm, he has a peanut allergy.* Laughing in response, I secretly hoped that he did order a satay next time. The thought of pressing my mouth to his for the sole purpose of successfully breathing life back into him excited me very much. *Oh, no you don't, you little tramp.*

'So, Alexis, I want you. I don't want anyone else. What is it going to take?'

Without any control, I pretty much spat the tomato and bean shoot I had just placed in my mouth back out and onto the plate. 'I'm sorry?' I spluttered, grabbing my napkin. *Oh, that was classy, Alexis.*

He seemed amused with my disgusting display of table manners. 'I want you to be my PA. I won't take no for an answer, Alexis. What is it going to take for you to say yes?'

I quickly gained my composure after his clarification and thought back to the questions I had earlier that day. 'The thing is, Mr Clark, I trained very hard to be a Concierge Attendant. I was starting to like my career change.'

'If you want your position back when Lucy returns, it's yours.'

'Okay, my children always come first. So, with that being said, what hours would you require of me?'

'7 a.m. to 6 p.m.'

I placed my fork down and counter-offered: '8 a.m. to 6 p.m.'

'Deal. What else?' he asked, seemingly quite eager.

I picked up my fork again and nibbled on a piece of calamari, murmuring my next question. 'What is the salary?' *Alexis, you are on fire, this is going well so far.*

'What do you want it to be?'

Once more, I nearly spat out the contents of my mouth. I honestly didn't know how to respond to that question. In the past, if I'd been in a sticky situation I would fake it until I made it, so to speak.

Swallowing, I bit down on my empty fork and looked directly at him. He fidgeted in his seat, then broke my gaze and reached for a glass of water. *Did I just unnerve the infamous Bryce Clark?*

It was in that moment that I decided I would work for this man for free if I had to. There was just something about our chemistry that drew me to him. Deep down, I knew this could spell trouble for me, but I didn't care, or at least I didn't think I did.

'Okay, Mr Clark. I'll be your PA.'

He smiled at my acceptance then stood up, walking to his desk and picking up the phone. 'Lucy, can you let Michelle in, please?'

Almost instantly, the door opened and a stunning, dark-haired Amazonian goddess walked in, pushing a garment rack full of clothing. She carried herself impeccably and seemed to be just as fond of Bryce's blue eyes as I was.

'Michelle, thank you, as per usual you are a treasure,' he said kindly. He was extremely charismatic and knew just what to say to a woman.

'You're welcome, Mr Clark,' she replied with obvious affection.

It seemed she did not want to leave because she stood there a moment, waiting for further instruction ... or, perhaps, praise. It wasn't until Bryce returned to the conference table that she sullenly said 'thank you' and left the room.

I glanced at the rack, noticing the silk mesh dress I had fantasised about earlier that morning; next to the dress were approximately ten other garment bags, not to mention the Versace I had left with dry-cleaning. My jaw dropped and I turned to Bryce.

'All yours, Ms Summers. Think of it as an addition to your salary, which you still need to propose.'

Standing up, I walked over to the rack, my mouth still agape. It not only contained clothing but also held matching shoes and bags. 'This really is too much,' I whispered, my face red with embarrassment.

'Alexis, it's non-negotiable.' He moved to the other side of the rack. 'Now, Lucy will begin your training straightaway, and I will need your salary figure by the end of the day, or

I will decide for you. I have spoken to Abigail and she has found another CA to fill your place. Also, Alexis, when you speak to me, please call me Bryce.'

He held out his hand. I grabbed it and went to shake but he turned my hand over and put it to his mouth, gently kissing the top of it. I swear I nearly convulsed on the spot.

'Thank you,' he said sincerely, his lips lingering a bit longer than necessary.

It was in that moment I realised he had feelings for me.

CHAPTER

5

My hand was still tingling as I looked at myself in the bathroom mirror. *You are imagining this, Alexis. No, no, you're not. You're thirty-five and have a pretty good idea when someone is coming on to you.*

Taking a deep breath as I stared at my reflection, I fixed my hair and patted my cheeks with some cold water. *Maybe he is just a very flirtatious guy? Of course he is, just look at him. He'd have women falling at his feet on a daily basis. No wonder he likes to flirt.* I mentally kept trying to justify his actions, but the more I thought about his behaviour, the more certain I became that he had feelings for me. *It doesn't matter if he has feelings for you, Alexis. You are married. End. Of. Story.*

Agreeing to be his PA was inevitable; I was simply drawn to him. But I knew I would need to tread carefully, especially if he was so brazen with his flirting and because I was enjoying it immensely.

Stepping back from the mirror, I smoothed my dress down, then taking another deep breath, I gave myself a quick pep talk. *Get a grip, Alexis, you can handle this. It's just a little harmless chemistry.* Feeling a new sense of empowerment, I walked out of the bathroom and headed back to Lucinda.

'So, where to start?' Lucinda mused. 'Okay, I'm not going to bore you with instructions on how to meet and greet, answer telephones, or take messages. You already know how to do all that. I think what is most important is to educate you on the "who" of my brother, Bryce Edward Clark. And we can do that by invading his privacy. Follow me,' she grinned mischievously, while forwarding all calls to her mobile and directing me out of the room.

* * *

The door to Bryce's private residence opened when Lucinda swiped her card through the security scanner. As I stepped inside his apartment, the decor that greeted me was very different to what had been in his office. Instead of the cream, mahogany and gold colour scheme, the theme in his private quarters was very masculine: greys, whites, blacks, deep blues. But what mostly drew my eye, were the windows and the quantity of glass ... incredible.

The apartment appeared to be very open plan, making the view the star attraction, and rightfully so. As you walked in, you automatically stepped down into a lowered living area, containing white leather sofas and stunning black and deep-blue silk drapes with silver sheers.

'Wow!' I exclaimed. 'This is just gorgeous, he has great taste.'

'Yes, he does. He knows what he likes.'

Continuing to scan my surroundings, I scoffed when noticing the shiny, black grand piano near the opening to the balcony. 'Can he play?' I asked, gesturing toward it.

'Yes, we both can, but Bryce prefers the guitar.' *Of course he does; the sexy rock god.*

Lucy led me past the sofas and over to the bifold glass doors where I could sneak a peek outside. The balcony was enormous, equipped with a pool, spa and outdoor gym. It then continued right around to the other side of the building.

Amazed by the extravagance, I turned back to face the entrance of the apartment, my eyesight being snagged by something up above. Tilting my head to get the full effect, I admired a glorious, glass spiral chandelier hanging from the ceiling — approximately three levels high. There was also a staircase, running adjacent to the wall near the entrance, leading up to the second floor. I assumed this was where the bedrooms were. The feeling of butterflies churning in my stomach developed as I thought about *his* bedroom. *Get your head out of the gutter, Alexis!*

'Just round here to the left is the kitchen. Bryce loves food and cooks whenever he gets a chance,' Lucinda explained, unaware of my wayward thoughts.

'He cooks, are you serious? All the money in the world and the man cooks?' *He has just escalated from sexy rock god, billionaire, boss-man, to* perfect, *sexy rock god, billionaire, boss-man.*

Following Lucinda into the kitchen, I found myself having cookery-envy. His kitchen was to die for with black marble benchtops that looked like they could have spanned the length of my entire house. *Well, maybe not quite.* There were stainless steel appliances and sleek glossy white cupboards.

But what stood out the most was a single photo of Bryce and Lucinda stuck to the fridge. It made me smile; it was such a sweet sentiment.

'A kitchen is not quite a kitchen without something stuck to the fridge. That's a lovely photo of you both.'

'Pfft, I look terrible. I had awful morning sickness that day. Bryce took me down to St Kilda beach to get some fresh air then pulled out the iPhone and took a selfie of us. He seems to like it though. That, or he is deliberately tormenting me by having it on his fridge.' She screwed up her face as she walked past the photo and back into the living area.

I followed her up the stairs, amazed by how agile she still was for being nearly eight months pregnant. When I was at that stage in my pregnancy with Nate, I had been pretty much couch-bound. With Charlotte though, I was a little better, but nothing compared to Lucinda.

'The second floor is made up of bedrooms,' she explained as she opened a door. 'This is my room for when I stay. I live in Richmond with my partner, Nic. Sometimes I can't be bothered going home, and sometimes I just like to keep "big bro" company.'

Lucinda's room was spacious and feminine, with a pale-pink bedspread, white sheer curtains and decorative cushions. In the far corner of the room was a brand new cot, and in the cot was a stuffed blue dog.

I turned to Lucinda. 'You're having a boy?'

'Yes, we are,' she beamed and, on cue, gently rubbed her belly.

At that very moment, I couldn't help but think of Nate. He was my special little man and I adored him unconditionally. 'That's wonderful, boys are so sweet.'

'And girls aren't?' Lucy asked with curious joviality.

I laughed. 'They are sweet too, just in a completely different way.'

We moved along, quickly perusing a few more guest rooms before stopping at the very end of the hall.

'And this is the master bedroom, Bryce's room,' Lucy explained, holding the door open for me to step inside.

I almost felt intrusive as we entered his private space. In the middle of the room and in front of a feature wall was a king-sized bed. The bathroom was hidden behind the feature wall and it was huge, to say the least. His shower was generous enough to fit a family of four and the spa was deep enough to disappear into entirely. He certainly did have superb taste when it came to his surroundings.

I noticed his aftershave on the vanity next to the sink — Jean Paul Gaultier's Le Male, one of my favourites. I just loved aftershave and perfume, it being a another secret fetish of mine. I must own at least forty bottles of perfume myself. I picked it up and had a sniff ... *mmmm.*

Lucy giggled. 'You right there?'

'Am now. I love this one,' I explained, putting it back down with an expression of just-getting-my-fix.

To my delight — as I kept scanning my surroundings — I could not see any evidence of a Mrs Clark, or a soon-to-be Mrs Clark, there being no woman's perfume, toiletries or clothing. Nor did I see any photos of him with a significant other. Of course, this did not rule out that he could very well be a ladies' man, a player, and have absolutely no intention of tying himself down to anybody. So, I plucked up the nerve to ask Lucinda. After all, this tour was simply a means to get to know the real Bryce.

'Is there a Mrs Bryce?' I asked casually, trying to sound as professional as possible and not the slightest bit interested either way, other than for factual gain, of course.

'No, Bryce is as single as they come. At first I thought he was afraid of sharing what he has ... and himself, for that matter. You know, afraid of the whole "commitment" thing,' she explained, making the quotation gestures with her fingers. 'That, or he was simply too selfish for a relationship. But I've come to realise in recent years that he just hasn't been tempted yet. Hasn't found the right woman to wholeheartedly give himself to. I think that is what he's waiting for. My brother doesn't do things by halves. If Bryce sees something he wants, he goes for it and gets it — professionally and personally.'

I considered what she'd just said as we left his room; it made perfect sense. He was a very powerful man. Money meant power and he had a lot of it. I guess he would be dubious about women and their true intentions. One couldn't really blame him for that.

Once again, I continued to follow behind her until we reached the staircase and began to descend. 'You would think he'd have an elevator in here. How are you coping with these stairs?'

'I'm fine. And he does. It's his personal elevator. It starts at his private basement and accesses every floor of the hotel, every level in his private residence, the helipad and the observatory.'

'Observatory?' I asked in an unnaturally high-pitched voice. *Next I'll find out he has his own personal zoo!*

'Yes,' Lucinda giggled. 'Bryce dabbles in astronomy. It really is magical on the perfect night.'

Nate would love to see the observatory, being obsessively mad for planets, stars and more importantly, *Star Wars*. I'd been meaning to take him to the planetarium at Scienceworks, but I had never gotten around to it. 'Wow! That is pretty impressive. My son would love to see an observatory.'

'Oh, you should tell Bryce! I'm sure he would show Nate. Just between you and me, I think he would thoroughly enjoy explaining all the "blah blah" of what's up there to someone who actually cares.'

I laughed ... not that her mocking was very nice, but it was a typical sibling thing to say.

We reached the lower level and Lucinda opened the doors to the balcony. The fresh summer air hit my senses, a welcome delight. It was a stunning day, and it seemed a shame that this spectacular outdoor space was unoccupied. I wanted nothing more than to kick off my pumps and take refuge on one of the comfortable-looking sun lounges.

Inwardly pouting as we walked past the inviting lounges, I paid attention as Lucinda pointed out various things. 'Pool, gym, and just around this corner is the helipad.'

Following her toward the helipad, we turned the corner to find the large space occupied. Placed beautifully on a large, white letter H was a black helicopter with R44 printed on it and, in gold lettering, the words 'Clark Incorporated'.

'This is the company helicopter. It is mainly used for scenic flights and transportation of VIP guests. Bryce does take it out every now and again, though. However, all flight requests need to be approved by him. Abigail will email you the request forms when a VIP is scheduled, and you will need to get him to sign them off.'

'That sounds easy enough, but backtrack just a couple of steps for me. I'm sure you just said that Bryce takes it out. Do you mean he actually flies it himself?'

'Yes, he is a fully qualified helicopter pilot.'

'Is there anything your brother can't do?' I asked, smiling, yet blown away by his lifestyle.

'Uh huh, he can't sing.'

I couldn't help but laugh. 'Well, there you go. Nobody is perfect.' *But fuck, he is close to it.*

* * *

We sat on the balcony for the rest of the afternoon and in between answering her mobile calls Lucinda filled me in on what would be required of me. Basically, it was whatever Bryce asked for. If he needed room service; order it. If he needed housekeeping; organise it. Schedule meetings, book flights and accompany him to events and appointments if required.

Lucinda and I also got to know each other a lot better. Lucy — as I was now told to call her — was a little younger than me. She was thirty-two and lived in Richmond with her partner, Nic, who was actually a Nicole. They had been together for eight years and had been part of an IVF program. They were over-the-moon in love with each other and it was clear from Lucy's words that she idolised Nicole.

Nicole had rescued Lucy from an extremely dark period in her life. Bryce and Lucy were two of three children to Stephanie and Lindsay Clark. Tragically, both their parents and their youngest brother, Lauchie, died in a car accident when Bryce was nineteen. Lauchie had been only eleven.

Bryce had inherited Clark Incorporated from his father, who at the time had a small chain of hotels in Melbourne and Sydney. Lucy inherited her parents Toorak mansion, but could not bring herself to remain living there, so sold the mansion and bought a couple of smaller properties around

Melbourne. Sadly, Lucy drank and smoked a lot of her inheritance down the drain, sinking into a huge hole of depression and anger after her parents and brother passed away. Bryce, on the other hand, had been determined to make the most of his life, and innovatively expanded and changed the direction of Clark Incorporated into the multi-billion dollar company that it was today.

Bryce and Lucy's cousin, Gareth, was the son of Lindsay's brother, Charles. Charles had had a love-hate relationship with his brother and, according to Lucy, Charles had been extremely jealous of his brother's money and achievements. When Lindsay died and passed the company on to Bryce, Charles was furious and exceedingly bitter towards Bryce — their relationship was still on thin ice. Bryce and Gareth, however, were close, hence Gareth being in the position of vice-president.

Pondering the enormity of Bryce and Lucy's loss, I couldn't help but express my sincerest condolences. 'Lucy, I'm terribly sorry for the passing of your parents and brother, especially when you and Bryce were so young. That must have been unbelievably hard?'

'It was. I hated the world and everyone in it, and I hated the fact that my uncle became my guardian ... not that he had any control over me whatsoever. Bryce objected to the guardianship and fought it in court, but as he was only nineteen years old, he wasn't successful.

'He did everything he could to keep me from getting into trouble, but I was selfish and made his life a living hell. I didn't realise at the time that my actions were causing him more pain and that it was all adding to his not being able to grieve his own loss. I think what also assisted my rebellion and anger was the fact I was subconsciously denying my own sexuality.'

Lucy twisted a ring on her wedding finger and smiled. 'I met Nic in a bar. She was like a ray of sunshine. I'd been in the dark for months and she was the first thing that made me smile after Mum, Dad and Lauchie's death. I was a mess and broken, and she ... well ... she repaired me.'

It was beautiful to bear witness to the depth of Lucy's love for Nic. 'I'm so glad you found your Princess Charming,' I smiled coyly at her.

She laughed. 'That she is —'

'I'm so glad she found her as well,' Bryce interrupted.

Both Lucy and I looked up to find him leaning against the folding door with his arms crossed over his chest and his feet crossed at the ankles. He pushed off from the door with his shoulder and walked toward us, taking a seat next to Lucy. 'So, what has my dear sister been revealing to you?' he questioned, giving her a gentle nudge.

'Nothing, nothing at all,' I offered just a little too quickly, feeling as though we had just been busted gossiping.

My childish response reminded me of Nate when he'd been caught playing with his PlayStation after it had been banned.

Lucy slowly stood up, stretching her back with an uncomfortable scowl. 'Excuse me for a minute, the toilet calls yet again!' she explained, before waddling off.

My heart rate quickened as I met Bryce's eyes. He was smirking at me, so I looked away. That goddamned smirk would be my undoing.

'Your apartment is breathtaking, Mr Clark.'

'Bryce,' he said with a firm yet pleasant tone, reminding me not to call him the former.

'Sorry, I mean Bryce.'

He smiled at my correction and stood up, wandering over to the glass balustrade. 'Do you like heights, Alexis?'

'Sure, they are fine when I have solid ground under my feet,' I replied, standing up slowly and hesitantly making my way over to meet him at the balustrade.

As I took in the distance from my position in relation to the ground forty-three storeys below, my stomach literally dropped to my feet, a sensation of a little light-headedness washing over me. *Okay, maybe not.* I stepped back when Bryce grabbed my arms and placed them back on the railing.

'It helps if you don't look down straightaway. Start by looking directly ahead,' he said softly, positioning himself behind my back and pointing toward the Rialto building. I could feel his breath on my neck, and I found myself clenching my thighs once again. *Oh, holy fuck.*

'Now move your eyesight down to something just a bit lower, then lower again, until you are looking at the ground,' he instructed as I followed his arm, nodding my head lower like a puppet. He was right. It wasn't so gut-wrenching once you allowed yourself time to adjust.

Taking in the view around us, I understood why he lived up here. You felt as though you were on top of the world and looking down upon it. It was empowering.

He moved from behind me and positioned himself to my side with his back against the balustrade. The sight of him looking comfortably cocky and extremely sexy had my mouth parched.

'So, Ms Summers —'

'It's Mrs, Mr Clark, not Ms.'

'So, Mrs Summers ...' he paused. 'Nah, doesn't have the same ring to it,' he said, turning to face the view while gifting me his sexy smirk. *You cheeky bastard.*

With his arms crossed and completely ignoring my gaping jaw, he continued. 'Have you thought of a figure yet, for your salary?'

I hadn't even given it a thought. *Shit. Crap. Balls.*

I quickly glanced at my watch, noticing it was past 6 p.m. *Great! That's my cue to leave.*

Stepping back from the balustrade and mustering enough courage to play his cheeky game with him, I spun on my heel and started to walk inside. 'I don't think you can afford me, Mr Clark,' I called back, before making my way home.

CHAPTER

6

The following weeks went by quite fast. Lucy was a great teacher, and I loved hanging out with her. The job so far was quite easy, actually. The CA's handled Bryce's room service and housekeeping, and apart from politely meeting and greeting his appointments there really wasn't much more to it. If it weren't for the fantastic perve, the electrifying chemistry between us both, and the smirk he threw me countless times a day, it would easily be the most laid-back job ever! Then again, it was quite possible that this was the calm which preceded the storm.

Bryce hadn't talked to me about my salary figure since I so mischievously told him that 'he probably couldn't afford me'. Truth is, I'd happily perve and flirt with him for free. Although I was quite sure my family would not appreciate that notion, especially not my husband. Then again, Rick was a pretty good flirt himself, so technically, we were sort of even. *Yeah, nice rationalisation, Alexis. You keep telling yourself that.*

Rick had asked me what my new salary was going to be after I explained that I'd accepted the promotion. But at the time, I could only tell him was 'a bit more'. This answer had displeased him, and he said I hadn't negotiated 'properly'. But, at the end of the day, I hadn't returned to work for the money. Yeah, the money is undeniably a big help toward bills and for extra spending, and I did want to be well and truly compensated for the time I was giving up with my children; however, my main reason for returning to work was for my social life. I *needed* to get out of the house and amongst other adults in a working environment. I *needed* this for my sanity.

* * *

Sitting behind the reception desk and sipping my hot white-chocolate, I was scanning through the morning's emails. Lucy had not yet arrived at work and Bryce was at the self-defence class, at which he was instructor, for hotel guests. He must be some kind of martial arts guru as well — I wouldn't put it past him.

Noticing an email from payroll addressed to me, I discovered that my payslip was attached. *Finally.*

A small smile crept across my face at the thought of what Bryce had chosen for my salary. And if I was going to be honest, I had liked feeling that small sense of power when I threw that particular ball back into his court.

Biting the inside of my lip in anticipation, I clicked on the attachment and opened it. *Holy fuck! $500,000 annually, minus tax, gives me ... just over $5,000 clear a week. This is* *insane! On second thoughts, Rick will be over the moon. No ... no! It's too much, far too much. Shit, he really can't take a joke, can he? Or is this his idea of a joke. Argh! The man is utterly infuriating.*

As I groaned in frustration, Lucy stepped out of the elevator, looking a little off-colour.

'Good morning, Lucy. You all right?'

'Yeah, just feeling a bit icky today,' she grumbled.

'That's no good. Would you like me to go out back and make you a cup of tea? Tea used to help settle my stomach on the icky days.'

'Thanks, but I need the toilet for like the fifth time this morning. I'll make one when I'm done.'

'Okay, but if you need anything, just yell. I'm only too happy to help.'

She placed her bag down next to me and waddled toward the toilet.

I felt sympathetic for her obvious discomfort, remembering the last month of both my pregnancies being extremely uncomfortable. The aches and pains, and the feeling of pressure on your uterus, were not pleasant at all. Then there was the back pain and tiredness. I had to hand it to her though, she was doing really well, although she should also be resting. Not making the trip into work every weekday.

Making a mental note to try and convince her I was ready to tackle the job alone and that she should start her maternity leave, I looked back at the computer screen and the evidence of my new promotion ... I couldn't possibly agree to that much money, it certainly didn't correspond with the job description. Not to mention that he had to be playing a game with me.

Closing my eyes and running my fingers along the bridge of my nose, I sucked in a long-winded breath just as the elevator doors opened.

Bryce stepped out in his jaw-droppingly sexy work-out gear and already, I felt my resolve diminishing. *Be strong Alexis. Don't let his toned legs, biceps and arse distract you.*

'Good morning, Ms Summers,' he smiled seductively.

That's it. He not only said 'Ms' but he's smirking at me, too. Right, here goes.

'Mr Clark ...' *Oh, he looks HOT! Focus, Alexis.* '... I don't know what game you are playing with me, but $500,000, really? That's absurd. I can't possibly accept that.'

He suddenly picked up his pace as he made his way toward me, stopping and sitting on the edge of my desk. *Does he seriously need to do that?*

'Is it not enough, Alexis? I'm sorry, just tell me what you want and I'll pay it. I don't want anyone else for my PA. So, whatever you want, it's yours,' he pleaded, a worried expression on his face. His almost distraught demeanour made it clear that his exuberant offer was, in fact, a serious one. *Shit! Now I've come across as demanding and ungrateful.*

'Bryce, it's enough. It's more than enough. It's far too much. My job description doesn't warrant $500,000. I'm sorry, I should've just been professional and upfront with you in the first place.' I grabbed a piece of paper and scribbled down $85,000, folded it and placed it in his hand. 'Here, this is more than enough,' I smiled apologetically at him.

He opened the piece of paper and shot up from the desk. 'Absolutely not!'

Instantly, I felt that I had offended him. 'I'm sorry I —'

'It stands at $500,000, Alexis. And if you think you are not doing enough to "warrant" it ...' he said, even performing the little quotation actions with his fingers — *how cute* — '... then I will have to give you more to do. Starting with tonight, I'll need you to stay back and attend a meeting with me. I am renovating some of the rooms in the City Promenade building to be more family-friendly and, seeing as you are a mum, your input would be perfect.'

Feeling terrible for offending him, I had the incredible urge to want to run my hand through his luscious blond hair and tell him, 'It's fine. I'll do whatever you say'. How he could turn me from being so angry and infuriated with him one minute, to wanting to nurture him like a child the next, was beyond me.

Before I could say anything in response, Lucy appeared in the doorway of the conference room. She was standing awkwardly and looked very distressed. 'Um, I think my waters just broke,' she blurted out.

At Lucy's sudden confession, Bryce was up like a shot and by her side in no time. 'Right, we'll take the chopper. Where is your hospital bag?' he asked, panic written over his face, but despite his clear anxiety, he remained calm.

'It's in my room ... oh, crap, that hurts,' she winced, squeezing his hand.

Instinctively, I looked at my watch. 'Tell me when the contraction stops, Lucy. We need to time them. Just breathe, hon. Nice deep breaths and it will ease shortly.'

Moments later, I noticed her body language suggesting the contraction was easing, her tense form beginning to relax. 'Okay, that was just over thirty seconds long. Tell me when the next one begins, okay?'

'Okay,' she nodded as Bryce helped her over to one of the sofas in the waiting area.

'Here, take a seat. I'll go get your bag and prepare the chopper. Alexis, stay with her and clear my schedule, please.'

I placed my hand on Lucy's back. 'Bryce, it's fine. Go and have a quick shower. I'll ring the birthing suite and speak to a midwife. Lucy, what hospital are you booked in at?'

'The Royal Women's ... argh!' she cried out in pain, her body tensing underneath my hand.

Bryce stilled, seemingly unsure of what do to. I looked down at my watch again, taking note it had been six minutes since her last contraction. 'Breathe through it,' I explained as I rubbed her back and, keeping an eye on the duration of the contraction, I noted once again that it was just over thirty seconds long. 'Okay, you've got time, Bryce. Go, I'll let the hospital know you're flying her there shortly.'

He nodded and took off toward his apartment.

'Lucy, do you want me to call Nic for you?'

'No, I'll do it. My phone is in my bag.'

I stood up and fetched it for her. 'Your contractions are just over thirty seconds long and six minutes apart, so you're doing really well,' I encouraged as I handed her the phone and went back to my desk.

Picking up the phone, I dialled the Royal Women's Hospital and spoke to a midwife.

'Hello, I'm here with Lucinda Clark, a patient who is booked in to give birth at your hospital. She has gone into labour and her contractions are approximately five to six mins apart and between thirty and forty seconds long. Her waters broke nearly twenty minutes ago. Lucinda's brother is Mr Bryce Clark, and he will be flying her in by helicopter,' I explained.

She hesitated when I informed her that their mode of transport was to be by helicopter. 'He can drive her in. By the sounds of it, she's in early labour.'

'I understand that, but Mr Clark will not take no for an answer. What helipad does he have clearance to land on?'

She placed me on hold just as Lucy started her next contraction. The space of time from the last one had now decreased to five minutes, and this particular contraction lasted an extra ten seconds longer.

When the midwife finally came back on the line, I informed her of the change. She advised that Bryce had clearance to land on helipad two.

Thanking her, I hung up.

In the meantime, Lucy had dialled Nic and was explaining the situation. While she was distracted, I took a quick look at Bryce's schedule. It was not too busy, thank goodness. He had an appointment between 11 a.m. and noon, then a Jessica at 3 p.m. *Hmmm, Jessica, I didn't make that appointment!*

Lucy sighed as she hung up from Nic. 'She's a worrywart. I just hope she drives safely.'

'Is she far from here?'

'No, she is an interior decorator with a firm on Collins Street.'

'Oh, good. Lucy, I need to cancel an appointment Bryce has made with a Jessica. I don't know who she is or her contact details.'

'Jessica is ... oh, shit!' She gripped the couch. 'Shit! This one is ... arrrrggh ... stronger.'

I ran over to her and rubbed her back. 'Just concentrate on your breathing. I know it's hard but it helps.'

Lucy looked up at me intently and took deep breaths. In and out. In and out. Soon enough, the contraction eased. However, they were definitely lasting longer and were now consistently five minutes apart.

'Alexis, I am so glad you are here,' she stated, sincerely.

'I'm glad I am, too. I know it's scary the first time. But I promise you, you are doing really well.'

'Thank you, I'm just doing what you tell me,' she said as she closed her eyes. Just as her lids fell shut, they quickly opened back up again. 'Oh, you asked about Jessica? She is Bryce's therapist, remind him about the appointment and he will call her and cancel it himself.'

'Oh, okay.' I smiled a little half-heartedly. The fact that she mentioned he had a therapist shocked me for the slightest of seconds. But, after allowing my brain to process the information, I guessed it was not so surprising really, considering his loss.

Bursting through the door like a madman and breaking into my inner thoughts, Bryce entered the room, undoubtedly looking more anxious. 'How is she?'

Anxious or not, he looked glorious. His hair was slightly towel-dried, and he had thrown on a pair of jeans, Nikes and a t-shirt.

'She's fine,' I reassured him, trying not to stare too long at the way his t-shirt clung to his biceps. 'Her contractions are lasting a bit longer and are more frequent, so whenever you are ready. You have clearance to land on helipad two.'

'Good. Come on, sis,' he directed, helping Lucy to stand up and allowing her to completely lean her weight on him.

I put her handbag in his free hand. 'Don't worry about anything. I've got everything under control here. I'll cancel your appointments and reschedule them. Now go. And good luck, Lucy, you'll be fine. Soon you'll be holding your beautiful little boy and this will all be worth it.'

I kissed her cheek and stepped back, which was when she grabbed me. 'Please, come with us. I need you, Alexis. Please?' she begged me, her expression quite panicked.

I looked at Bryce, hesitantly.

'Alexis, you're coming,' he confirmed.

Grabbing my bag, I took back Lucy's handbag from his arm, and we made our way out to the helicopter.

* * *

Moments later, we were sitting in the chopper, Lucy next to me while I held her hand, offering her as much reassurance as I could. It was clear she was now highly agitated as her contractions were stronger.

'Just breathe through it, Lucy. Big, deep breaths. Suck the air in through your nose and breathe out through your mouth ... yes, like that ... good.'

Trying to keep my focus on Lucy, I was barely aware that Bryce was talking to someone, somewhere, through his headset. Honestly, I had no idea what he was saying and didn't pay much attention. Which was why when we lifted off the roof, the sudden escalation surprised me.

The next thing I knew, we were headed toward the hospital. I took in the view of the city. It was simply amazing. For me, the flight only took what seemed like a few minutes, partly because I was enjoying the aerial view, and partly because the Royal Women's Hospital was on the outskirts of the city. So, by chopper, I guess it *was* only a few minutes.

Bryce gently placed the helicopter down on the helipad. His piloting skills were good, really good. Unfortunately though, it was not the time to admire those skills as Lucy was currently panting and not far from making noises similar to that of a whale's song.

Helping her into a waiting wheelchair, Bryce held her hand as the nurse wheeled her from the rooftop and into the hospital. I tailed behind, but then paused as they entered the birthing suite.

'I'll wait outside,' I said as they went through the door.

'No, Alexis. Please come in. Arrrggh!' *Here come the whale impressions.* I knew better than to argue with a woman in labour, so I followed closely behind.

'Ms Clark, would you like some pethidine for the pain?' a midwife asked as she placed the foetal monitoring straps across Lucy's stomach.

'No! No drugs,' Bryce declared, glaring at the midwife. 'She has a history with addiction, so NO drugs.'

'It hurts, it hurts, give me something ... anything! God-damn it, Bryce, if I don't have something for this pain, I will rip your fucking head off,' Lucy screamed.

Bryce looked at me in horror, and all I could do was smile at him sympathetically.

'Epidural?' she asked the nurse. 'What about a bloody epidural?' Lucy looked pleadingly at the midwife, but I had a feeling it was a bit too late for an epidural.

The midwife positioned herself between Lucy's legs, then stood back up and proceeded to move around the room like this was any other day to her. She then casually answered the question I already knew the answer to.

'You are too far dilated for an epidural. If you don't want the pethidine injection, you can have gas.'

'What's in the "gas"?' Bryce sternly asked.

'Give me the freakin' gas. I don't care what's in it, just give me the gas,' Lucy spat out.

I let go of Lucy's hand and walked over to Bryce. He was clearly starting to lose his shit, so I put both hands on his shoulders. 'Bryce, the gas is fine. It's nitrous oxide. It's a form of anaesthetic. It won't hurt her.'

He glanced over my shoulder toward his sister, trepidation in his eyes.

'Hey, you're doing well. Just hold her hand and let her yell at you and hate you for being a male. She will love you again when it's all over, I promise.' I lightly pushed him over to the side of her bed and asked the nurse for a face washer.

Making my way back around to the other side of the bed, I placed the dampened cloth on Lucy's forehead. 'There you go, Lucy. You're doing so well. Deep breaths, suck that gas in and try to relax. Your son will be in your arms soon, just focus on that.'

A second midwife came into the room and announced that Nicole Smith was outside.

'There you go. Nic is here,' I reassured her. 'I'll go and get her, okay?'

Prying my hand out of Lucy's tight grasp, I gave her shoulder a squeeze then looked up at Bryce and smiled. The poor guy could only manage a half-grin. I realised that this must've been extremely hard for him.

I let myself out of the birthing suite and found Nic pacing just outside the door. She gave me a who-the-hell-are-you look before I introduced myself.

'Hi, Nic. I'm Alexis. You can go in now.'

Leaving no time for thanks, she burst into the birthing suite.

* * *

After one of the nurses directed me to a waiting room, I made myself a cup of tea. Then, taking out my phone, I made a few calls.

Firstly, I needed to call Abigail and advise her that the penthouse was unattended. Secondly, I cancelled Bryce's 11 a.m. appointment. Then I called housekeeping to attend to the mess Lucy had left behind in the bathroom. I also left Bryce's five o'clock appointment as it was, figuring I'd talk to him about it when he came out, together with the appointment he had with Jessica. I also decided to give Rick a quick call and let him know about my exciting morning so far, together with the over-exuberant salary increase and the fact I could be late home.

'Melbourne Mortgages, you're speaking with Rick.'

'Hi, it's me.'

'Hey me, your number didn't come up?'

'Oh yeah, sorry. I'm calling from my work mobile.'

'What's up, did you find out the salary figure?'

'Yeah, I did. Steady on, I'll get to that in a minute. I'm just letting you know that I'm at the Royal Women's Hospital. Lucy has gone into labour.'

'Oh, nice, so why are you there?' he asked, sounding a little confused.

'She was anxious and didn't want me to leave her. I think my experience in the whole pushing out babies department was comforting for her. We flew here in the company helicopter!'

'Fair enough, well, why wouldn't you?' he stated, his blasé attitude rolling from him.

I shook my head at his nonchalance. 'Anyway, I negotiated my salary with Mr Clark this morning. He wants to pay me, and wait for it ... $500k, but it will mean I need to attend out-of-hours meetings and events, possibly starting with tonight.'

'Fuck! $500 grand. Are you for real?' he asked, his voice escalating a few octaves.

'Yes, I know, it's ridiculous, but that's the figure and conditions. Thought you'd be happy.'

'Happy! Maybe I should get you to negotiate with my boss. Shit, I'm speechless. Wow! Lexi, the breadwinner. Never thought I'd say that.'

Rick began to laugh, or more to the point, mock me.

I rolled my eyes. 'Is that right, Mr Summers? Well, seeing I am the new household breadwinner, I expect a hot, roast dinner on the table waiting for me when I get home. And an hour-long foot rub, because I hate to admit it, but these shoes are starting to punish me.'

'A foot rub? Really?'

'Yes, I'm feeling brave.'

'Your wish is my command, Miss Half-a-mil.'

I laughed. He really did know how to make a joke about pretty much anything.

'Yeah, and don't you forget it. I'll call you later when I know what's happening. Love you, bye,' I said, hanging up just as Bryce walked around the corner and into the waiting room. He literally collapsed into the chair.

I stood up, walked over to where he was slumped, and sat next to his seat. 'Is everything all right? How is Lucy?'

He remained quiet and didn't answer me at first, seemingly a little shocked.

'Bryce?' I probed again, starting to feel a little worried.

Snapping out of his trance, he met my eyes with his own. 'Yes, yes, she's fine. She's terrifying, but fine. Guess what?' he asked, piercing me with his emotion-filled, blue windows-to-his-soul. I could see his eyes start to well with tears, the sincerity and pure love he held gripping at my heart.

'I'm an uncle. I'm a bloody uncle, Alexis. Uncle Bryce.'

Jumping up, overjoyed, he pulled me into his arms. *Geez, he's strong.*

He hugged me so tightly then practically spun me around, repeating his happy news. 'I'm an uncle!'

In that moment, our eyes met yet again, and my body welcomed his embrace. My heart also welcomed his emotion, so I smiled brightly in return.

He gently put me down and apologised, then ran his hands through his hair. *Oh fuck. He looks so hot when he does that.* 'Sorry, I'm just so ... so ... shit, unprepared,' he groaned, slumping back down on the seat. 'I don't know the first thing about being an uncle.'

The man before me was like no other. He was rich, powerful, strong, obnoxious — a force to be reckoned with. Yet he was also kind, caring, selfless, scared and unsure of himself.

Sitting down on the arm of his chair, I offered some reassurance. 'I'm not an uncle, but I am an aunty, and all you need to know is how to love your nephew. Bryce, I think you've already got that pretty much taken care of.'

Instinctively, I touched his leg and gave him an encouraging look. At my touch, we both turned our gaze toward my hand, my hand which lay upon his leg. For a second, the electricity that surged through my body was almost too hard to bear, the chemistry between us recognisably obvious.

Instantly, I retracted my hand and stood up, then turned my back to him in the hope he couldn't sense my embarrassment. 'I don't know what the coffee is like here, but the tea is all right. Can I make you one?' I offered, silently cursing myself for being so stupid.

'No, I'm going to need something stronger. Come on,' he stated, while standing up and gently grabbing my arm.

He then led me out of the room.

CHAPTER

7

'Where are we going?' I asked as he ushered me along the hospital corridor.

'I need to take the chopper back. They don't allow long-term parking on their helipads. Chopper parking fines are a killer,' he advised while waggling his eyebrows.

I scoffed at his lame joke, but admittedly, I liked his sarcastic sense of humour. It was fun to play with.

'Fair enough, that makes perfect sense.'

He led me out to the helipad, keeping his hand on the small of my back the entire time. Then, as I was propping myself up on the step of the helicopter, he placed one of his hands on my hip and the other one on my arse in order to boost me up. *Not that I really needed boosting.*

I ignored his inappropriate grope, not wanting to make a big deal of it. But that sweet feeling in between my legs was hard to overlook.

Once seated, Bryce reached over to buckle me in and I let him, without pointing out that I had done it myself earlier. He positioned his head only centimetres from mine. I sucked in a breath, taking in his luscious scent. *Oh, please hurry up and get that freaking buckle in, I'm about to hyperventilate.*

Noticing my unease, he smirked, so I glared at him. 'You're enjoying this, aren't you?'

'Yes, but your safety is my utmost concern, Ms Summers,' he said with a wink. 'There you go, all buckled in.'

He leaned over again and reached for something underneath my seat, his head now basically in my lap. *Seriously Bryce, you are killing me.* I clenched my thighs together as hard as they would go. *Think about poo, and snot, and baby vomit. And all things disgusting, Alexis.*

This man was getting the better of me. I wasn't sure if I liked him getting the better of me. Let's face it, I did like it, but did I like him having the upper hand? No, I didn't think that I did. Maybe I could quite possibly step it up a little and try and beat him at his own smirking, flirting and groping game. But would it work? Or would it just fuel his fire? Also, was that crossing the line? I was married, and he wasn't. *For the love of fuck!*

I was dwelling on it far too much, probably because I'd just had an emotional couple of hours. *It's easy, Alexis, go with the flow, but don't cross any lines.*

Taking in his close proximity to my lap, I raised an eyebrow. 'Do you know what it is you are looking for down there, Mr Clark?' I asked with a seductive undertone, while opening my legs a little to allow him easier access and find whatever it was he needed to find under my seat.

Although I had opened my legs just slightly, I made damn sure I kept my knees well and truly together while waiting for his response.

He gritted his teeth and didn't look at me for a moment or two. Then, when he finally met my gaze, his eyes burned with lust. 'I always know what I'm looking for down in this vicinity, Ms Summers.'

He removed his hand from beneath my seat and placed a headset in my lap. It took every ounce of my willpower to keep my knees together as we stared at each other intently.

'I should hope so, Mr Clark,' I said quietly, while putting the headset on.

He took one look at me and burst into laughter.

Mortified by his sudden change of attitude, I asked why he was laughing, hoping it had nothing to do with my obvious flirting. 'What's so funny?'

He leaned in, took the headset off my head and turned it around, putting it on the correct way. He then continued to laugh and shook his head as he closed my door. *Oh, Alexis, give up now. You are embarrassing yourself.*

He was still laughing as he climbed into his seat.

* * *

On our way back to the hotel, I had a better opportunity to take in the aerial view of Melbourne, this time not having a woman in labour panting next to me.

City Towers stood towering over the Yarra River, its reflection in the water mirroring its impressiveness.

Circling the magnificent building once, I shouted through the headset as we began to descend, although I forgot I didn't need to shout.

'Admiring your handiwork, Mr Clark? Your building really is sensational, and the view is just beautiful.'

'The one next to me is far better,' he said softly through the headset.

Shocked, I looked over at him, but he didn't return my gaze. Instead, he focussed his attention on placing the helicopter down safely.

Once we were landed on the roof, I realised just how much skill and accuracy was needed to fly and manoeuvre such an aircraft, especially when such limited space was on offer. He really was a talented man.

After the rotor blades had slowed, Bryce helped me out of the cockpit. The awkwardness from his declaration moments ago was hanging loosely in the air and, because of this, I purposely didn't linger for long, instead choosing to head inside.

He followed and offered me a seat. 'Please, take a seat, Alexis. Would you like a drink?'

'Yes, please, I'd love one.'

Walking over to his bar, he retrieved two glasses from a cupboard then poured himself a Scotch and me a gin.

'Thank you,' I said, accepting the drink and shaking my head at the same time.

He sat down on the lounge opposite me and raised his eyebrows to question my head shake.

'You and your creepy research, Mr Clark.'

Gin was my alcoholic drink of choice. *How does he know these things?*

'It's what —'

I knew exactly what he was about to say, so cut him off mid-sentence and mimicked his voice. 'I know, I know. "It's what I do, Ms Summers."' I raised my glass. 'Cheers, congratulations, Uncle Bryce.'

He squinted his eyes at me, and I reckon if we were a lot younger, he would have probably poked his tongue out or stuck his thumb on his nose and twiddled his fingers. Instead, being the mature, respectable businessman that he was, he leaned forward and clinked my glass with his own. 'Thanks. What a morning! I've got to hand it to you ladies, that is one hard act to follow,' he admitted before taking a swig of his drink.

I laughed. 'What? Childbirth? Ha, that's not an act. She did a great job, and so did you, by the way.'

He looked upon me with sincerity. 'I wouldn't have been able to do it if you weren't there. Really, Alexis, you were amazing and you kept me grounded. That's ...' he hesitated for a small moment, '... that's not something I'm used to.'

Leaning back on the couch, he put one arm up on the headrest and the other arm — Scotch in hand — on his leg. He looked so comfortable, and so incredibly sexy in his jeans and t-shirt.

Slowly, I allowed my eyes to rake over his body, taking note that his t-shirt was designed to be loose. Except, due to the size of his pecs and biceps, the material clung to him in all the right places.

I took a much needed sip of my drink and swallowed heavily. 'Thank you, but it was nothing really. It pays to have experienced it yourself, that's all,' I said dismissively, trying to evade his compliment.

Honestly, I was not very good at accepting compliments, and that wasn't because I was never on the receiving end of them — because I was. Rick had a habit of telling me he loved me and praising me for different things, in his own kind of way. No, the reason I was unable to handle such flattery was because I didn't think I deserved sentiments for merely being me. Now, if I had physically delivered Lucy's son, well, yes, I'd accept the praise.

Changing the subject — in the hope of avoiding any further awkwardness — I remembered to mention his appointments. 'Oh, by the way, you have Jessica scheduled at 3 p.m. I didn't know who she was or how to contact her, so I was unable to cancel. Also, I didn't cancel the five o'clock meeting either.'

He nodded in approval. 'Don't worry about Jessica, I'll deal with her.'

I sensed that he had no idea that Lucy had, in fact, filled me in on who Jessica was exactly. And that was okay. I completely understood why he would see a therapist and why he would want to keep that to himself — the trauma he'd been through as a young man was terrible.

I decided not to question him any further about Jessica. If he was protecting his pride, or privacy, then who was I to bring that protection down.

'So, Alexis, did Lucy give you a tour when you were here last?'

'Yes, just briefly. Your apartment is amazing, you have wonderful taste. She showed me around this level and pointed out you had a private elevator and an observatory. It was only a quick tour, mainly just to familiarise me with ...' I gestured to him, '... yours truly, so that I can do my job more efficiently.'

I could hear myself starting to sound defensive, not wanting him to think I had snooped around his place.

'And rightly so. You will need to get to know me *very* well in order to do your job properly, which is why I have configured your keycard to allow access to my apartment.'

'Oh ... thanks,' I replied sheepishly, while taking another sip of my drink and feeling a blushing wave of what-the-fuck roll over me. *Shit, access to his private residence.*

'So, what else has my darling sister told you about me?' he asked, casually.

I glanced at him over the rim of my glass, taking in how relaxed he looked as he lounged back in his seat, foot resting on top of his knee. His posture screamed a touch of arrogance. I liked it.

When I didn't answer straightaway, he ran his hand through his hair, and it was this display that seemed to trigger my inner naughty-Alexis.

'Who says she's told me anything? I may have my own talent in creepy research,' I replied just as casually, deciding to mimic his relaxed position by wiggling back into my seat, crossing my legs and putting one arm behind my head. *Alexis, you probably look ridiculous!*

Bryce's stare penetrated my body to its core, and the immense physical and sexual tension in the small space between us made my heart pound vigorously within the confines of my chest.

I noticed his free hand clench into a fist then release again. *Alexis what are you doing?* It was only now that I began to understand just how much I was affecting him and possibly even torturing him. *This isn't me. I'm not normally like this. It's just ... I can't help myself around him. I think he does this to me, surely?*

'Well, let's hear it ... your creepy research that is,' he requested, his tension easing.

Taking a deep breath, I vocally exhaled what I had learned thus far. 'Okay. You are incredibly wealthy and innovative, and you have created an empire of luxurious hotels worldwide. You're thirty-six years of age and adore your sister and baby nephew. You have impeccable taste in decor. You are a helicopter pilot, guitarist, pianist, astronomer and martial arts guru. You like to cook, conduct creepy research and you have an allergy to nuts.'

He leaned forward and placed his empty glass on the coffee table between us while displaying a conceited expression. 'Is that all?' *Grrr, the arrogance of this man.*

With just as much confidence, I placed my empty glass down on the coffee table also. 'No, I have more. You suffered a devastating loss when your parents and younger brother died in a car accident. You have an estranged relationship with your uncle, yet seem to get along with his son. You are highly desirable to women, yet you remain single. Why? Because you haven't met your match yet.'

As the last word fell from my tongue, I realised what I had just said aloud and sat there frozen with shame. *Oh fuck, did I just say all that? Shit, shit, he is going to have me thrown out.*

Shooting straight up from my seat, I put my hands to my mouth and mumbled my apology. 'Shit, I'm so sorry. I, I, I didn't mean to say ... shit!'

Turning around, I then practically ran for the front door.

I had made it across the room when seconds later I felt his hand on my arm. He spun me to face him and pinned me against the entryway wall, placing both hands against the wall on either side of my head.

Pinned in and with nowhere to go, I had no choice but to stare into his heated eyes. 'I'm sorry, Bryce. I shouldn't have said any of that. It was inappropriate and rude. I'm so sorry.'

He leaned in closer, only centimetres from my face. 'Don't be sorry, you were right, except for one thing. I have found my match,' he whispered, then moved his hands from the wall and placed them on the sides of my face, closing the distance between us and kissing me passionately.

I was momentarily stunned, my hands splayed on the wall behind me. At first I wanted to fight him off, but he tasted so good. He truly was a superb kisser, his lips so soft and his tongue, incredible — it possessed mine entirely.

Opening my eyes, I gently pushed him back. 'Stop,' I whispered, 'I can't do this.'

He didn't argue, just rested his forehead on mine.

'I'm sorry. I can't do this, Bryce. I'm married, and I love my husband. I'm not the kind of person to cheat, ever,' I explained, fighting back the tears.

He moved aside to provide some space between us, then put one hand in his hair and the other across his mouth. 'Shit, Alexis. No, I'm sorry. Fuck!' he growled, remorse clearly present in his eyes. He turned away from me and headed toward the kitchen.

Standing there with my back against the wall for what seemed like an eternity, I began to understand the gravity of what had just happened. *This is all your fault, Alexis. You flirted with him knowing he had feelings for you. You crossed the line and led him on, and now you have hurt him and fucked up your job.*

Angry with myself and determined to make things right, I pushed off the wall and cautiously made my way to the kitchen. As I entered, I found Bryce leaning against the bench with his head in his hands.

'Bryce,' I said softly, my voice trembling, 'this is all my fault. I shouldn't have flirted with you. I was enjoying it a lot — maybe too much — but I let it go too far. I'm sorry. I never thought you would want to take it any further. I'll go and clear out my desk.'

His head shot up from his hands. 'Alexis, no,' he said firmly, yet with a fragile manner. 'Please, don't leave. I should never have kissed you without your consent. I promise it won't happen again. I want you to stay, and I think you want to stay, too.'

I did want to stay, more than anything. The past couple of weeks had been amazing. I had felt energetic, exhilarated, and a bit like the Alexis of old; the Alexis I once was before deciding to stay home and raise my kids. Don't get me wrong. I love my kids, and I love being a mother and wife, but I gave up my single life very early on, and sacrificed my career for a family. I would never go back on those decisions, nor do I regret any of them. It was just ... this was now the time to get a little bit of the old me back, and I needed that for my own sanity. *Alexis, you just lost control a little bit, that's all.*

'No, Bryce, you're right. I don't want to leave. I love being here, I feel like I was meant to be here. But I am married, and I have two beautiful children who depend on me. They depend on me to make decisions in their best interest. What happened moments ago was *not* in their best interest.'

'I know. I'm sorry. Just don't leave, I need you to stay.'

'I'm not going anywhere, Bryce, not if you don't want me to, but I do need some air. You're about to see Jessica, and I need some lunch.'

He appeared to sigh with relief. 'All right, in that case, take as much time as you need. Although tonight's meeting will still go ahead. So I'll see you back in the office at five?' he asked, giving me an unsure smile.

I nodded my head and exited the room, leaving his apartment and heading for the elevator. I had to get some fresh air and dissect what the hell just happened. What I did know is that what had just happened was horribly wrong ... but somehow it felt right, it felt very right.

How could that be?

CHAPTER

8

Stepping into the elevator, I pressed level two and headed for what felt like my sanctuary in the hotel — the sun deck. Unfortunately, though, it was far too busy and certainly not the place I should be in order to clear my head. So, instead, I decided I would go and check out the aquarium.

The City Towers aquarium was built like a cylinder, standing two storeys high. It was surrounded by a spiral staircase that traversed levels one and two, allowing you a 360 degree view of the tank.

Peering through the glass exterior, I watched an array of different tropical fish swimming around. I wasn't sure what species the majority of the fish were. However, I could identify the small sharks, the stingray and the Nemo lookalike.

As I stood there, I felt as though my mind was swimming about just like the fish — in and out, up and down, around and around. A feeling of terrible guilt surged through me as

I remembered having allowed Bryce to continue his kiss. But most of all, I felt awful for wanting him to do so. If Rick ever found out what had just transpired, he'd be furious, but more importantly, hurt.

Many years ago, Rick had become very close to a family friend, and although they never ended up in a passionate embrace, it still hurt me terribly. I think I was more disappointed that he had allowed himself to get into that type of situation in the first place. Yet here I was in the same position with Bryce, and it had happened so easily.

I was positive I didn't want to resign from my new job. Clearly, I wanted to stay. I wanted to resume the friendships I had made with other employees, and I wanted to continue to earn good money. Easy money ... really.

As I watched the colourful aquatic picture before me, I realised that the reason I wanted to stay was for the simple fact that I loved it at City Towers. I loved my surroundings, loved my new sense of freedom and I loved finding my feet in the working world again.

However, things had changed. One thing was now abundantly clear; I had to be stronger. I had to maintain a professional — and professional only — relationship with Bryce. I simply had no choice if I was going to stay.

Stopped on the landing between the two levels, I gazed at the Nemo, the little orange and white clownfish, swimming back and forth. I could've sworn he even twitched his fin at me in a show of boldness. *Don't judge me, Nemo. I really am a good person.*

He swam off — probably in disgust, or in search of his dad — so I peered deeper into the tank, hoping that I could lose myself in the underwater world of weightlessness. That's when I noticed someone returning my gaze, the magnified male face scaring the absolute shit out of me. It wasn't long before I realised it was, in fact, Gareth, and he was around the other side of the tank.

He smiled, waved, and started to climb the steps toward me. 'Alexis, it's nice to see you again. So, how have you settled in?'

Gareth was attractive, in a scruffy kind of way. He wasn't as tall as Bryce, but you could see a very faint similarity in their appearance; it was obvious they were related in some way. Gareth's hair was light brown and short, and he had deep brown eyes. I didn't know what it was about him, but he gave me the creeps. He was pleasant enough. He just gave me the heebie-jeebies.

'Hi, Gareth, I've settled in just fine. Although I'll be without my teacher now.'

He looked at me, quizzically. 'Oh?'

'Lucy gave birth this morning,' I answered, regretting the words the moment they left my mouth.

A look of disappointment appeared across his face, displaying that he had no idea she had gone into labour. *Shit! Did I just put my foot in it?*

He replaced his initial look of shock with a fake expression of delight. 'Lovely! What did she have? A boy or a girl?'

Again, he seemed to have no idea.

Not wanting to share any further information with him — as it wasn't mine to share — I tried my best to flip him off. 'Um, I'm not too sure, Gareth. Listen, I hate to be rude, but I really have to be somewhere. It was nice to see you again,' I offered, smiling uneasily before climbing the stairs to level two, all the while feeling his stare pierce deep into my back, leaving me with an unwelcome chill.

* * *

I made my way to the hotel kitchen in order to seek refuge from Gareth's probing questions, but also because I was starving hungry. Looking at the contents of the staff fridge, I opted to grab myself a salad sandwich and a much needed cup of tea.

As I was about to head back to my desk, Abigail walked into the room. 'Alexis, how are you, dear? How's Lucy doing? Did she have the baby?'

'Yes, Abigail, she did. She did a wonderful job. I'm hoping to go and see her tomorrow sometime.'

'Oh, that's good news. So how are you settling into your new position?'

'Just fine, thanks. Mr Clark is a lovely person and very easy to work for.' *He is also incredibly irresistible and tempting, and I was lip-locked with him just over an hour ago.*

'That's wonderful, Alexis. I'm so glad you are enjoying the change, considering it was not too long after your employment began. You must have made quite the impression on him.'

I nodded, gingerly.

'If you do see Lucy tomorrow, please pass on my congratulations. Babies are such wonderful gifts,' she cooed.

I knew only too well what she meant. My babies were the greatest gifts I'd ever received, and I missed them terribly. I felt awfully guilty for not seeing them as much as I would have liked of late, adding that guilt to my now ever-growing list of culpability.

The Alexis Summers List of Shame ... Item number one: kissed a man who was not my husband. Item number two: abandoned my two children to work for the man I kissed who was not my

husband. Item number three: enjoyed the kiss from the man who
was not my husband.

It was obvious to me — and to make up for my time
away — that I needed to do something special with Nate and
Charli on the weekend. The thought of bringing them with
me to see Lucy and the baby was definitely an option. And
then maybe I could swing past the hotel afterward so that they
could see where I worked. This notion made me smile, knowing that they would wholeheartedly enjoy that.

'Yes, of course, Abigail. I'll be sure to pass on your congratulations. And you're right, babies are the greatest gifts of all,'
I said with fond accord. 'I'm sorry, but I really must go. I've
been summoned to a meeting with Mr Clark to brainstorm
ideas for the new family-friendly rooms in the Promenade.'

Abigail raised her eyebrows. 'Really? That's quite impressive, Alexis. Good luck,' she said with a smile, while moving
aside so I could pass.

I pushed on the swinging door of the staff kitchen with my
backside and smiled at Abigail. 'Thank you.'

Then I headed for the elevator.

* * *

Ascending to the penthouse floor with a drink and sandwich in hand, I pondered what Abigail had said. *Impressive?*
What did she mean by impressive? The fact that the Promenade
is being renovated? That I'm helping with ideas? Or something
else entirely?

It was obvious to me that there was so much more going
on in and around the hotel than I was aware of. Then again,
the fact that that notion surprised me was, in itself, surprising.
After all, I had only been employed with Clark Incorporated

for a short time. And regardless of my employment time length, I couldn't shake the sense I was stepping into a world of well-kept secrets. *You're such a drama queen, Alexis.*

Looking down at my sandwich, I lightly shook my head at my own nonsense as the elevator doors opened. With my head down, I was in a world of my own, trying to figure out the unanswered questions plaguing my mind, when Bryce startled me. He was standing waiting for the elevator with a sophisticated-looking redhead who was wearing a grey, feminine business suit. Her hair was up in a tightly twisted bun, and she had glasses perched on the end of her nose. *Who is this toffee-nosed carrot-top?*

Bryce placed his hand across the elevator door for Ms Carrot-top and smiled, looking somewhat relieved when I stepped out of the lift.

'Thank you, Jessica. I will see you next month,' he said to the woman, while keeping his eyes on me. *Of course ... Jessica. Okay, maybe I was a bit quick to label her Ms Carrot-top.*

Jessica tilted her head down just a little so that she could see me over the frames of her glasses, sizing me up it seemed.

'Yes, Bryce, you will,' she stated as an obvious matter of fact.

Stepping into the elevator, she then pushed her glasses back up to her eyes and continued. 'Afternoon, Mrs Summers.'

Her tone of voice was not warm, friendly, or 'pleased to meet you', and it felt as though she had deliberately left out the 'good' part of that sentence on purpose, insinuating that I was the reason she had, in fact, left it out in the first place. Unable to bring myself to smile at her — due to sensing a bit of hostility on her part — I replied with the same contempt she had given me. 'Afternoon.'

Confused by her demeanour, I watched as the doors slid shut then turned to Bryce, his smile now replaced with a look of irritation, which I assumed was directed at Jessica.

'Alexis, you came back,' he said a little warily as he leaned up against the glass window. 'I thought you might decide to leave.'

'I told you, I'm not going anywhere. What happened before lunch was my fault, and I won't let it happen again.' I continued to walk toward my desk, not wanting to talk about it any further. 'Have you eaten anything, Bryce?'

'Yes, I ordered afternoon tea during my appointment with Jessica.'

I nodded in acknowledgement and placed my bag, sandwich and drink on my desk. 'Ah, Jessica, who is she exactly?' I asked with faux curiosity. 'She obviously knows who I am.'

Bryce cocked his eyebrow. 'Alexis, are you telling me your creepy research did not extend to Jessica?' he asked with a sexy, suggestive voice.

I sat down and looked up at him, sighing in surrender. 'Okay, Bryce, let's not play dumb. You told your therapist about me. She obviously knows something, because I now have frostbite as a result of her icy reception.'

Turning my gaze back to my sandwich, I removed the plastic wrap, deliberately refusing to meet his eye and looking unfazed at the same time.

He leaned over and put his hands down on my desk, placing himself only centimetres from my head. 'Not bad, Ms Summers. I may need to employ your creepy research services in the future.'

Never having had much luck in the willpower department, I was unable to stop looking up at him. 'I doubt that, you are very well equipped with those skills yourself.'

He smiled, held my gaze for the smallest of seconds then stood up. I figured this was a good time to change the subject before the little challenge between us led to something it shouldn't. Plus, I was curious as to exactly what our upcoming meeting would be about. I also wanted to know what was required of me so that I didn't look like a deer in the headlights.

'Who are we talking with at this meeting, and what do you need from me? Are you sure you really need *my* input?' I asked, biting into my sandwich.

Oh, thank goodness. Closing my eyes for the smallest of seconds, I enjoyed the feel of finally having some food in my mouth. My stomach had been aggressively telling me to feed it not long before I stepped out of the elevator. Thankfully, it had not repeated its growling and gurgling demands in front of Bryce.

I opened my eyes and took a sip of my cup of tea, washing down my mouthful of food before following with another bite of my sandwich. *Don't worry about your stomach rumbles, Alexis. You probably resemble a hungry little piglet right now.*

Suddenly realising I had been unapologetically wolfing down my lunch, I slowly looked up to meet Bryce's gaze once again, noticing that he had begun to smirk at me.

His obvious amusement at my expense forced the corners of my mouth to turn up into a small smile. 'You really need to stop doing that,' I mumbled at him before swallowing.

His smirk grew even bigger. 'What?'

'You know what.' I glared at him, scoffing more of my sandwich. 'So, are you going to answer my question?'

Bryce continued to smirk. 'We are meeting with my head designer, Patrick. I want you to give him ideas of what you would expect in a hotel room which is labelled family-friendly. He will be here in around fifteen minutes time, so finish your sandwich and escort him in when he arrives. Okay?' He smiled then disappeared into his office.

* * *

Patrick arrived promptly and, after introducing myself, I escorted him into Bryce's office.

As Patrick laid out a number of sketch boards on the coffee table and produced his iPad, Bryce gestured for me to sit beside him on the sofa. Not wanting to be so close to him after the earlier happenings of that day, yet also not wanting to cause a scene or appear hostile, I decided not to argue and took my seat.

'Well, Mr Clark, as you can see from the sketches, the transformation is not diabolical. We can add some extra walls here and there and take some out. I'd like to change the colour palette to neutral, as contemporary doesn't suit the demographic. We will also require some furniture modifications in the form of bunk beds and sofa beds,' Patrick stated, giving me the impression that he had no children in his life, his suggestions far from 'child-friendly' to my mind.

'Very good, Patrick. I'm sure you met out in reception, but I'd like to formally introduce you to my personal assistant, Alexis. She is a mother of two, and I think her thoughts and expectations on what should constitute a family-friendly room could be paramount in deciding the design changes,' Bryce very casually informed his head designer from his sexy seated position beside me.

Patrick sat back on the sofa opposite us and rested the iPad on his lap. 'I see.' He then looked at me, expectantly.

Oh, that's my cue. I cleared my throat. 'Okay, um, all right,' I stuttered, nervously glancing at Bryce. 'If I was sitting at home behind my laptop, looking up hotel rooms to book for a family holiday and came across a hotel advertising or promoting family-friendly rooms, I would expect safety to be a given. It wouldn't be a selling point; it would just be expected.

'First of all, I'm not sure what levels of the Promenade building you are thinking of renovating, but I would assume high-rise levels would freak most parents out. None of us really want to be ten, fifteen or twenty storeys high when holidaying with our small children. So the levels closer to the ground would, more than likely, be a better option.

'Secondly, rooms with accessible balconies: again, this would freak parents out. So, either no doors to the exterior, or provide doors that are key-locked. That way, parents can then make the choice to acquire a key or not.'

Bryce relaxed, sat back, and put his arm behind me on the headrest of the couch. This simple move heightened my alertness and sent strange sensations through my entire body. It made me feel both uncomfortable and comfortable at the same time, if that is at all possible.

He smiled at me, so I smiled back and continued.

'If you're promoting family-friendly, you need to accommodate families with children from infants to teenagers. If you can configure the walls in the rooms to give you two- or three-bedroom apartments, then that would definitely be a selling point. Rooms with microwaves and dishwashers are great selling points too, as mums don't want to be doing dishes on their holiday — trust me!

'Washing machines and dryers in the apartments are also great incentives, as it means you would need to bring less luggage. Also, in terms of furniture, have nothing with sharp, pointy edges. TVs should be braced to walls ... but you probably already know that. Oh, and provision of highchairs and portacots ...' I said eagerly, knowing these were essential items for families with babies.

Now that I was comfortable offering my ideas, I kept listing them as they came to my head. 'Heavy-duty and easily cleaned carpets — children are feral, you know. Bunk beds, sure, but not in all rooms, as families with children aged between one and five will find them a nuisance and dangerous, therefore a variety of sleeping and bedding configurations would be best.'

I was far from finished with my offerings so continued on. 'I think neutral colours predominantly, yes, but kids love colour, colour plays on mood and a good mood equals a good holiday.

'Have things like Nintendo Wiis, and maybe big coloured dots on the carpet to resemble a Twister game. And those wall-play gadgets and thingies you find in family feeding rooms in shopping centres — kids love those things.'

Finding myself starting to ramble in a very unprofessional way, I decided to bite my tongue and wait for Patrick and Bryce's reaction.

'I'm sorry, I've babbled on too much,' I apologised, grabbing a glass of water and sitting back in my chair.

I hadn't noticed during my spiel that Patrick had been taking notes. 'Twister carpet,' he murmured, while finishing his scribbling. He looked up and smiled. 'I love it! That's a lot of useful information, Alexis. There are certainly many things we can implement that would definitely fall within budget.' Patrick seemed impressed.

'Great! Work with the information Alexis just gave you, Patrick, and then get back to me with new sketches, designs and figures. We'll go from there.' Bryce stood up, so I followed suit. 'Alexis, I'll also need you to organise a meeting with Chris from marketing.'

Patrick packed up his things, stood, and extended a hand to me. 'It was a pleasure meeting you, Alexis. I'm sure we will be seeing more of each other in the near future.

'Mr Clark, again, thank you for your time.' He shook Bryce's hand then exited the room.

Turning back around, I found Bryce had seated himself again and was staring at me. 'You really are a piece of work, Alexis.'

He was smirking the smirkiest smirk of all smirks to date. I couldn't help but laugh, even that smirk was hard to ignore. *Fuck, maybe I should call him Mr Smirk.*

'Why? Did I hijack your meeting? I'm so sorry. It's just when I thought about what you were trying to achieve, the ideas just tumbled out,' I explained.

I felt exhilarated; the meeting had been fun. I just hoped that I hadn't come across as a know-all.

'Exactly, you really are the perfect person to work with in relation to these renovations.' He seemed thrilled with my input. So much so, that I thought I was now a vital part of the project.

'Well, I'm glad I lived up to your expectations, Mr Clark,' I said, smiling and nervously smoothing down the front of my dress.

'You surpass them, Alexis,' he murmured as the undeniable sexual tension began creeping in between us. *Nip it in the bud, Alexis.*

Noticing it was past 8 p.m., I headed for the office door. 'If that is all you need from me tonight, I should head home.'

'Actually, if you don't mind staying a little longer, there is something I want to show you,' he said quite quickly, sliding forward in his seat.

He looked like an excited child, and whatever it was that he wanted to show me had me curious.

'Sure, what is it?' I asked.

Bryce jumped up with such enthusiasm, he resembled a jack-in-the-box. 'Follow me,' he instructed, holding his arm out and gesturing toward the apartment door. *Oh, my goodness! His hands are gloriously strong, masculine and large. You know what they say about men with big hands, right? Alexis, you need to slap yourself.*

He led me into his apartment and over to his private elevator. 'In you go,' he commanded while placing his hand on the small of my back and gently moving me into the elevator. *Oh, holy fuck. I'm in this tiny little confined space with a man who has big hands, tastes divine and obviously wants to get down and dirty with me. Breathe, Alexis, breathe.*

I watched intently as he hit the button labelled 'Ob'. *Ob? Of course ... Observatory. Ooh, how exciting?*

'Have you ever been in an observatory?' he asked with raised eyebrows as the doors opened.

I shook my head. 'No, never.'

We stepped into a small dome-shaped room. An extremely, *really* cosy, dome-shaped room. Bryce flicked a switch on the wall and the dome-shaped roof began to open. As it slowly separated, each half of the dome moving away from the other, the starry sky came into sight. *Oh, my God! The stars look enormous.*

I wasn't sure if the stars looked so big because there were no clouds in sight, or if it was because we were so high in the air, being forty-three floors high in the atmosphere.

I arched and bent my head all the way back as I performed a pirouette. 'Wow, this is amazing!'

'You have seen nothing yet. Here, take my hand.'

I placed my hand in his, and I swear I nearly passed out. I had never felt anything like it before. The feelings I got when he touched me were indescribable, and I couldn't for the life of me figure out why.

He helped me step up on a ladder that led to an enormous telescope. There were only a few rungs on the ladder, but I think he felt the need to stand right behind me in case I fell.

Bryce's body was hard against my back, making it increasingly difficult to breathe. *You shouldn't have agreed to this, Alexis. This is what will get you in trouble.*

He gestured to an eyepiece on the telescope. 'Look through here.'

I leaned forward and looked into the lens.

Bryce then basically hugged my body in order to reach and adjust a few knobs on the telescope. 'What can you see, Ms Summers?'

'It's the moon. A big, ginormous moon! I feel like I can just reach out and touch it,' I said in awe. *Stupid me does in fact reach out. Der, Alexis.* 'This is great. I can see why you like this hobby.'

Without thinking I twisted around to see his expression, causing our faces to be only centimetres away from each other. *Oh shit, not again.* I was about to object to the pending kiss when he spoke first, his voice dangerously low.

'Don't worry, Alexis, I'm not going to kiss you again. Every single entire ounce of me wants to grab you and kiss you until our mouths are dry. Then, I want to rip your dress from you, take your underwear off with my teeth and kiss every inch of your fabulous body ... paying a lot of attention to your sexy arse, gorgeous tits and wet —'

'Bryce —' I began, thinking that my heart had stopped beating, even though I was panting ... and well and truly lubricated in the very underwear he wanted to tear off me.

He didn't let me finish though and continued: 'But, I'm not going to, Alexis. Not until you tell me you want me to. I will never cross that line again and kiss you without your permission. That doesn't mean I don't want to though. That will not change.'

CHAPTER

9

I was speechless and utterly craving what he had just declared. He was smirking at me, though, which I would normally find completely irritating but endearing. This time, however, his confidence and smugness made me mad and more to the point, extremely pissed off.

I placed both my hands on his chest and shoved him, forcing him to stumble back and nearly fall on his arse. 'You can't just say that and smirk at me, Bryce. What am I supposed to do with that confession? What do you want me to do?'

I stepped off the ladder and stomped like a child to the elevator door. He followed and stood with his back against the wall facing me, his hands in his trouser pockets, looking quite casual and relaxed.

'I know you feel it, Alexis. You want me between your legs just as badly as I want to be there.'

'Bryce, stop it! You are so far out of line, it's not funny.'

He started to laugh, so I turned to face him. *Is he for real? He is so infuriating — yet adorable — yet maddening — yet delectable. Oh my God, he is turning me into a freaking yo-yo.*

Without thinking, I slapped him across the face. He rubbed his cheek and smiled at me, impressively. Trying desperately to keep my furious expression, I glared at him, but I was very slowly losing the battle with the muscles in my face.

Noticing my defeat, he laughed again, and I could only follow suit.

'I hate you right now,' I blurted out, looking away from him. I was beyond being polite and stepping on eggshells where our employer-employee relationship was concerned. He had overstepped that mark well and truly.

'No, you don't.'

'Yes, I do,' I bit back. It dawned on me suddenly that the elevator was not moving. 'Bryce, I need to go home before I punch you. Press the bloody button.'

He laughed, but this time he was mocking me.

I shot him a challenging look. 'Oh, you don't think I can punch you?'

He shook his head in response.

'Go on, kiss me again, I dare you,' I goaded him.

He was on me like a flash, pushing me hard up against the wall, ravaging my mouth with his own and sending pure intense passion through his tongue onto mine. I aggressively ran my hands through his hair as he lifted me up, allowing me to wrap my legs around his waist. *No, no, no! Stop it, Alexis. What did you say that for, and where is that punch you so boldly threatened him with?*

Releasing my legs from around his waist, I dropped them to the ground and punched him in the arm. I tried to get in a second blow, but he caught my fist and brought my arm down, spinning me around and trapping my arms across my chest and perfectly securing my body to his abdomen.

He held me there for a few seconds, then whispered softly into my ear, his breath hot and paralysing. 'You gave me permission, Alexis. You can't then attack me, not that I'd call that an attack. In fact, you need a lot of instruction on attack and self-defence. So, on Monday morning you are coming to my self-defence class. Wear some clothes you don't mind working up a sweat in.'

'Let me go, I need to go home to my *husband*,' I hissed at him.

He released me and hit the button to his apartment. The doors opened and I stepped out, making my way to my bag. I quickly picked it up and turned to meet his face, finding him leaning up against the entryway wall where we had first kissed earlier that day. It felt as if that kiss had happened days ago, but I guess that was because so much had happened in such a short space of time, and it had not really all sunk in yet. Thank God the next day was Saturday. I wanted the entire weekend to recover from the head-fuck that this day had been.

I began to talk, but he cut me off.

'I can't help myself, Alexis. You ... you are like no one I have ever met, and I want you.'

'You can't have me, Bryce. I'm taken.'

He stared deep into my eyes. 'I don't believe anything is absolute. Things change, people change. *Circumstances* change.'

I can't believe him. Lucy was right when she said 'if he sees something he wants, he goes for it and gets it'. Well, I was something he was not going to 'get'.

I put my hand up to indicate that he shut up. 'You've had an emotional day, and you are probably still high on adrenaline.' *You don't honestly believe that, Alexis.* 'I'll see you Monday.' With that, I turned, let myself out, and headed home.

* * *

'Mum, wake up ... Mum, it's Saturday. You need to make us pancakes!' *What? Pancakes?* I opened my eyes, forcing a slow return to reality. There in front of me was Charlotte, virtually nose-to-nose. She was waiting very patiently, but not patiently enough to let me wake without her assistance.

'Charli, it's too early, let mummy sleep longer,' I groaned into my pillow.

Rick moaned and turned over.

'But Mum, I'm hungry, and you always make pancakes on Saturday.'

She was right, I did. Every Saturday I would cook up a batch of pancakes before Nate and Rick left for the football, and Charli and I left for her dancing class.

Urgh, I grumbled then basically rolled out of bed and into a vertical position. 'Slippers, where are my slippers?'

Charli was already on bended knee, placing my slippers down so that I could step into them.

Gradually, I came back to earth as I sipped my cup of tea and poured the batter into the pan. Charlotte was sitting at our breakfast bar, waiting eagerly. Nate had not yet surfaced. And Rick? Well, he had made that animal sound when Charli woke me, but he had not made a peep since.

'So, Charli-Bear, how was school yesterday?' I asked, feeling shattered that I had arrived home after she had gone to bed the night before.

'Good. Guess what? We are going on an excursion to the zoo in a few weeks,' she sang.

Charli loved animals. She had already decided she wanted to be a vet. But that was after she had decided she wanted to be a princess, a teacher, and the next Rachel in *Glee*.

'That will be nice, sweetheart. You'll get to see the baby elephant.'

She did a little happy dance in her seat, making me laugh. She was such a delightful child.

'Here you go. Maple or lemon?'

Not knowing why I asked, I shook my head in disbelief. Charlotte always chose maple.

After handing her the plate of maple syrup-covered pancakes, I watched with amusement as she demolished them rather quickly. 'So, would you like to see where Mummy works? We could also visit my friend, Lucy, and her baby boy.'

'Can we?' she mumbled through a mouthful. 'That would be awesome. What's his name? Can I hold him? Can I feed him a bottle?'

'Whoa, settle petal. Yes, we can. And no, you can't hold him or feed him, he's only one day old.'

Charli pouted, so I stuck my finger out and flicked her protruding lip, making her giggle.

Turning back toward the stove, I then finished up cooking the pancake batter, stacking each fluffy, non-circular flat cake on a plate. I then got Charlotte ready for dancing.

'Rick, Nate. Get up! Or you'll be late for football,' I shouted from the living room.

Nate made a stirring noise from his room, but I knew from experience that Rick would need further persuasion. When he was fast asleep, you could set a firecracker off in the lounge room, and I kid you not, he would sleep through it.

Creeping up to him as he lay looking comatose, I spoke softly in his ear. 'Rick ... Rick, get your arse out of bed.'

He opened his eyes and grabbed me. 'You get your arse into bed,' he coaxed as he pulled me on top of him.

I tried to break free. 'Stop it, you horny shit, we are going to be late.'

'We've got time, come on, babe. You were barely awake when you finally got home last night.'

I leaned down and kissed his forehead. 'I know. I had a big day.' *That was an understatement!* I felt terribly guilty and did not want to elaborate on my day's events in any detail. 'Come on, we really don't have time.'

Surrendering unhappily, he let me go and got out of bed.

'So, I was thinking that after footy and dancing, I might head into the city and see how Lucy and the baby are, then show Charli City Towers,' I advised as we both got ourselves dressed.

'Sounds good, I wouldn't mind checking out your half a million dollar office myself,' he said while bending over to tie his shoe. *Oh shit, I hadn't bargained on Rick actually wanting to come along. I hope Bryce is out doing whatever billionaires do.*

* * *

A couple of hours later, we were standing outside of Lucy's hospital room. I told Rick and the kids to wait in the corridor while I checked to see that she was not in the middle of feeding.

'Knock, knock,' I asked as I peeped into Lucy's room. To my delight, she was cradling the most beautiful little bundle of joy. 'Aw, look at him, he's adorable.'

'Come in,' she beamed.

I entered the room and made my way to her bedside, giving her a kiss on the forehead.

'This is little Alexander,' she said, beaming, and then popped her finger on his tiny nose, giving it a very gentle wiggle.

He was peacefully wrapped up like a cocoon. 'Hi, Alexander,' I cooed. 'I like his name.'

'It was going to be Jack up until yesterday, but I wasn't a fan of the name Jack. Nic really liked it though. So, Alexis, not only did you help bring him into this world —'

I interrupted her, 'Pfft, I didn't help bring him into this world. You did that by yourself.'

She continued as if I hadn't interrupted her. 'Not only did you help bring him into this world, you gave me the perfect excuse for an alternate name for him.' *Alexander ... oh! She has named him after me! No, don't do that, I didn't do anything.*

I was both humbled and embarrassed by her sentiment, and I did not deserve the acclaim she was giving me. I didn't want to come across as rude or ungrateful, so I smiled thankfully and tried to bury the emotion from the past day's events as it was about to boil over within me again.

'That's lovely, Lucy. It really is. Thank you.' I didn't have anything else to say.

'No, thank you, Alexis. I mean it. You really were a godsend yesterday, not only for me, but Bryce too. It's the least I can do. Anyway, I really like the name Alexander. It is the name of kings.'

I smiled sheepishly but felt extremely uncomfortable. I didn't want any recognition. 'Lucy, Rick and the kids are with me. They are just outside the door. Do you mind if I introduce you and Alexander? Charlotte is very excited to see the baby.'

'Sure, of course, bring them in.'

I introduced my family to Lucy. She was great and had a knack for speaking to you as though she had known you for years. Charlotte was instantly smitten by baby Alexander, and Lucy let her sit up on the bed for a cuddle. Charlotte gave baby Al — as she so aptly named him — the blue teddy she had picked out in the gift shop, then we said our goodbyes, not wanting to stay long due to Alexander's next feed not being far away.

* * *

As we walked into the City Towers lobby, I spotted Liam talking on the phone at his desk. I smiled at him when he gave me an over-enthusiastic wave.

Rick nudged my shoulder. 'He sure is excited to see you.'

'Shut up. He bats for the other team, stupid,' I whispered, giving Rick a little hip bump. 'So, who wants to see the aquarium?' I asked eagerly, diverting the conversation.

'The aquarium? Sick!' Nate exclaimed.

'Sick' was Nate's word of the month. Last month it had been 'totes', and the month before that, 'epic'. I didn't mind the word epic so much, and found it had somehow crept into my own vocabulary. Still, I didn't think 'sick' was going to do the same.

After a tour of the impressive aquarium — which the kids thought was sick — I showed them the sun deck. Charlotte displayed her disappointment at not being able to have a swim by pouting her lip and dropping her head.

'There will be plenty of chances to come for a swim, Charlotte, just not today. Anyway, didn't you want to see what a penthouse looked like?' I offered, hoping to turn her frown upside-down.

Her little eyes lit up at my question.

I laughed. 'Come on then.'

* * *

As we all ascended by elevator, I was nervous as hell, antici-pating an awkward encounter with Bryce. Luckily, when the doors opened and there was no sign of anyone else around, I found I could finally breathe easily again.

'So, this is where Mummy works,' I said proudly as I walked over to the large mahogany desk.

'It's so high up, Mum, don't you feel height-sick?' Char-lotte asked, her face planted against the window and looking down. *Lol ... height-sick. I love how her little mind works.*

'Only when I look down, sweetheart.'

Stepping away from the window, Charlotte crossed one leg over the other. 'Mum, I need to go to the toilet.'

'Of course you do. Nate, do you need the toilet too?'

He shook his head.

'Good. Stay here with Dad, and we'll be back in a minute.'

I led Charlotte through to the toilet.

'Mum, this place is so cool. I want to work here when I grow up,' she admitted while sniffing her clean hands.

'I thought you wanted to be a vet?'

'I changed my mind, this is so cool,' she squealed.

I loved how, at such a young age, children could flip from one thing to another without a second thought. If only life was that simple for an adult.

I laughed to myself as we made our way back through the conference room, considering the irony of what I had just thought.

As we approached the foyer, I could hear Rick talking and soon realised the voice that was reciprocating belonged to Bryce. *Oh shit! He's here.*

I took a deep breath and opened the door.

'Alexis, can't get enough of the place?' Bryce said, with a hint of complacency. *Oh, of course you are smirking, Mr Clark. How could I possibly think you would not?*

I managed a fake laugh, maybe too fake. 'Yeah, you just can't keep me away. No, Charlotte was very keen to see where I worked. Charlotte this is, Mr Clark, Mummy's boss. And this is my son, Nate, and my husband —'

'Rick ... yes, we have already introduced ourselves. Hey, Charlotte, have you ever seen a helipad?'

'No, what's a helipad?' She looked at me wide-eyed.

Nate tutted and rolled his eyes. 'It's where helicopters land, silly,' he said, trying to act cool in front of Bryce.

Bryce gently scruffed Nate's hair. 'You're right, Nate, it is. Come on, then, come with me and meet the Crow,' he said smiling and gesturing us toward his office.

I gave him a snide glare, but quickly corrected it to a smile when Rick looked my way.

* * *

Do you know that feeling you get when you're about to enter a situation you want nothing more than to avoid? Well, that's how I felt the moment Bryce led us out to the helipad and introduced the kids to the 'Crow' — which I now realised was, in fact, the helicopter.

'Do you fly it?' Nate queried, with a look of wonder at the piece of machinery in front of his eyes.

'Yeah, all the time. Would you like to go for a ride?'

At this point, I jumped in very quickly. 'No, no, not today! Maybe some other time.'

'Aw, Mum, can we go, please?' Nate begged.

I shot Bryce a look to say don't-even-think-about-it. 'No, not today. Mr Clark is a very busy man, maybe next time.'

He registered my expression and offered a compromise. 'That's all right, maybe next time, Nate. Your mum tells me that you like astronomy? Maybe you'd like to have a look at my observatory instead?'

'Sweet,' Nate declared, clenching his fist and bringing his elbow into his side. He was very quickly becoming Bryce's biggest fan.

Rick leaned in and put his arm around my shoulder. 'So, how often do you take her out?'

Fuck, where did this come from? Was it that obvious? 'Never. Why?' I asked defensively, eyes overly wide open as I looked at Rick.

His return gaze was one of confusion.

'At least once a week,' Bryce replied, and then grinned at me.

I screwed up my face, but then realised they were talking about the helicopter. *Oh, stupid me.*

Bryce's gaze flicked to Rick's new position by my side, but what I found even stranger was the feeling that Rick had moved closer on purpose — he never staked his claim like that.

Feeling a tightened pressure on my shoulder, I noticed Rick's grip had tensed. *Seriously, Rick! Why not mark your territory by cocking your leg and peeing on mine.*

'Must be nice and quiet up in the air with no other traffic,' Rick said, continuing to tighten his grip. His tone suggested he was trying to make out his comment was a joke. But I knew him, and I sensed he was having a stab.

'That's one of the reasons I love it, Rick; no other *idiots* to contend with,' Bryce replied. *Hmm, this is starting to feel like the beginning of a cockfight. Okay, time to leave.*

Still eyeing Rick's arm on my shoulder, Bryce turned back toward the apartment. 'Come inside and I'll fix us all a drink.' *No. Ah ... shit!*

'No thank you, Bryce. We won't take up any more of your time,' I politely declined, nudging the kids ever so slightly toward the door.

Rick stepped up in Bryce's direction. 'We are not in a hurry, babe. Thanks, I'll take you up on that drink, Bryce.'

I'm going to kill Rick. Then again, I could kill them both. They are both pissing me off.

We followed Bryce inside where he moved to the bar and grabbed a bottle of gin. *Oh no, you don't!*

'Take a seat,' he gestured to the lounge.

We both sat as directed, Rick with his back to Bryce.

'What's your drink of choice, Rick?'

'I'll have a JB if you've got it.' *Rick! Yes, you are first on my hit list.*

Bryce sniggered and raised his eyebrow at me. I wasn't able to respond because Rick was staring at me and would have noticed if I had.

'Do you like Scotch?' Bryce asked and, without waiting for Rick's answer, began pouring two glasses of Glenfiddich 50.

Now, I'm not a drinker, but I know that is one of the most expensive bottles of Scotch in the world. While studying for my Bachelor degree, we did a brief module on exclusive luxury items, and I vaguely recall a bottle being worth approximately $20,000.

'And a gin for you, Alexis?' he inquired, with a nonchalance that could only be described as confidently cocky. *You smart-arse. Now you are definitely on my hit list, too.*

I struggled to give a polite smile. 'No, thank you.'

'Perhaps you'd like a cup of English breakfast or a hot white-chocolate?'

That's it. They may as well flop their dicks out on the coffee table and get it over with.

'Water is fine,' I responded with gritted teeth. All I wanted was to get the hell out of there.

Bryce poured me a glass of water and picked up the phone. 'Grace, yes, fine. Can I order two milkshake mountains, please?' He looked over at Nate and Charli. 'What flavours would you like?' he asked them.

Both my children's faces lit up and they spoke at the same time over the top of one another. 'Blue. Chocolate. Heaven.'

'One chocolate and one blue heaven thanks, Grace. Yes, straightaway, please. Thank you.' He ended the call and I had to hand it to him; he knew just how to impress my children. He also seemed quite pleased to have us as guests. Either that, or he enjoyed playing games and fucking around with my head.

I walked over to the bar and picked up my water, and the look in his eyes had me squirming on the spot. So I quickly retreated to the lounge and sat next to Rick, although the usual comfort I took when nestled into my husband's side was not currently present.

Bryce handed Rick the Scotch and sat opposite us in his laid-back, sexy couch position, which — by the look on his smirky face — he knew I had taken a liking to.

'We paid Lucy a visit this morning and met baby Alexander, he's amazing,' I offered, wanting to change the topic of conversation and ease the tension in the air. Tension that not one of us was willing to admit — out loud — was there.

Bryce's eyes gleamed and he boldly replied, 'Yes, Alexander Bryce Clark, he even sounds perfect.'

At that moment, I could have leapt over the table and hit him. *Right, if he wants to play games, then I will play games, too.* Leaning back, I put my hand in Rick's hair. It was something I did a lot, so Rick would have missed the attempted crack at Bryce.

'So, have you been back to see Lucy since yesterday?' I asked, casually.

He tilted his head to the side and took a swig of his drink. *Take that, Mr agonisingly hot Clark!*

'Yes, first thing, earlier this morning.'

A buzz sounded through a speaker near the door to his office, prompting Bryce to stand up from his chair and leave the room. 'Please excuse me for a moment.'

He returned moments later with what looked like two massive glasses full of cream, chocolate, sprinkles and blue topping.

'Two milkshake mountains coming your way,' he smiled, offering the drinks to Nate and Charli.

Both my children's eyes nearly bulged out of their heads. *Oh great, that's just what I need. Sticky, milky, drinks spilled over his rug, which probably cost more than our house alone.*

I pointed toward the kitchen. 'At the dining table, please.'

Bryce led the way and placed the drinks down on the table.

'No mucking around and no mess. What do you say to Mr Clark?' I prompted my kids.

Both Nate and Charli chimed in with gratitude. 'Thank you.'

'Good, now behave.' I turned and headed back toward the lounge, Bryce not far behind me.

As we passed out of the kitchen, he pressed himself against my back, and whispered quietly in my ear: 'Ms Summers, your arse in those jeans is making me hard.'

CHAPTER

10

Lust-filled heat ran from the spot on my neck that his breath caressed, right down to my pussy, my body's reaction betraying my moral compass. The kids had their backs to us and were not in earshot, and there was a wall in between the kitchen and lounge which had become a useful shield.

I walked the extra steps it would take us to become completely out of my children's vicinity, then turned around abruptly and got right up into his personal space.

Heated anger flaring from my pores, I shoved my finger at his taut, muscled chest. 'You need to cut this shit out, now! My husband is in the other room and deserves better than this. Do you want me to walk? Walk away from being your PA?' I whispered harshly.

'You won't,' he said, very sure of himself.

'I love my husband, and he is good to me. Really good. So, enough, Bryce. Or I will walk!'

I turned back around and continued into the lounge with a sneaking suspicion he was watching my arse. With curiosity getting the better of me, I quickly glanced back over my shoulder; confirming my suspicion. He quickly raised his eyes to meet mine, a hint of satisfaction glazing over them. I glared at him in response, but couldn't deny the fact I enjoyed his appreciation of my assets. And, although I was furious with his not so subtle forthright behaviour, the knowledge that he was yearning for me was more than a turn-on.

I gave Rick's leg a firm squeeze as I sat down beside him on the sofa. 'Drink up. Don't forget I am going out with the girls tonight.'

* * *

For the remainder of our time at the apartment, my threat appeared to have subdued Bryce — he had chosen to play nicely. He also followed through with his compromise and showed Nate the observatory, which apparently was 'the sickest'.

We politely thanked him for his hospitality — *and indecent suggestive game playing* — and then said our goodbyes.

As we were entering the elevator to head back down to the lobby, Bryce called out from his position in the doorway to his office. 'Don't forget your gym clothes on Monday.'

'Why do you need gym clothes?' Rick asked, his tone sounding slightly suspicious.

His question had me feeling that he was more than just curious. 'Oh, it's nothing. I'm just having a lesson in self-defence. The hotel runs a course for guests, and I need to check it out. Apparently, it's the boss's orders,' I said with a shrug, giving him the impression it was non-negotiable — which it sort of was — but I was actually really looking forward to it.

* * *

As we headed back to the car, Nate and Charlotte were on a high, which one could rightly assume was the result of mixing high altitude, large fish tanks, black helicopters and a shitload of sugar. Rick, on the other hand, was a lot quieter than usual. And it appeared our interaction with Bryce may have had an impact on him, but as to the actual effect of that impact at this point in time, I wasn't sure. Knowing Rick, I would be in receipt of the effect sooner rather than later. He would either opt to turn on the silent treatment, or fix or clean something that didn't actually need it.

'I soooo can't wait to have a ride in the Crow,' Nate said with surety. *Over my dead body you will, young man.*

I smiled the smile that mothers do when they hope their child will just forget and move on. Unfortunately, I was quite sure Nate was not going to forget Bryce's offer anytime soon.

Out of the corner of my eye, I spotted Samantha as we entered the car park. I was just about to yell out and make ourselves known when a man appeared behind her, pinching her arse and kissing her neck. At first glance he looked somewhat familiar. However, from my distant position, his face was unrecognisable. It wasn't until he walked around to face her that I became aware of exactly who he was. *What is Samantha doing with Gareth?*

For some reason, seeing them together left a strange feeling in my stomach, and I figured it best not to make them aware I was standing there bearing witness to their affection-ate display. So, putting my head down and attempting to be inconspicuous, I headed for the car.

* * *

Going out with the girls for a night of fun could not have come at a better time. I hadn't seen them since returning to work and was really looking forward to letting my hair down and distracting my thoughts away from a particular tall, blond, tasty billionaire.

Flicking through the outfits in my wardrobe, I settled on a pair of shiny, black denim skinny-cut pants, black glitter heels, a red silk blouse — which gathered at my breasts — and a black satin blazer. My hair was down and straightened; my make-up, subtle. I opted for some tinted moisturiser, eyeliner and red lipstick as I felt that less was more where I was concerned.

After glamming myself up, kissing the kids goodnight, and leaving Rick sitting comfortably on the sofa fully immersed in the evening's televised football match, I made my way outside and into the waiting taxi.

It wasn't long before the taxi I was riding in pulled up to my best friend Carly's house. Carls and I had known each other since we were toddlers — having been neighbours for eighteen years.

Carly knew me better than anybody but, sadly, we didn't get to see each other as often as we would've liked due to our life-styles being somewhat different. I had married young and had children, whereas Carly was still single and enjoying her free, unencumbered life. In hindsight though, our inability to catch up often was not detrimental to our friendship ... because when we did eventually get together, we definitely made the most of it.

Carly opened the car door and climbed in. She had curled her ash-blonde hair and it fell in loose ringlets past her shoulders. Carly Henkley rocked a smoky eye better than anyone, and she had opted for a little black dress that covered one shoulder and left the other bare.

'Look at you!' she squealed excitedly as she leaned over the back seat to give me a hug. 'You look totes glam, Lexi!'

'What?' I asked in confusion while smiling and shaking my head. 'You sound just like Nate.'

She laughed. 'Good, I'd rather sound like him than you, you old fart,' she joked.

I hit her on the arm. I was only six months older than she was, but still, she liked to remind me of that.

'You look pretty smokin' yourself,' I replied, admiring her appearance. 'Love those strappy heels.'

'I know, right? My Jimmy Choos and I are like this.' She held up her hand and crossed her fingers. 'So, how's the new job, babe?'

'Yeah, good, although I feel like I'm in over my head most days, and that has nothing to do with the actual work!'

'Oh? Do tell,' she said curiously while taking a sip of her Red Bull.

I knew I could tell Carly anything, it was what I held so dear in our friendship. No matter what we shared with each other, we never judged; we were brutally honest. Sometimes too honest — which could lead to a speaking famine, the worst having been five months long.

'Okay,' I sighed. 'So, my boss is a billionaire, the sexiest man I have ever laid eyes on, and he wants to fuck me senseless,' I rattled out quickly.

She spat the Red Bull she was about to swallow across the back of the passenger seat, causing the driver to shoot us a dirty look via the rear-view mirror.

'Fuck off, you aren't serious?' she asked, searchingly. I didn't flinch. 'Shit, you ARE serious.'

Grabbing a tissue out of her bag, she leaned forward and wiped the back of the seat. 'That's freaking hot. Why can't this shit happen to me? It's a waste on you,' she said dismissively.

Carly paused in her attempted Red Bull clean-up and squinted her smoky eyes toward me. 'Alexis, you little whore,' she said with a highly amused expression. 'What have you done?'

I could tell she was enjoying the drama that was creating havoc in my life. I also hated how she could read me so easily.

'Nothing. I wouldn't do that, you know me. He just kissed me, that's all. Really, it was nothing.'

She raised an eyebrow at me and pursed her lips. 'I hate you. Ask him if he'd like a threesome?'

I shot her an evil look.

'Okay, I'm kidding. Right, I'm putting on my serious-Carly face now.' She pulled a face that was anything but serious. 'So, does Rick know that your boss kissed you?'

'God, no. It was an accident and a once-off. There's no point in telling him. It's not going to happen again.'

She nodded then raised her eyebrow at me. 'Are you sure?'

Knowing that she could see straight through my uncertain facade, I relented. 'I'm struggling, Carls. He's smart, cheeky, kind and loving. He's also arrogant, infuriating and direct. And, when he talks dirty to me, I almost orgasm on the spot. I'm really not sure I can resist him.'

'You have to,' she said, right before taking another sip.

'I know. But the problem is, I love my job, and he's paying me half a million —'

She spat her sip out again and turned to face me, her eyes bulging out of her head while she mouthed the words half a million.

I leaned my head against the glass window of the car. 'I hate backing down, Carls. It's just not in me. But when I stand my ground, it only fuels his fire.'

'Serious-Carly' was well and truly with me now. 'Lexi, be careful, hon. You are not used to this shit.' *Don't I know it?*

'I know, hon. Anyway, no more talk of hot bossman. The last thing I need,' I said, gesturing toward Tash's house as we pulled into her driveway, 'is Tash finding out about this and giving me a hard time.'

Tash was another close friend of mine. Our children were the same age and attended the same school, so we had seen each other on a daily basis before I had returned to work.

Opening the taxi door, Tash climbed into the front seat, wearing a dress with shimmery, black, three-quarter length leggings, and black patent pumps. *Damn it! I should've worn my navy, sequined shift dress. Shit! Crap! Balls!*

Tash had long dark-brown hair, was olive-skinned and could pull off the most vibrant full lips I'd ever seen. 'What's up, bitches?' Tash was also filterless; as in never filtered the words that came out of her mouth.

'Hey, Tash, where's Lil?' I asked curiously, having been under the impression that we were supposed to be picking up both Tash and Lilly.

'She's meeting us there. Seth has tonsilitis so she's waiting until he's settled before heading out.'

Lilly's son Seth was also one of Nate's friends.

'Did you hear back from Jade and Steph as well?' I asked, hoping that she had. Jade and Steph also had children who attended the same school as ours. In fact, our children got along remarkably well and, as a result, we all became quite close, too.

'Yeah, they'll meet us there,' she replied.

I honestly loved having friends with children. Our mutual interests always led to great discussions and they were always helpful when advice was needed. But I also loved having a friend like Carly — she was a breath of fresh air.

Smiling as I settled back into my seat, I relaxed and let the tension I harboured ease, once again allowing myself to very much look forward to the evening ahead. It was going to be great and just what I needed to get my mind away from Bryce.

'The Metro better brace itself tonight, girls. Because I am in the mood to go off,' Tash hollered, sounding fully charged-up.

I loved her energy and her ability to make the most of every situation she was in. I also loved watching her take control at our usual club of choice — the Metro — with its trendy black and white disco floor. And in addition, the '70s and '80s music was right up our alley.

'Let's ditch the Metro and go to Opals?' Carly suggested quickly. *You bitch, Carls!*

Opals was one of the nightclubs at City Towers.

'I haven't been to Opals in years. Yeah, sounds good. I'll text the others and let them know.' Tash started typing away before I could protest. *Shit!* Carly, however, smiled and poked her tongue out. She did that a lot.

* * *

As we walked into Opals, it became quite obvious to me that the style and decor bore a striking resemblance to Bryce's penthouse apartment. Blacks, whites, silver and lime-green.

The stage was against the far wall and directly ahead of us. The bar was to our left and ran along the wall in an 'L' shape. Sleek was a word that came to mind when describing the bar, illuminated by bright lime-green lights which were fitted under the bench lip. Silver lights also hung over it from the drop ceiling suspended above.

Not quite in the centre of the room was a staircase leading up to level two and, along the walls — to either side of the stage — were booths and small tables with stools. Jade and Steph were already seated in one of those booths and, when they spotted us, they waved to get our attention.

'How the hell did you get here so fast?' I asked in amazement as we approached the table.

'Jade drove,' Steph said, as if no further explanation was necessary — it wasn't.

Steph was the epitome of a rock girl, sporting short brown hair with highlights of red, femininely styled to frame her flawless face. She had on a silver, sequined tunic dress, a cropped, black leather jacket, and loose, black knee-high boots.

Jade, however, was my saviour, having also gone for a pair of pants. *Okay, I feel much better now.* She was also wearing a cream-coloured, drapey top and matching cream-coloured peep-toes. Her shoulder-length red hair was straightened and looking quite different from when I last saw her.

'What's up, bitches?' Tash bellowed as we sat down at the table.

Anyone would think Tash had already downed some drinks, but she hadn't; she was merely on fire and ready to get the night underway. 'Schnappies!' she sang at the top of her voice.

'I'm on it. Drinks are on me tonight, lovelies,' I declared, as I turned for the bar. *Why not? I was well and truly in the money now and more than happy to share my new-found wealth with my beautiful friends.* They objected to my offer, but Carls very cheekily assured them that I was now rich.

I got us a round of schnappies — also known as Cocksucking Cowboys — and some cosmopolitans. My plans were to have a big night of drinking with pretty-coloured, fruity cocktails and shots — lots of shots. The variety of alcoholic drinks I had chosen was sure to help ease the built-up tension that had formed since meeting my extremely delicious employer. Well ... that was the plan anyway and I was sticking to it.

* * *

Lil joined us almost an hour later, she too having gone for black dress pants but with a baby-blue blouse, her dark brown wavy hair pinned up into a loose bun.

Not wasting any more time, I quickly brought her up to speed with a row of shots. 'How's Seth, hon?'

'He's got tonsilitis. I'm over it,' she sighed, looking exhausted.

I felt her pain; there was nothing worse than having sick kids.

'And, to top it off, Lex, I think I am getting it, too. My throat is killing me. I feel like I have a huge, prickly hard cock stuck in the back of my throat.'

I laughed at her. 'Well, we can't have that then, can we? Come on, drink up and forget about it.'

She did just that and slammed all four shots in rapid succession.

'Lil, you're an animal!' I praised her, and gave her shoulder a tight squeeze. She responded by giving me a thumbs-up.

* * *

Opals nightclub had three levels. The lower level atmosphere was more laid-back and had a bar-like feel about it. The band that was playing was awesome, and I thoroughly enjoyed the songs they covered. I was a rock girl at heart and loved Def Leppard, Guns N' Roses, Kings of Leon, Pearl Jam, U2, Foo Fighters, the list goes on. Steph shared my love of rock, and we both did our best version of Eddie Vedder when the song 'Better Man' was covered. I couldn't help but feel guilty as I sang along to the words. *It's karma, Alexis, and you know it!*

Level two of Opals was centred around current pop music. Tash and Carls had their dancing shoes on, so we spent the night switching between both levels. Level three was hardcore techno, but it was a no-go zone for us since none of us liked that genre.

* * *

Since we were at a club in the City Towers precinct, I couldn't help but look over my shoulder for most of the night, sensing that I was being watched and having a good idea of whom. *You're paranoid, Alexis, get over yourself.*

I couldn't shake the feeling though, because a few times when I was very stupidly dancing Gangnam Style with Tash and Jade, I could have sworn I spotted Bryce leaning against the wall. But when I looked back, he was gone. It had to be my imagination; there was no possible way he could have known I was there. City Towers Entertainment Complex was enormous, and even his creepy research skills could not have revealed that we had changed our plans to go there at the last minute, surely?

Putting aside my warranted, or not so warranted, feelings of being stalked, you knew that you'd had a crazy fun night when the table you were sitting at was topped with empty glasses. Not to mention you'd laughed so extensively that a trip to the toilet eventuated numerous times. Your voice was somewhat missing. Your eyes were constantly pounding. And you'd danced so much that your feet no longer had feeling in them. All these indications were of a night well had, and I loved having shared them with my friends.

So, after copious amounts of pretty cocktails, shots and terrible dance moves — including watching Tash's infamous bum dance — the clock was fast approaching 1.30 a.m. My feet had gone past the stage of numbness and were now at the point of reminding me just how much they hated heels. I had to give them credit where credit was due though, because they had been very good to me lately. I had obviously taken them for granted this particular night and now they hated me.

Carls, Tash, and Steph were still in dancing mode, so they continued their dancing to non-existent music all the way out of the nightclub, through the casino, and toward the car park. Lil and Jade, on the other hand, looked as punished and exhausted as I was.

'What are they on?' Jade asked with astonishment as she shook her head at our three crazy dancing friends.

Lil started rubbing her throat. 'Fuck, whatever it is, I want some.'

'How's that cock going, Lil? The prickly one that stuck in your throat,' I giggled.

She cleared her throat and winced. 'It's still fucking there.'

Jade stopped, propped herself against the wall, and proceeded to remove her shoes. 'I'm too old for this shit.'

Fuck it, I'm doing it too. I figured it was the early hours of the morning and there was a slim to no chance that anybody I knew would catch me being a drunken bogan.

'You are not too fucking old, Jade,' I mumbled as I stopped just short of her position. 'Maybe we just need to lower our heel height a bit ... or drink and dance less.'

I attempted to pry off my left heel and stumbled into her.

'Lexi, did you have enough to drink tonight, luv?'

Now that was an understatement! My telltale signs of stumbling, increased foul language, and the constant need to smile, were slowly becoming apparent.

'Just a bit. Shh,' I giggled, and put my arm on hers for balance, trying my shoe removal again and bending over in the hope that if I did fall, I wouldn't fall far.

An intoxicated sleazeball obviously thought in passing — as my arse was highly accessible in my bent over position — that he had the right to pinch it.

'Hey! Piss off, prick,' Jade warned while eyeballing the guy.

I would normally just ignore idiots like him. But, after so many drinks, I somehow thought I was a lot tougher, inevitably stepping up my aggression, which wasn't always a good thing. 'Keep your fucking filthy hands to yourself, arsehole,' I offensively yelled at him.

We started to walk again, but he stepped in front of us, blocking my path. I went to go around him, but he stumbled and blocked me once more.

Clenching my heel in my hand, I prepared myself for an attack. 'Piss off, dickhead.'

'Oh, come on, darlin'. With an arse like that it's begging to be felt.' He went for another touch and, as he did, his arm was subdued in mid-grope and bent so far up his back that he groaned loudly with pain.

'The lady said "piss off", not touch her arse again.'

I groggily looked up to see Bryce standing behind the drunken arsehole, looking furious and ever so slightly inching the guy's arm up higher. The arsehole's friend went to throw a punch in Bryce's direction, but Bryce saw it coming and wrenched the arsehole round to block the incoming attack.

It was actually quite funny — sort of like a Jackie Chan movie, and I'm sure I let out a woozy giggle as Jade and Lil moved me back and away from the action. Two security guards appeared almost instantly and helped Bryce to subdue both arseholes. In the meantime, Tash, Carls and Steph had stopped dancing and doubled back to see what had happened.

'Ladies, are you all right?' Bryce asked, while keeping his eyes locked solely on mine.

He had moved closer and was now by my side. I couldn't help smiling at him. He was my sexy knight in shining armour and I wanted to pat my hand down his face and coo at him like a puppy. *Alexis, you're drunk. He is not a beautiful puppy!*

'Jackie Chan, what a coincidence. Thank you for saving our lives,' I stated, unable to sound any more sarcastic and unappreciative if I tried.

He smirked at me — of course — so I continued to stare at him. Partly because I loved looking at his immaculate face, but also because I was, in fact, quite intoxicated and found it difficult to look away.

He cocked an eyebrow and smiled broadly. 'Jackie Chan?' *Oh shit, did that come out of my mouth? That was supposed to stay in my head.*

'Alexis, earth to Alexis,' Carls sang.

I tried to answer her, but couldn't, and when I didn't respond right away, she decided to introduce herself.

'I'm Carly, you must be Mr Clark. I've heard so much about you,' Carls explained as she extended her hand. *Carly Josephine Henkley, I am going to kill you.*

'You have, have you?' Bryce replied, smiling at me then at Carly before politely shaking her hand.

After hearing Carly's knowledge of who he was, he seemed quite pleased with himself. I, on the other hand, silently witnessed his now overly-cocky expression and made a drunken mental note to carry out my homicide attempt on Carly when I was not so inebriated.

'How are you ladies getting home tonight?' Bryce asked, directing his question to the other girls.

Noticing that Lil, Tash, Jade and Steph were all speechless and pretty much drooling, Carls seemed to be the only one who could formulate words. 'Alexis is driving,' she said stoically before cracking up laughing and playfully hitting Bryce on the arm. 'No, just kidding. We are catching a ... Maxi Taxi,' she hollered, practically singing the stupid name. It made me giggle again.

Bryce reached into his pocket, removed his phone, then put it up to his ear. 'Danny, can you bring the limo round to exit door eight. Thank you.'

Carly had now joined the rest of the girls, becoming speechless as she stood there with her mouth gaping open.

I, however, found my tongue after his request for the limo. 'It's fine, Bryce, we can get a ... Maxi Taxi.' This time I did, in fact, sing the stupid name. Everyone laughed, including Bryce. *Urgh! You are going to hate yourself tomorrow, Alexis.*

Subduing his chuckle, Bryce's demeanour turned somewhat serious. 'It's not negotiable, Alexis. Danny will take you all home safely. It's the least I can do after that creep gave you a hard time,' he informed me, remorse and anger filling his eyes.

Seeing the obvious concern he was feeling, not to mention that he also seemed to be enjoying the power he had over me and that he could show it in front of my friends, I decided not to argue with him.

Exit door eight was only metres from where we had been standing. Bryce opened the door and gestured the girls to go through and enter the car park where there was a limo waiting. I followed, but stopped beside Bryce in the doorway, only to find Danny standing by the limo and holding the door open as all the girls stepped inside.

I waited till they were in and seated before I turned to Bryce and screwed up my face. 'Thank you,' I said with surrender. I was too tired and frankly too drunk to argue or interrogate him as to how he just happened to be there at the exact moment to intervene.

'You're welcome, Alexis.'

He eyed me up and down and ran his hand through his hair. *Oh, that is so sexy. I hate yet love it when he does that.*

'Fuck,' he groaned, taking another sweeping look over my body. 'You look good tonight. I can't really blame that arsehole for wanting to touch you. It's taking every single bit of my strength not to touch you myself, especially your tits. You have great tits, Alexis.'

I couldn't help but burst into laughter. It had to be the alcohol, there was no other explanation. Not knowing how to respond to his declaration of admiring my 'tits', I smiled at him and got into the limo.

* * *

Sunday morning was sleep-in day — my favourite day of the week. But this particular morning was far from fun. Unfortunately, I decided I agreed with Jade; I was too fucking old for this shit. My head was throbbing, and every time I took a breath, it felt as though I was sucking in a mouthful of dust.

Not wanting to open my eyes — already anticipating the blinding light that would shine through when I did — I opted to just lay there and thought back to the night before. How had Bryce known I was there? Surely he hadn't just happened to be at the nightclub when we walked in. No, I didn't believe that for a second. It had to be some form of his creepy research. To be honest though, I was glad he had come to my rescue. Looking back at it now, I realised I may not have had the coordination, nor the strength, to ward those arseholes off. Realising this, I genuinely needed to thank him the next time I was at work.

Eventually, when I opened my eyes, I found that Rick was no longer lying next to me. The house was quiet — which was very unusual — so I got up to investigate the rarity.

Upon entering the kitchen, I found a note Rick had left on the dining room table, informing me that he had taken the kids to the football. *Rick, you wonderful man!*

We were members of the Essendon Football Club and went to as many games as we could. Nate loved the footy and was lucky enough to have his jersey signed by all the players.

Happy to have the house to myself, I thought I would use my new-found alone time to get the washing, vacuuming and my personal grooming done.

By the time everyone returned home, I had a roast lamb in the oven, the washing folded and ready to put away, and not a skerrick of hair on my legs, bikini line or underarms. *A Sunday well utilised, Alexis!* I mentally gave myself a pat on the back.

* * *

Later that night, I heard my mobile phone ring from within my handbag. I quickly retrieved it to see Tash's smiling face on the screen. *Shit! No, go away. I don't want a grilling. Argh.*

Hesitantly, I answered the call. 'Hi, Tash, what's up?'

'How's the hangover, luv?'

'Behaving. And yours?'

'Don't worry about mine, because you, missy, have some explaining to do.'

'I do not.'

'Yes, you do. You fobbed us off during the limo ride home last night, but there is no way in hell I am waiting any longer. Right, so Mr sexyarse-Jackie Chan-Clark. Explain! Now!' *Jackie Chan? That wasn't a dream. Ah, shit! Crap! Balls! It was inevitable. I had been busted.*

I managed to spill only half the beans to Tash, basically confessing to having an extremely sexy boss who liked to flirt with me. I had brushed her off by explaining that he was a filthy rich bachelor who made a habit of flirting and that I was no one special.

Thankfully, she left it at that and just cursed at me for ditching our coffee dates to go and work for the 'Super-hot god'!

CHAPTER
11

Still sporting a slight hangover, I groaned as I pulled myself out of bed in order to get ready for work. *Sleep, I need more sleep!*

Remembering Bryce's request to come in my gym clothes for a self-defence lesson, I was glad I needn't worry about spending half an hour putting on make-up. To be honest, his request was both bitter and sweet. Yes, there was no need to fluff about with cosmetics, but instead, I was soon going to be punished for having no idea how to participate in a martial arts class. Bryce was going to love my lack of coordination, not to mention have a really good laugh at me at the same time — he seemed to enjoy getting one up on me.

Pulling my hair into a ponytail, I grabbed my make-up bag and Burberry shirtdress. 'I hope the two of you are both ready and waiting by the time I get out there,' I yelled to my children.

Lucky for them, as I walked into the lounge Nate and Charlotte were both ready and waiting like soldiers at attention.

'Ahhh ... very good, at ease, soldiers,' I smiled, before bundling them into the car and heading off.

Thankfully, the school drop-offs had become less harrowing, Nate having discovered that before-school care was not as awful as he had originally thought. My instincts told me that this had something to do with a particular nine-year-old girl named Chantal who also attended the before-school program.

Smiling to myself at the thought of Nate trying to impress her, I blew both him and Charli extra kisses as they walked into the office building. 'Bye, ratbags, love you. I'll see you tonight.'

* * *

Initially, the thought of self-defence class had worried me. But as my session with Bryce approached, the idea of it had actually grown on me ... until I bore witness to the abundance of women who were waiting in the hotel gymnasium. Just seeing them gathered around, waiting for the class to begin, made me feel intimidated and unsure.

I was the proud owner of a gym membership, but I only ever used the weights or the cardio machines. Plus, I hadn't actually exercised once since starting my new job. So I knew the class was going to be a challenge, not only physically but from my lack of coordination as well.

It really shouldn't have surprised me that there would be a lot of women in attendance. In fact, I could've confidently bet money that none of them actually gave a shit about self-defence nor paid any attention to the learning aspects of the class. Judging by the whispered giggling and obvious excitement when Bryce entered the room, they were only there for one reason — a bloody good perve!

Sneaking into the class two rows from the back, I was sure the spot I had chosen was the most inconspicuous position. Surely, I couldn't embarrass myself in this little pocket of space.

'Good morning, ladies. Did we all have a good weekend?' Bryce asked the class in his charming and alluring tone of voice.

The women agreed in unison, and I couldn't help but playfully roll my eyes at their spellbound display. It was as though I was in the middle of a bunch of schoolgirls.

'Good, now that your fun is over, we need to get serious.'

A lady behind me murmured, 'I'd like to get serious with him.' Another laughed and agreed.

'Do I have any newcomers today?' he asked, scanning the room.

A couple of women put their hands up, so he directed them to stand in the front row. I figured I'd stay where I was and hide near the back — but he was onto me. Before I had a chance to look elsewhere, our eyes met and locked.

'Ah, Alexis, my lovely assistant. I'd like you all to meet Alexis. She is going to help me demonstrate a few defensive moves today,' he explained smugly, holding out his hand and then pointing to the empty spot next to him. *Oh shit, you didn't just do that! And you're freaking smirking at me.*

Hesitantly and very slowly, I made my way to the front, giving a sheepish wave to the class. Which, from the looks on their faces, impressed none of them; in fact, I'd hazard a guess and say they all secretly hated me.

Bryce placed his hands on both my shoulders and positioned me next to him, causing my cheeks to redden. I knew that once again, I looked like the beetroot I so often resembled when I was around him.

'Okay, ladies, shall we begin?'

They all nodded eagerly.

'I want you to remember the following six soft spots: eyes, ears, throat, groin, fingers and toes. Inflicting pain to these very sensitive areas can help to give you the best chance of disabling your attacker,' he advised as he began pacing the stage.

As he spoke, every pair of eyes in the room followed his every move. Including mine.

'No matter how big your attacker is, his eyelids are always going to be just a thin layer of skin. This makes them a very vulnerable target to attack. A simple eye gouge with your thumb is all that is needed to cause your attacker pain and quite possibly allow you to get away.'

He moved to face me and demonstrated the action of sticking his thumbs into my eyes, although he didn't actually touch me.

'Or, you can make a quick hard jab to the eye sockets with the fingertips, like this.'

I flinched instinctively as he thrust his finger toward my eye, stopping just short of my face. My flinch made him laugh. *Oh, you are hilarious.*

'Either of those two actions are great techniques to assist you in breaking a hold your attacker may have you in, especially where your arms are not restrained.

'Okay, the next soft spot you should learn about are the ears. The ears are usually easy enough to grab onto and, if yanked hard enough, will cause your attacker a great deal of discomfort. Another effective tactic is giving both ears a hard slap at the same time with your palms, creating such air pressure that it could potentially rupture an eardrum.'

With him still facing me, he instructed me to perform the last technique on him. 'Alexis, with both your palms facing inward, slap both my ears in unison.' He quickly put his hands over his ears before my hands reached his head. *Damn it! He was onto me. Oh well, my revenge will have to wait.*

I did what I was told and slapped his ears. 'Excellent, hitting both ears at the same time is paramount in this situation.'

Bryce moved quite close to me and placed his two fingers to my throat. I tried not to look directly into his eyes as his face was not far from mine, but my attempt was futile. Upon eye contact with each other, my chest began to rise and fall quite obviously.

He, too, picked up on my sudden change of heart rate, noticeably swallowing hard. 'What I call the trachea well is the little patch of soft flesh here,' he said gently as he massaged my lower throat with his fingertips, 'at the base of where the Adam's apple on a man would be.'

I couldn't help but close my eyes for the smallest of seconds, the whole ordeal nearly proving to be too much to cope with in a room full of onlookers.

'Just like the eyelids, this area is only one thin layer of skin protecting a vital and sensitive body part. You attack the trachea well in the same manner as the eyelids, with a thumb gouge or sharp, finger jab like this.' He repeated the quick jabbing move, prompting me to reopen my eyes.

'The second part of the throat area to strike is the carotid artery.' He removed his fingers from my lower neck and firmly replaced one of his hands higher up, squeezing gently. 'Grabbing in a claw-like motion to either side of the Adam's apple area, and squeezing hard, will cause your attacker a great deal of pain,' he explained.

This particular demonstration made me feel quite uncomfortable, not to mention vulnerable — I didn't like my neck being squeezed. Unable to stop myself from looking up at the roof, I silently prayed this demonstration would not last long.

Bryce, noticing my unease, immediately relaxed his fingers, then walked round to stand behind me. He left his hand resting on my shoulderblade and gently flexed his fingers, which gave me a sense of relief.

'Most of you will already be aware that the groin is always a popular attack point. I probably don't need to explain why, but let me assure you, if enough force is inflicted on this area, it does cause a male a severe amount of pain,' he continued to explain.

There was a snigger around the room, and I noticed one of the ladies in the front row licking her lips. I wanted to slap her, hard! Better still, I wanted to slap both her ears at the same time and poke my fingers into her trachea. I found myself glaring at her.

'If you are being attacked from the front and he has your shoulders pinned, a swift kick to the groin with the top of your foot as hard as you can will be effective. Or, if he is closer to your body, a knee into the groin, nice and hard, can be just as successful. If you are able to grab his ears when you do this, it will not only give you more control and balance when kneeing him, but it will also cause pain in a second area at the same time.

'Now, as you are aware, men will not always attack from the front. In fact, attacking from behind is more likely as it enables them the element of surprise. If your attacker has you from behind in a bear hug, there are many things you can do to break his hold. One of the things you can do is simply step to the side and perform a hammer punch down into the groin, like this.'

He demonstrated the move by raising his arm to his shoulder with a clenched fist, then swinging down hard behind him. Then, walking up behind me, he whispered into my ear before the commencement of our next demonstration. 'Don't even think about making contact.' *Is that a threat, Mr Clark?*

I felt this was a good opportunity for revenge, but thought some more about his words — and he did have the power to make me squirm at the best of times. So I figured that obeying his request was the smart option.

Suddenly, he grabbed me hard from behind, causing my instincts to kick in. I stepped to the side and swung my arm down firm and fast, stopping just in time to gently brush his groin. I couldn't help but keep my hand there, as if magnetised to that very spot.

He twitched his dick ever so slightly to indicate he felt my hand, sending a hot flush right through me. Every fibre in my being wanted to grab him and feel his hard cock in my hand, but I couldn't ... I wouldn't. Instead, I kept my hand still, not being able to move it.

After several seconds had elapsed, Bryce cleared his throat and stepped to my side. 'Instead of a hammer punch, you could also grab the groin with force, squeeze really hard, and pull your handful forward.'

The lady who had licked her lips earlier smiled and batted her eyes at Bryce's suggestion. *That's it, bitch! It's on! You and me, right here, right now.* She was just so blatant in her desire to stroke his body with her tongue and it made me mad.

'Can everyone grab a partner, please?' Bryce instructed.

The women shuffled around until they were paired up.

'Thank you. Finally, I want to demonstrate how to break an attacker's head-hold. One of the most common ways a man will grab you is by the head. When someone restrains a victim's head, they gain control of most of their victim's body. This is why attackers tend to grab your head first. Now, facing Alexis, I'm going to grab the back of her head.'

He placed his hand quite firmly on the back of my head and looked me straight in the eyes.

'Your attacker will try to lower your head as it will enable him to gain the control that he's after. I want you to push back against his hand and keep the control yourself. Now, the ladies on the left will be the attackers and the ladies on the right, the victims.'

They all moved into position.

'Good. Attackers, you are going to grab your victims at the back of their head with the intention to bring it closer to you, or with the intention to lower it. Victims, you are going to push back with your head. However, before you practise this, remember to not put too much strength into your moves, we don't want any injuries. Use just enough force to allow you to feel how to perform the manoeuvre. Alexis and I will demonstrate first.'

He looked at me and nodded. 'Are you ready? Push back against my pull.'

Replacing his hand on the back of my head, I automatically wrenched up and back. I didn't think he anticipated my strength, as he smiled in surprise and kept his grip. 'The next thing you need to do is break this hold once you have gained some control over your head. You can perform many of the soft spot tactics I mentioned before, or if he has grabbed you with his left arm, you can swing your right arm around to hit him in the elbow joint with your palm. This will also break his hold on your head, and vice versa if he has used his other arm.

'Hitting an attacker with force on the elbow joint is always a good defensive move to try at any point, as the elbow is weak, regardless of how strong your attacker actually is.'

Releasing my head, he came around behind me and pressed himself against my back. This time his dick-twitch was not so subtle and, as I felt its hardness, tingles ran up and down my spine and together with his close proximity, my body unravelled in a quiet frenzy.

'Now, as you hit him in the elbow, turn slightly in the direction you have hit his arm. This allows the grip to release easier on your head.'

Bryce picked up my arm ever so gently and swung it around in a swift punching motion, like I was a puppet under his command. 'Just like that,' he motioned to the class and performed the move with my arm again. 'Everybody got that?'

They nodded in agreement.

'Good. Now, Alexis, are you ready?'

This time I was the one smirking at him and, in that split second before he grabbed the back of my head again, I noticed his apprehension when he spotted my cocky expression.

Feeling his hand on my head, I instantly jerked up and back then quickly swung my arm around hitting him directly in the elbow joint, forcing his grip away from my head. I then finger-jabbed his trachea — not too hard — but enough to catch him by surprise. *That felt great! Take that, Mr Use-me-as-a-guinea-pig Clark.*

He grabbed his elbow with his other arm, rubbed his throat, bent over slightly, and then looked up at me in shock. *Shit, did I hurt him?*

Giving his arm a shake, he praised my efforts. 'Very good, Alexis.' Although his tone sounded somewhat tense and I got the sense he was slightly annoyed but, quite possibly, slightly turned on at the same time. It gave me a surge of excitement and accomplishment. I grinned a little and stood back in my position.

'All right, ladies. Everyone give that a try please, minus the finger jab,' he explained while shooting me a you're-going-to-pay look.

Bryce began to circulate around the room to assist the women with their moves, almost every single one of them needing some form of help. 'Excellent, keep practising and taking turns for a minute,' he advised with obvious praise.

Watching him step back up on the stage, I noticed a renewed look of interest in his eyes. It both worried and exhilarated me at the same time.

'I like it when you are feisty,' he whispered seductively into my ear. *Oh, you do, do you?*

I turned to face him. 'Good, what's next then?'

I was ready for more. I had a sudden surge of adrenaline and wanted to kick his arse. Partly because he irritated the hell out of me in a cheeky way, but partly because we were getting up close and personal. And I liked the feeling of his twitching dick.

CHAPTER

12

The last of the women in the class were starting to get the idea that it was, in fact, time to leave. Bryce had been very polite to the ladies who hung around him like flies and didn't once give the impression they were pestering him. I was almost certain he received this reaction from women all the time. And I could only imagine it would have to be hugely annoying and draining. Then again, maybe it's different for men, I don't know. Still, if it had been me, I would definitely not have been as accommodating as he was.

Not wanting to hang around any longer, I grabbed my bag and headed to the change room. Bryce was still held up by the licking-lips lady, so I gestured to him that I would see him back in his office.

'Thank you, Chelsea, I'm glad you enjoyed it, but I'm sorry I really must go,' he said quickly, dismissing their conversation. *Brush-off of the century. Take that, lip-licking bitch.*

He picked up his pace, catching up to me and gently securing my arm. 'Alexis, where do you think you're going?'

'I'm going to have a quick shower before I see you up there,' I explained, now worried that my decision to do just that was somehow against the rules.

'Not down here you're not. I have five showers upstairs in my apartment. You can use one of those.'

'Oh,' I said, slightly surprised. I hadn't even thought to ask to use one of his. 'Thank you, I'd much prefer that.'

It was true, I really would prefer it. I didn't fancy gym showers at all; they completely grossed me out.

As we walked off, I noticed licking-lips lady snatch up her towel and bag while giving me a sarcastic smile. Again, I wanted to mow down the bitch and gouge her eyes with my thumbs. She really looked like a nasty piece of work. *Alexis, calm down, you adrenaline-infused martial arts wannabe.*

* * *

Bryce and I headed up to the penthouse via his private elevator, and I discovered it wasn't that much different from the main ones used by the hotel patrons. He punched in a code, and it took us directly to the second level of his apartment.

We stepped out of the elevator, and Bryce led me to one of the guest rooms, politely opening the door for me.

'Please make yourself at home and take as long as you want. I'll be in my room if you want me.' He stepped backward from the door with a smug look on his face.

This man never ceased to amaze me. He was just so upfront and goddamned cheeky and, if I wasn't married, I would happily take him up on the disguised invitation written all over his face.

Walking into the room, I noted it was — like every other room in his apartment — immaculate. However, it was also remarkably different from the others. It reminded me of a country cottage bed and breakfast room, with a neutral and green colour palette. The view of Port Phillip Bay from the window was magnificent, and I could see the *Spirit of Tasmania* docked at Station Pier in Port Melbourne. I thought back to a family holiday to Tasmania. We'd crossed Bass Strait on that ship and I had become terribly seasick. The memory made me shudder and, to this date, I have never been able to bring myself to attempt another ocean journey like that again.

Moving away from the window and suppressing my seasickness memory, I made my way to the bathroom, being met with a double-sized shower. There were also brand new bottles of shampoo, conditioner and body wash in the shower's caddy. Seeing this had me slightly puzzled, as the bottles matched the ones I used at home. *No, he couldn't possibly know what toiletries I use. That is just beyond creepy research: that is disturbing.*

I told myself to quiz him about it later, being more than happy to put it down to a weird coincidence, because the alternative was unnerving.

Stepping into the shower, I welcomed the glorious hot water as it slid down my neck, soothing my breasts and washing away the sexual frustration I had endured at the hands of Bryce during his self-defence class. *Ah, that's so nice. Would he notice if I just stayed in here all day? Of course he would, Alexis. He is probably watching you now on CCTV.*

Suddenly, I looked up, frantically searching every corner of the room. *Don't be stupid, that would be completely crossing the line.* The thing was, I couldn't entirely put it past him. From what I had learned so far, Bryce having CCTV was a definite possibility. *No, Alexis, you're an idiot. Hurry up and wash your hair.*

Now in a rush to get out of his guest shower, I reached for the shampoo and conditioner and washed my hair, following with the body wash. The steam from the hot water enhanced the scent of rose and jasmine, filling my nostrils with the familiar aroma. My body started to relax all over, so I closed my eyes and enjoyed the moment.

Not realising how long I had been standing there with my eyes closed, I opened them hastily, anxious to get my bearings back. As my eyes and brain adjusted to the sudden scenic change, I found Bryce standing directly in front of me — completely naked. Before I could comprehend my situation, he grabbed hold of my face and pressed me up against the shower wall.

I gasped at the chill from the tiles combined with the shock of him actually being in front of me ... up against me. 'Bryce! No!'

'Shut up, Alexis.' *Oh, okay.*

I didn't argue any further. I was completely overwhelmed with sensation, and having his extremely sexy, hard, naked body up against my bare skin was totally disorientating.

He spun me around with hungry passion and cupped my breasts, groaning with vigour into my ear as he kissed my neck. His obvious desperation to have me already had me close to climaxing, coupled with the dangerous and forbidden nature of our involvement. I knew it was wrong but it felt so fucking exciting and hot — my body was literally on fire and ready to combust.

He trailed his hand down to my clit and took control of it instantly, forcing me to groan and completely lose myself in the moment. I was utterly riled, provoked and so incredibly turned on.

Spinning back around, I grabbed the back of his head and pressed my lips to his, kissing him aggressively, almost like we each had to take control of each other's mouth.

Gripping my arse ferociously, he lifted me up. *Holy fuck!*

I was breathing hard as I yanked his head back and looked deeply into the depths of his eyes. We stared at each other silently for several seconds, both yearning for more. His expression was so honest, and I could see how much he wanted me, how much he had wanted this, and how I was no longer capable of saying no to him, regardless of what it cost me. I was totally addicted to him.

Patience obviously not one of our strongest virtues, we resumed our passionate kissing, but the intensity had eased ever so slightly, and now we were savouring the moment and exploring one another's body with our hands, fingers, lips and tongues.

I felt myself stretch as he entered me, the feeling exquisite as he penetrated me further. I couldn't hold back any more, and exploded with pleasure all the while falling back against the tap.

Suddenly, I felt a stream of cold water spray my body. I opened my eyes, and it took me a moment to become aware of the explicit and highly forbidden daydream I had just concocted in my head and greedily endured. *What. The. Fuck. Alexis?*

Standing there completely overwhelmed and feeling dazed and embarrassed, I realised I had actually masturbated and orgasmed in Bryce's bathroom. *You shameless little bitch!*

Having no option but to let the cold water bathe me, I stood there, needing the icy chill after what I'd just envisioned and physically experienced.

What was this man doing to me? And more importantly, what was I doing to myself?

CHAPTER
13

Staring in the vanity mirror, I observed my flushed cheeks. I couldn't help but smile, having never in my wildest dreams done anything like that before. *Well, you have now, you wanton hussy. Go ahead, Alexis. Add it to your list: masturbate in the shower while you daydream about the man of your dreams fucking you!*

I sheepishly laughed at my reflection, a reflection that was so different to what it had been weeks ago. The Alexis looking back at me now was sure of herself — maybe too sure — and she was dressed immaculately in a black Burberry shirtdress with a gorgeous garter and stockings. I had even developed a knack for make-up and could confidently say I was definitely changing for the better. Or was I? Was fantasising about infidelity really for the better? No, it wasn't.

Bending down, I opened the vanity cupboard. *A hairdryer, brilliant!* Also, sitting in an elegant basket in the vanity, were a number of perfume bottles that were brand new and still in shrink-wrap. I recognised a few and picked up Dolce and Gabbana, Rose The One — my favourite. *What can I say? I seriously do love roses.*

Perusing the basket again, I became aware that it was, in fact, full of my favourite perfumes: Chanel N°5, Lady Million, Chloé, even White Musk from The Body Shop. *This is crazy! How does he know this? It's not like it's written on my résumé or plastered across my Facebook page.*

Unease surfacing from the pit of my stomach, I knew I had to get to the bottom of this creepy research once and for all. But first I needed to dry my hair and spritz myself with Chanel. *Hair and perfume … priorities.*

* * *

Cautiously, I made my way down the stairs, my caution partly due to the fact I was new to heels this high and partly because I had no idea where Bryce had gone. When I reached the bottom step, he came out from the kitchen, holding two plates and stopping momentarily to look at me before resuming his original course.

'Breakfast is ready, Alexis. How was the shower?' *Did he just smirk at me? Oh, holy shit! He does have CCTV! He watched me, he fucking watched me!* I was ready to take a dive over his forty-third floor balustrade.

'Alexis, are you okay? You look like you've just seen a ghost. What's wrong?' Bryce put the plates on the coffee table and rushed over to me. 'What's wrong? Please tell me?' he asked, looking horrified. 'Was the shower okay? It should've been fully equipped with everything you'd need.'

I took in his concerned face and watched him wait eagerly for my response, getting the impression that maybe I'd been too hasty and made the wrong assumption in regards to the CCTV. But, as I had him there squirming, I figured I might as well utilise the situation.

'The toiletries and the perfume, how did you know? This is way past creepy, Bryce. This is more like spine-chilling, stalker-like research.'

His disposition suddenly relaxed, and he very subtly murmured, 'Phew'.

Spine-chilling, stalker-like research aside, he is just so adorably cute sometimes.

'Lucy,' was all he said.

'Lucy what?' I asked.

'Lucy figured that you would one day need to use the guest room. Let's just say the creepy or "spine-chilling, stalker-like research" as you put it, runs in the family.'

'But how does she know?' *Gee, they're as bad as each other.*

He walked back over to the coffee table, picked up the plates, and proceeded out to the balcony. 'She rang and spoke to your daughter.'

I began my pursuit, calling out after him. 'But you can't do that! That's an invasion of privacy, not to mention harassment and taking advantage of a six-year-old with a big mouth.'

I sat down at the table he had set up.

'It's what we do, Ms Summers.'

Oh, please! I rolled my eyes. *Give it up, Alexis, you are not going to win this one.* I let out a surrendering sigh then surveyed the table. Salmon and dill omelettes, orange juice, fresh berry salad with yogurt, and a hot white-chocolate topped with none other than a single marshmallow. It looked amazing and smelled incredible.

'Eat, Alexis, you need to build up your protein after a work-out.' *I've had a work-out all right, just not the one you are referring to.*

Not waiting a second longer, I dug into the omelette. It was delicious. 'Yum, I hope you pay your chefs more than me,' I said with awe while my tastebuds went to heaven and back. I wolfed down another mouthful, prompting him to laugh quietly. *What? Was I making a pig of myself?* 'What's so funny, Mr Clark?'

I knew I wasn't the most elegant eater in the world, but surely I wasn't laughable.

'You could say that,' he answered, still amused by something unknown to me.

'Could say what?' I spoke, with my mouth full. *Okay, scratch that last thought. I was laughable!*

'You could say that I pay the chef more than you.'

'Oh, good. Because he deserves it. This is wonderful.'

'Thank you.'

Ding goes the light bulb! 'You cooked this? Bryce, you are sensational.'

He grinned sheepishly, put his head down, and continued to eat. *A blushing billionaire. Who would've thought!*

* * *

After breakfast, Bryce had me schedule his itinerary for the upcoming Tel V Awards, which were to be held in the Queen Victoria Ballroom the following Monday evening. This was very exciting for me because I enjoyed watching the event on TV every year from my couch at home. The Tel V Awards were the Australian equivalent of the American Emmy Awards, and everyone who was anyone would be at the hotel in a weeks' time.

City Towers had hosted the prestigious event for many years and was highly renowned for its attention to detail and extremely high-security protocols system. City Towers also had a total of four hundred and eighty-one rooms and suites, and thirty villas — the perfect set-up to host the VIP guests from Australia and other parts of the world.

I had spoken to Clarissa from Versace — lovely lady that she was — and she assured me Bryce's tuxedo would arrive in time for the event.

Bryce was so busy in the lead-up to the Tel V Awards that he had meetings booked all weekend with numerous heads of department: Dale, Head of Security; Maria, Head of House-keeping; Vincent, Head Chef in the complex's catering kitchen for large events; and Joyce, Head Media Liaison Officer. The last meeting I had to arrange for him was with Abigail, so picked up the phone and dialled her mobile.

'Abigail, it's Alexis. How are you today?

'Alexis, sweetheart, I'm assuming this is a business call?'

'Yes, I need to schedule a meeting with you for Friday regarding the Tel V Awards. Mr Clark wants your overview delivered here, preferably today, so he can peruse and then discuss it with you at the meeting. As you can imagine he has back-to-backs from Thursday onwards, but I have reserved a time slot for you at 9.30 a.m.'

'Certainly, I'm one step ahead of you though. Samantha and Chelsea are on their way with the overview now.'

'You're one of a kind, Abigail, thank you.'

I ended the call, realising that I missed Abigail. I really could have learned a lot from that wonderful lady. She was extremely diligent and professional and, as the elevator doors opened, I could add efficiently organised to that list, too.

Samantha stepped through the doors, and a tall leggy blonde followed behind her. Seeing Samantha reminded me that I still needed to have a chat with her about Gareth; he simply gave me the creeps and I wanted to find out whether I was being unreasonable or not.

As they approached my desk, I realised that I had seen the blonde before, becoming more annoyed when I realised where. Chelsea was licking-lips lady. *What is that bitch doing here?*

'Alexis, long time no see. Are you snubbing me now that you are up here in the penthouse?' Samantha said with a pout.

'Of course not, sweetie. Actually, I wanted to catch up for lunch sometime this week.'

'Sounds good. Listen, have you met Chelsea? She has filled your position.'

Are you shitting me?

Chelsea stepped up to stand beside Samantha and towered over me as I sat in my seat. 'We haven't met as such, but I was witness to Alexis' self-defence skills this morning.'

Ms Chelsea fucking-licking-lips-bitch was hopeless at trying to cover up her contempt for me with a smile.

'Oh, that's right, Chelsea. Mr Clark asked you to take the class so that you could promote it to guests. Do you know self-defence, Alexis? I didn't know that you knew self-defence?' Sam said with an unsure smile as she looked between Chelsea and me.

'No, Sam, I don't. Mr Clark apparently needed a guinea pig and chose me.' I raised my eyebrows at her.

Just as Samantha was about to respond, Bryce opened his office door, then entered the foyer.

Samantha smiled nervously in his direction. 'Good morning, Mr Clark. Here is the overview you requested from Abigail,' she advised as she went to hand him the brief.

'Thank you, Ms Taylor, but you can leave that with Alexis. Ms Hogan, can I have a moment in my office, please.'

Chelsea smiled sweetly at him. 'Of course, Mr Clark.'

He motioned her toward his office and as she walked past he placed his hand at the small of her back and followed her in.

That small insignificant gesture had me fuming. I wanted nothing more than to army-roll across my desk, kick down the door, pounce on this Chelsea bitch and scratch her brown freaking eyes out. Then I wanted to demonstrate to Bryce exactly just what it would feel like if my hammer punch had, in fact, connected with force to his groin. *Alexis, bury your WWE alter ego and get a grip.* I closed my eyes, then took in a breath.

'Argh! I hate her, Alexis.' *What?*

Samantha had dropped her head on my desk. *Don't worry, hon, I hate her too.*

'Why? What's been happening?' I asked with interest. I missed the interaction with her and Liam; their gossip sessions were always amusing.

'She thinks her shit don't stink. Just because daddy owns a helicopter charter company out in Essendon. She has a pilot's licence, you know. She is also six foot tall, and can speak fluent French, Italian, and Greek, and blah, blah, blah.'

Her voice trailed off like a whinging toddler. *Pilot licence? I hate her unconditionally now.*

Samantha slowly got up from her slumped position at my desk. 'Anyway, I've got to go. We have so much to organise for the Tel V Awards this week. It's such a huge event, I had no idea. Did you know 4Life are performing and staying in one of the villas? It's going to be crazy!'

4Life were the hottest boy band in the world. The hotel was going to be swarming with hypersensitive teenage girls. And Charlotte, oh my God! Charlotte was going to drive me crazy. She adored 4Life.

'Okay, Sam. Lunch tomorrow?'

'Yeah, should be fine.'

* * *

Shortly after Samantha left, Bryce buzzed my phone.

'Alexis, can you please have Sebastian bring up a bottle of the Chandon Rosé, a club sandwich and a crab baguette,' he said briskly, and then he hung up. *Fucking crab baguette! You can stick your crab baguette up your arse.*

I dialled Sebastian and placed the order. I was mad — so fucking mad — but why? Bryce had done nothing wrong really, maybe it was just the fact that this Chelsea bitch was a cocky little stuck-up moll and was clearly making her moves on him. Then again, why would this make me mad? There's not one single woman on this planet who wouldn't want to make a move on him. I couldn't really blame her ... he was single. *Am I jealous? I think I am.*

It was obvious that I was jealous. But I think I was more angry at the fact he had declared that he wanted me and had made me cross a very strict line when we kissed. And now he was just moving on to fresh meat. So, yes, I was jealous and pissed off, and rightfully so. *I should have added peanut butter to his bloody club sandwich.*

Sebastian appeared as the elevator doors opened, stepping into the foyer and pushing a food and beverage trolley. 'Ms Summers, Mr Clark's lunch request.'

'Yes, thank you, Sebastian.' I got up and walked over to the trolley. 'I will take it from here.'

He gave me a strange look and almost hesitated. Poor thing, I must have broken protocol or something.

'It's fine, Sebastian,' I said, giving him a reassuring look before taking the trolley from him.

'Very well. Good day, Ms Summers.'

Oh, I like him, he is so polite and sweet, and I just want to give him a hug and tell him his mother would be proud.

After Sebastian left the foyer, I pushed the trolley over to Bryce's office door and caught a glimpse of myself in the mirrored panelling on the wall. I decided to let my hair down so that it fell nicely in waves across my back. My breasts were conservatively covered, so I unbuttoned the top of my dress to reveal just a small peek of my red lace bra. Being that I was wearing a shirt dress, I was also able to unbutton the bottom to allow a split which would slightly expose the lacy top of my stockings when I knelt. *Right, let us see how this settles with him.*

Taking a deep breath, I knocked on the door. He didn't respond right away, which only added fuel to my fire.

'Yes?' he answered in his arrogant, rich, pig-headed tone.

I opened the door and pushed the trolley through. Bryce and Chelsea were seated opposite each other at the lounge where Bryce and I had shared our first lunch together. I closed the door behind me and pushed the trolley further into the room, making note of his wide-opened eyes as he took in my appearance.

'Your lunch, Mr Clark. Where would you like it?' I asked as sweetly as I could, trying desperately not to pick up each cloche and launch them at the two of them.

Chelsea had her back to me and had not looked around. *Smug, ungrateful bitch.*

Bryce ran his hand through his hair, giving away that my small adjustments had, in fact, aroused his attention. *Whatever it is you wanted to achieve, Alexis, I think it's working.*

'Just down here, thank you, Alexis,' he choked out.

I pushed the trolley toward him, stopping it right next to Chelsea so that it was in between me and her and pierced him with my anger-filled stare.

From the moment I had walked in, Bryce had not taken his eyes from me, his intense stare penetrating my core as he took in every tiny move that I made. His heated gaze had me feeling sheer exhilaration in the knowledge that I had such a profound effect on him. This gave me the nerve to continue the punishment I was giving — a punishment I wanted him to remember.

I knelt down beside the trolley to retrieve the bottle of Chandon and, as I squatted in my dress, I revealed the top of my stockings, this rather bold exposure making him fidget in his seat.

He had one leg resting on the other, which was the same way he sat when he was arrogantly flirting with me. I looked up and yet again pierced him with my furious glare, which made him uncross his leg. *Yeah, that's right, squirm, Mr game-playing Clark, squirm.*

Leaning over to place the bottle on the coffee table, I deliberately exposed a small portion of my bra, prompting him to cross his other leg.

I stood back up upright and was about to produce their plates when Bryce cleared his throat. 'Thank you, Alexis.'

'You're very welcome, Mr Clark,' I said, with clear distaste in my tone, and in turning to leave, flashed him a triumphant expression. *Yes, let this be a warning to you, Mr Clark. Don't fuck around with me.*

Then, completing my turn, I walked to the door, making sure my arse shook the absolute shit out of him. And not once during my display did I acknowledge that Chelsea was even in the room with us.

CHAPTER
14

I closed his door behind me and fell back against it, sighing, frustrated and hurt. My teasing punishment had felt so good when I was in his office, but it also felt childish, and what moments of satisfaction I had just achieved were now gone. *What am I doing?*

Deciding I would take a lunchbreak and tie up a few loose ends in person, things I would normally do from my desk, I forwarded all calls to my mobile and I got the hell out of there.

* * *

I had managed to spend most of the afternoon out of the office and, just when I thought I was home free, a call from Bryce rang through to my phone.

'Yes, Mr Clark?' I answered, as casually as was possible.

'Alexis, where are you?' he questioned, with an annoyed tone to his voice.

You tell me, stalker! 'I'm with Chris, from marketing.'

'When you're done, I'd like to see you in my office, please.'
Shit!

'Certainly, we are nearly done here,' I bit out, still trying to remain pleasantly calm before hanging up. *Who does he think he is? Yes, he's my boss, but he doesn't have any claim on me whatsoever. And, after his cute display earlier today with Chelsea, he has no right to have such a possessive tone with me. I'm not a toy and, more importantly, I'm not his toy.*

Chris and I quickly finished up our discussion on marketing the family-friendly rooms at the Promenade. He was very nice and seemed quite interested in my point of view as a mother. I guess that was the point to our meeting though.

'Thank you, Alexis. Your insight has been a great help. I'll run a few of these ideas through an advertising submission and will contact you shortly to discuss with Mr Clark.'

'Great. Thanks, Chris, I look forward to it.'

I got up and hesitantly made my way up to the lion's den.

* * *

While in the elevator, I pinned my hair back up and double-checked all my buttons were fastened. I was not going to make a point by teasing him again like I had. No matter how good it had felt, it really was a bad move on my part. Still, I had absolutely no intention of apologising to Bryce. If he wanted to be the rich, playful bachelor that he obviously was, then that was his business and none of mine. I had a husband who I loved and who loved me in return, and I was more than happy with that.

Stepping out of the elevator as the doors opened, I headed straight for my desk. But before making it even halfway there, Bryce came out of his office and into the foyer.

'Alexis, a word please,' he demanded. *Hold your horses.*

Giving myself a moment to take him in, I noticed he seemed quite angry. *Shit! I'm in trouble. I've really pissed him off.*

Thinking that couldn't be good — because despite what had happened, I still wanted to keep my job — I diverted from my desk, walking past him and into his office. As I entered his space, memories of him seated comfortably with Chelsea-bitch filtered back into my mind, firing my anger once again to boiling point. *You know what, Bryce? Bring it on. I'm sick of these games as well.*

Stopping dead still, I placed my bag down on the table and spun around to face him.

'Have a seat, Alexis.'

'No thanks, I'll stand.' *Screw him.*

He walked right up to me, fury filling his features. 'Why the disappearing act?'

I decided to play dumb. 'What disappearing act?'

'Why have you spent nearly four hours away from your desk?'

Because you infuriate me! 'I had loose ends to tie up and a meeting with marketing.' *I'm not fourteen, Bryce, nor am I grounded. Back the fuck off!*

'I need you at your desk.'

I need you to take me on my desk. Alexis, you are angry with him, remember?

'Why?' I demanded.

He didn't answer, instead asking me his own question. 'Why are you angry with me?' His tone had now softened, and he seemed to have dropped the bad cop attitude. *He is a bloody yo-yo.*

'I'm not,' I retorted, blatantly lying. I just wanted to go home.

Glancing at my watch, I noticed it was just past 6 p.m. *Thank God.*

'You are, and it has something to do with Chelsea.' He stepped away and headed to the buffet where he poured himself a drink, then, turning back to me, he smirked. *That does it!*

I was physically and mentally fucked, filled with jealous and anger and not understanding why. No longer able to hold any of it in any longer, I walked toward him with my hands on my hips. 'You know what, Bryce? You're right, I am pissed with you, and do you want to know why?' I didn't give him a chance to answer. 'Because you have completely turned my world upside-down. Not only have you single-handedly changed my career path, you have continuously flirted with me, invaded my privacy, taunted me with playful games, but also lured me in with expensive gifts and a "non-negotiable", absurd salary increase.

'You have played on the obvious sexual tension we share and have forced me to cross the line. This might be a game for you, but it's not for me. So, if you want to play your little touchy-feely wine and dine games with Miss Hogan, go right ahead. I'm going home to fuck my husband.' I snatched up my bag and made for the door.

In a flash he had my arm once again, spinning me around and pulling me to him. *Geez, he was quick.*

'Let me go,' I demanded.

'No, Alexis,' he said calmly.

'Let me go, Bryce,' I repeated, this time with less resolve.

He looked deep into my eyes and pleaded with me. 'Ask me to kiss you. Please ask me, or so help me God, I will break my promise.'

'No, let me go. I am not your toy. If you want a toy, go and play with Chelsea.'

'I don't want a toy, Alexis. And I don't want Chelsea either. I want you. I want you so fucking badly that it is driving me crazy. I've never wanted anyone or anything more in my life.' His grip tightened on my arm. 'You're killing me, you know that? You walk into my office looking so fucking sexy, teasing me with your lingerie. Then you disappear for hours. You're jealous and you want me too, just admit it.'

I was close to tears. 'Let me go,' I shouted, wrenching my arms up and hitting both his inner elbows hard, breaking his grip on me. The successful defensive move he had shown me seemed to momentarily surprise us both.

However, I was so emotional at that point and on the brink of bursting — bursting with anger, with regret, with lust, with bloody everything — that my anger spilled over and I screamed at him.

'Yes, I want you! I want to fuck the living shit out of you.' I started to cry. 'Do I like to see you touch other women? No ... no, I don't. Do I feel a thousand tiny tingles spread across my body whenever you touch me? Yes ... yes, I do. Am I exhilarated and alive whenever I am with you? Yes. Do I want to take it further? Yes ... yes, I fucking do, but that's not the point, Bryce.' I lowered my voice and took in a deep breath. 'It doesn't matter that I want you, and it doesn't matter that you want me. I took vows — to honour, to respect, and to be faithful, and I can't break them. I won't go behind Rick's back, ever! So what we want doesn't matter. I'm sorry,' I sobbed, then touched his cheek and left the room.

* * *

My head was a mess. The look of shock plastered on his face when I confessed that I wanted him was still stuck in my head.

He had texted me on my way home, asking me if I was leaving for good and, once again, I had replied by telling him, 'I'm not going anywhere'. The problem was, if we both felt this way, it was inevitable that I would have to leave at some point.

Walking through my front door, I felt wrecked. My heels got kicked off, the bag got dumped and I collapsed onto the couch.

Charlotte was on me almost instantly, giving me a kiss and stealing my high heels. 'Whoa, these are hard to walk in,' she said as she stumbled around the living room.

'I know, munchkin, and they hurt, too.' I rubbed my feet. 'Where's your brother?'

'Here,' Nate murmured as he came into the room and flopped onto the couch next to me.

I kissed his forehead. 'Hi, gorgeous boy.'

'How was work, Mum?'

'It was ... interesting.' *To say the least!* 'Oh, guess what I learned today?' I exclaimed, standing up wearily, my body protesting the movement. 'Self-defence.'

I did a ninja pose and Nate laughed. I must have been in the moment, because when Rick came in and put his hand on my shoulder, I spun around and whacked him on the elbow.

'Shit! Jesus, Alexis.' He rubbed his arm, making Charlotte laugh.

'Oh, damn! I'm sorry, babe.' I went to help with his rubbing when he grabbed me, crossing both my arms behind me.

'Get out of this one,' he challenged.

'I can, you know, but I'll hurt you,' I honestly replied.

'Sure you will.' He let me uncross my arms, then bear-hugged me and kissed my cheek. 'So, what's for tea?'

All three of them were looking at me.

'Really? Um ... well your choices are, pizza, pizza, or guess what? ... pizza. I'm plonking my butt on this couch and I'm not moving.'

* * *

It seemed everyone was happy with pizza and sitting on the floor in front of the TV which suited me perfectly. I really was exhausted, not just physically but also emotionally.

After dinner, I decided a long, hot bubble bath was needed — that, or a girls' weekend away. And, seeing that a girls' weekend was not going to happen right at that moment, I opted for the bubble bath instead. The idea of a girly get-away did sound good though. So much so that I decided I would ring Tash and get her on it.

So, after slipping into my blissful bath — with my feet thanking me for the hot lavender soak, and after the tension that was radiating through my body had started to ease — I grabbed my phone and dialled Tash.

'Lexi, how ya goin, luv? Still drooling over that boss of yours? I hate you. You do realise that, don't you?'

'Love you too, Tash. Listen, I need a girls' weekend away, in our barrel.'

Our 'barrel' was a large wine barrel cut in half and filled with natural thermal spring water with a temperature of forty degrees. It was our little sanctuary away from the real world in a tranquil hot springs day spa down on the coast.

'I'm hearing you, luv,' Tash sighed.

'You busy this weekend? I need it, STAT! My treat. Get Lil, Steph and Jade on to it as well, yeah?'

'Your treat? Piss off. What about Carls?'

'I'm pretty sure Carls has work stuff on. And I'm serious, hon. It's a long story and an emergency. I know it's late notice but I'm desperate. Pleeeeeease?' I begged.

'All right, I'm on it. Barrel, here we come.'

She hung up, and I pictured her doing her ruffle butt dance. Smiling with visions of Tash dancing away, I sank lower into the water and soaked in the bath until I resembled a human prune. Then, finally dragging myself out of the tub approximately an hour later, I pulled on my nightie and collapsed face down onto my mattress. Minutes later, Rick was at the base of the bed rubbing my feet.

'That's great,' I moaned into the pillow — not normally liking anyone touching my feet. However, they were so sore and it felt good. So I made the rare exception.

Rick started rubbing not only my feet, but my calves and thighs as well. I soon felt him placing kisses on the back of my knees.

'That tickles,' I giggled.

The next thing I knew, he had hiked up my nightie, exposing my bare arse and slapping me hard. 'Ow, that hurt.'

Chuckling, he kissed it better then rolled me onto my back before lifting my left leg and trailing kisses up it, watching for my reaction. His attention felt so nice.

Rick then lifted my other leg and performed the same action, this time kissing all the way up and skimming my clit ever so slightly.

Kneeling at the base of me, he removed his shirt. I sat up and helped him unbuckle his trousers, yanking them down impatiently.

'In a hurry, baby?' he asked with a smile as he gently pushed me back on the bed before kissing my neck.

'I need you, babe,' I declared almost desperately.

I wasn't lying, I really did need him. I needed to feel the same excitement that pulsed through me when I was with Bryce. I needed to feel that with Rick; needed it for reassurance, maybe. Up until now, I had never in our twelve years of marriage doubted our physical connection.

He leaned forward and licked my nipple, stretching it with his lips. I put my hands in his hair and massaged his head, prompting him to come back up to my mouth where he kissed me passionately. The kiss was both sweet and loving, but it always was with Rick.

Wanting to create and fuel a fiery passion between us, I rolled him over and straddled him, climbing on top of his erection and slowly pumping with my rise and fall. He gripped my hips and helped with the motion, infusing me with excitement and prompting me to quicken my pace. I wanted his hardness as deep as he could go. I wanted to be fucked.

'Not yet, baby,' he groaned and sat up, lifting me off him.

Hungry for more, I got on all fours, positioning myself in front of him where he re-entered me softly. He now controlled the pace and started slowly pushing himself inside, gradually pushing faster and harder until his balls were vehemently slapping my arse. We both came together and he filled me, massaging my breasts with his large hands as I continued to orgasm.

'I love you, Alexis,' he groaned.

'I know, babe, I love you too,' I said, breathlessly, my mixed emotions a horrible mess. I was completely and utterly spent, falling asleep almost instantly.

* * *

The next morning, I was running late. Nate had spent more than enough time in the bathroom and, when he did finally come out, he smelled of Joop. The thing was, my nine-year-old son did not own a bottle of Joop — his father did. When he climbed into the car, Charlotte asked what the smell was, knowing very well what it was and simply trying to stir her brother.

When we reached the school and the kids climbed out of the car, I kissed Nate through my wound down window.

'Not so much next time, okay?' I whispered in his ear. He went pink in the face and sniffed his collar. 'One spray, dude, trust me,' I winked. He nodded back.

* * *

Thankfully, the traffic on the freeway was light, so it wasn't until I turned onto Kings Way that everyone came to a complete halt. Unfortunately, the car behind me had not noticed the traffic ahead had stopped.

Watching the imminent impact via my rear-view mirror, I braced myself for the collision. The smash was hard, so hard that it pushed my vehicle into the car in front, setting my airbag off. It happened quickly, and if it weren't for the big white balloon in my face and the loud noise from the impact I may not have realised that it had happened at all.

Sitting there in shock for what could have been several minutes — I wasn't really sure — I eventually gathered my wits when a man came up to my window. I opened my door, the creaking noise it made sounding awful.

'Are you okay?' the man asked with concern.

'Yeah,' I said, warily, fairly sure that I was.

I unbuckled my seat belt and went to get out of the car.

'No, stay there. I've called an ambulance.'

'I don't need an ambulance, I'm fine,'

'No, stay there. You've been hit quite hard.' *Great, this is just what I need.* I was going to be late and without a car for God knows how long.

I reached for my phone and called Bryce.

'Alexis, is everything all right?'

'I'm going to be late, Bryce. I've been in an accident. My car is fucked and they've called an ambulance. I'm fine but —'

'Where are you?' he interrupted, speaking really fast.

'I'm just on the Kings Way exit ramp, not even five bloody minutes away —'

He interrupted again, saying 'I'm on my way,' then he hung up.

'What? No, I'm fine ...' *Shit! I'm fine.* 'I'm just pissed off,' I started to yell, 'that some dickhead wasn't watching where they were going!' *Screw this, I'm getting out.*

I stepped out of the car, having to steady myself.

The man who had come to my window was by my side once again. 'You really shouldn't move, ma'am.'

'Thank you, but I'm fine,' I grumbled as the sound of sirens filtered through my ears. By the sound of their blaring horns, the ambulance was not too far away.

Taking a step backward, I inspected my car. *Shit! Fucking crap! Balls!* My poor, poor car. It resembled that cube thingy from the movie *Transformers*. The tailgate was completely pushed in and jammed. The bonnet had bent up and made its way closer to the windscreen, and the radiator was leaking fluid. *Fuck, this is going to be a pain in the arse.*

I was just about ready to go and give the guy behind me a piece of my mind when I heard a helicopter overhead. Looking up, I spotted a chopper fast approaching and circling to land in the nearby vacant lot next to the exit ramp. At first I thought it was a medi-chopper, but soon realised it was Bryce's Crow. *Oh, no! He flew here, really? Talk about an overreaction.*

Dumbfounded, I watched him jump out of the chopper and sprint along the road like a madman, stopping directly in front of me and cupping my face. Not knowing if I was in more shock from the accident, or from his over-animated dash to my aid, I just stared at him with my mouth gaping.

'Alexis, are you okay? Are you hurt? Is anything broken? You really shouldn't be standing here.' Before I knew it, he had swept me off my feet and was carrying me to the side of the road.

'Bryce! What are you doing?' I squealed, finally finding my voice. 'Seriously, I'm fine. Put me down and stop making such a fuss. I'm fine.'

People were now looking at me with the frantic helicopter pilot who had just run along the exit ramp to an accident scene and rescued the damsel in distress.

'Where's the bloody ambulance?' he growled, his expression clearly distraught.

It was in that moment that it struck me — the accident! The car accident! Of course. He was freaking out over the accident because of his parents and brother. *Oh, shit, I should never have called him. Alexis, you bloody idiot.*

Still in his arms, I reached up and grabbed his face with both my hands. 'Bryce, Bryce, look at me.' I turned his head to get his full attention. 'I'm fine, see? I'm fine.'

Searching my eyes, his panic started to slowly fade. 'Shit, Alexis, you scared me half to death,' he breathed out, holding me tighter to him.

'I know. I'm sorry. I shouldn't have called you like that. I didn't think. I'm so sorry.'

He knelt down and gently placed me in his lap. 'Don't be. Shit, if anything had happened to you, I ...' He stopped mid-sentence. 'Alexis, I'd die if anything happened to you. I, I think I'm in lo—'

'Ma'am, are you all right?' A paramedic interrupted, while kneeling down beside us both. *What?*

Holy shit! Was Bryce about to say the 'L' word? Oh, fuck, I hope not!

CHAPTER
15

The paramedic was a young man with ginger hair and an Irish accent.

'Hi, there. What's your name, ma'am?' he asked, politely.

I love Irish accents, so I smiled at him. 'Alexis.'

'Alexis, how are you feeling? Do you have any pain anywhere?' He started checking me with a mini-flashlight, shining it into my eyes then away, then into my eyes and away again. *Bryce was telling me he loved me, I'm sure he was in the middle of saying the 'L' word. Maybe I have a concussion, and he actually isn't here and I'm just imagining it, or maybe I'm daydreaming this whole accident. Now that is a possibility; my daydreams have been just a tad vivid lately!*

I pinched myself. *Ouch, that didn't work.*

I pinched Bryce.

He looked stunned. 'What is she doing? Alexis, what are you doing?

'Huh? I'm ... I'm ...' *Not a daydream!* 'I'm ... fine.'

Bryce looked at the paramedic with concern.

'Did you hit your head? Blackout for any time at all?' Mr Irish-ginger-hair asked as he placed his hands on my neck and felt the base of my skull.

I sat up straighter. 'No, really I'm fine.'

He asked me to perform a few movement and response tests then took down my details. Satisfied with my results, he was happy to let me go.

'If you notice any vision changes or blackouts, experience severe headaches, sharp pain or imbalance in any way, then please go directly to hospital. You may feel a little drowsy, and that's okay. You will also have some whiplash and bruising where your seat belt has restrained you.'

He lightly touched my shoulder and chest to indicate the redness already appearing. 'If the pain from whiplash becomes severe, then again, make your way to the hospital. Refrain from anything strenuous or any heavy lifting. And take it easy for a day or two,' he advised, with a reassuring smile before walking away.

I soon found out that the guy who had crashed into my car was not as lucky as I, suffering a broken collarbone and concussion. He was taken to hospital by Mr Irish-ginger-hair.

The police also attended the scene, interviewing me swiftly as to my version of events, then assessing the damage to the cars, and directing traffic around us. I rang my insurance company, and they arranged a tow truck to retrieve my crumpled wreck.

The traffic jam on Kings Way had thrown the connecting West Gate Freeway into chaos, and before we took off in the helicopter, Bryce had to wait for air traffic clearance due to a couple of news media choppers flying around.

I watched him closely as he flicked switches and looked at gauges. 'You really didn't need to fly here, you know,' I said quietly, still embarrassed.

'Yes, I did,' he responded matter-of-factly as he kept performing his checks.

'No, you didn't. I understand your concern because of your family, but not every accident will have the same horrible outcome. All I'm saying is, I'm fine, and I could've caught a taxi. This was all a bit much. I'm grateful that you came, don't get me wrong, it's just ... I feel like an idiot.'

I looked out the window, feeling completely mortified. I should never have told him about the accident. The part about being late, yes. But the accident, no.

'You didn't hear me, did you?' he said as the engine got louder and we took off.

Before I knew it, we were landing at City Towers, and I could now understand just how quickly he had reached the accident scene — it took us no time at all. The rotors started to slow as he flicked different switches and, after what seemed like minutes, he climbed out of the cockpit and came around to my door.

Unbuckling my seat belt for me, he lifted me out of the Crow and into his arms before setting my legs and feet down. I was standing flush against him, his arms still wrapped around me as the wind from the rotors blew around us. Staring at each other and soaking in his emotion-filled eyes, I started to feel a bit dizzy.

'I think I need to sit down,' I declared, my wooziness probably having more to do with his intense gaze rather than the accident, although I didn't tell him that.

He scooped me back up into his arms and carried me toward his apartment.

'Bryce, put me down. You can't keep doing this.'

'I can and I will.'

There was just no arguing with this man. He was the most stubborn person I'd ever come across. He placed me down on his lounge and knelt beside me.

'Bryce, you are going way over the top. I have legs, and I can use them —'

He interrupted me. 'I know you have legs, I want them wrapped around me again.'

I blushed. 'That's not going to happen. You know that, don't you?'

I was starting to feel sleepy.

'I know nothing of which you speak, Ms Summers,' he playfully answered.

If I had more energy I would've rolled my eyes, but I did manage a smile.

'Alexis, I'm pretty damn sure I'm falling in love with you.'

My eyes flew wide open. 'You're not, Bryce. You can't!'

'I am, I can, and I have.'

I couldn't stop staring at him, this gorgeous, handsome, sexy knight in shining armour was kneeling down beside me, confessing his love, and all I could do was stare.

My eyelids became quite heavy, and I found myself fighting to keep them apart then, before drifting into unconsciousness, I swear I felt him kiss my forehead.

* * *

Slowly returning to the land of the cognisant, I was vaguely aware of Bryce's voice in the distance. 'Sebastian. Yes, now, please.' But then his voice drifted away again.

Stirring once more, I heard footsteps and a gentle clanging not too far from my head. I gradually opened my eyes to find that he was sitting on the lounge opposite me. He had placed a blanket over my body and put a pillow under my head and, on the coffee table before us were some pain meds, a glass of water, a cup of tea and a food cloche.

'How long have I been asleep?' I asked, groggily.

'A couple of hours. Janette, the City Towers nurse, has been up here every half an hour, checking on you. She assured me you were just having a snooze. She also said you'd be hungry and would more than likely have a headache when you woke. So, please, take the painkillers and eat your soup.'

I sat upright and felt quite good. *Shit, I haven't called Rick.* 'I have to make a phone call.'

Grabbing my phone from my bag, I walked over to the balcony door and dialled Rick.

'Melbourne Mortgages, you're speaking with Rick.'

'Hi, it's me.'

'Hey, you sound tired. Did I wear you out last night?' *Last night? Oh, yeah.* I felt my cheeks warm, and turned ever so slightly to see if Bryce was watching me. *Of course, he was.*

'No, I had a car accident this morning,' I explained.

'Shit, babe, you all right? What happened?'

'Well, my car got hit up the arse and in turn I hit the car in front. The airbag went off which means the Territory is totalled. It was towed to a repairer in Airport West.'

'The airbag went off? What about you, did you get hurt? Why are you only telling me now? It's after lunch.'

'I'm fine, although I was a little drowsy from the whiplash, so I had a sleep. I feel fine now.'

'Where are you?'

'At work.'

'And you slept?' he asked with obvious confusion.

'It's a hotel, Rick!'

I felt like adding *Der!* Not that I occupied a hotel suite, but that was only a minor detail.

'Oh, yeah, well as long as you are all right. How are you getting home? Do you need me to pick you up?' *Oh, I hadn't thought of that.*

'Um ... no, you go get the kids, and I'll catch a cab. Okay, babe, I've got to go. I'll see you at home. Bye.'

I ended the call and made my way back to the lounge. Once seated on the sofa, Bryce lifted the lid of the cloche. *Mm, minestrone.*

'Have you eaten?' I asked.

He was watching me intently and nodded. 'Yes.'

I dipped my crusty bread in the soup and took a bite, finding it quite awkward to eat soup from a low coffee table. Not to mention the awkwardness I felt due to him watching me.

I put the spoon down. 'Stop it.'

'Stop what?' he asked with contrived innocence and a smirk.

'Stop staring at me.'

He leaned forward and rested his arms on his knees. 'I like staring at you.'

'I can't eat if you watch me.'

He laughed. 'Why?'

'Because, I'll drop some or spill it or something.'

'Do you need me to feed you?'

He was mocking me now, but something told me he would be pretty keen if I'd agreed.

'No. Oh well, if I make a mess on your rug or make a pig of myself, then stiff shit.'

He sat back with one leg resting on the other and one hand in his hair. *Shit, can you possibly make it any harder for me to eat right now?*

Deciding that sometimes it's best not to argue, I came up with an idea. *Okay, smartypants, enjoy watching this.* I started to slurp the soup really loudly and bite my bread like a hungry Viking.

Looking up, I noticed he hadn't even flinched. *Seriously? Right!* I went in for the kill and performed a marathon slurp, nearly choking on a bit of celery. I then did my best Cookie Monster impression with the last bit of bread. My blue, hairy *Sesame Street* character impersonation broke him, and he cracked up laughing.

'Are you sure you didn't hit your head?'

'No, not really!' *Maybe I did? It would explain this crazy display.*

'Hurry up and finish, I want to show you something.'

'I'm done,' I said as I grabbed the napkin and wiped my face, praying I had removed all the crumbs and soup spray.

He stood up and extended his hand. 'Your chariot awaits, my dear.' *What? What is he talking about?*

* * *

Bryce led me to his elevator, pushed the basement four button, and keyed in a code which allowed our descent. When the doors reopened, I was confronted by what could only be described as a view of a luxury car dealership: easily twenty cars, both new and old.

'Are these all yours?' I asked, completely blown away by the machinery in front of me. 'On second thoughts, don't answer that. Of course they are.'

I loved cars. LOVED cars. I was my father's daughter when it came to anything with an engine on four wheels. Dad had taught me to drive a manual transmission in a stock car at the age of sixteen. He had strapped me into the harness and pointed me toward the racetrack, saying, 'Off you go. Go get 'em.'

I can vividly remember the adrenaline rush I had experienced as I flew down the gravel track for the first time. Our division of motor car racing allowed contact with other vehicles, so with my father and brother's influence, I didn't hold back. Unfortunately, that had been my downfall in my inaugural race. Over the years, I did improve, earning myself a Victorian title and second place Victorian championship, and I competed in the ladies division for a further three years until a bad accident left me with hairline fractures to my C1 and C2 vertebrae. Unfortunately, after that I could no longer race due to the chronic headaches resulting from the accident.

* * *

Standing in his private car park was like being a kid in a candy store. The gold McLaren F1 caught my eye first. *How could it not?* Next to that was a Ferrari Testarossa. *Oh my God! Just like the Barbie Ferrari I had when I was little.* I couldn't help myself and made my way over to have a closer look — it was immaculate in all its bright red glory.

My cargasm didn't stop there though, because side-by-side were none other than an Aston Martin One-77 and a Lamborghini Reventón. *Holy fuck! That's over $3,000,000 just there, between those two.*

I looked up at Bryce, and he was boasting a very big smile, so I shook my head at him in disbelief and kept walking. A bright yellow Porsche Cayman, black Jaguar, white Mercedes-Benz, dark blue BMW, silver Lexus, blue Cadillac — the list went on. It was truly beyond words, the calibre of motor vehicle parked in front of me.

Rounding a concrete pylon, I stopped dead in my tracks. I was, without a doubt, impressed with the luxurious models I had just passed, but I was a classic girl at heart, therefore, when I saw the '69 purple Dodge Charger, I froze — just froze.

It was accompanied by a '66 Ford Thunderbird, a '79 Trans Am, and a '57 Chevy Bel Air.

Finding my legs once again, I practically ran up to the Charger. It was sensational. Obviously not factory colour, but the restoration was immaculate. Unable to help myself, I ran my finger along the front guard and peeked inside the window. What I saw had me awestruck — I'd always wanted a Charger.

I turned back to Bryce who was leaning against the pylon and biting his thumb nail as he watched me.

'You had me literally speechless there for a minute,' I said.

He smiled, knowingly. 'It's open, hop in.'

'Really? Argh!' I squealed with delight. If I could have performed a series of backflips, I would have been tumbling right through the garage.

Pushing in the button on the door handle, I pulled it toward me and climbed inside. The black leather was pristine, and I could pretty much see my reflection in it. I placed my hands on the steering wheel. It wasn't small, thick and chunky like they are made nowadays. It was large, round, thin and hard.

Closing my eyes in sheer contentment, I put my head back while gripping the wheel. *Oh, this is so good. I'm in heaven.*

Almost instantly, I felt Bryce's hand on my neck and involuntarily let out a soft cry of pleasure. The warmth from his fingertip left a burning trail up and down my throat. I kept my eyes closed, not daring to open them.

With the utmost delicacy, he moved his finger across my lips and dipped it into my slightly opened mouth. I bit down gently and swirled my tongue around it, savouring the taste of his skin. He removed his now damp digit from my mouth, trailed it back down my throat and in between my breasts, where he slipped it into my bra and gently massaged my nipple.

My eyes remained tightly closed and my breathing became quite ragged. Wanting nothing more than to open my eyes, I found that I couldn't, for if I had opened them, I would've stopped him. It just seemed that closing my eyes made it more acceptable.

He removed his hand from my breast, the anticipation of his next touch simply excruciating. I gripped the steering wheel quite hard as I waited for him to place his hand — which he did — on my knee, slowly moving it up my leg and underneath my skirt. I had stockings on again, and when his hand reached the bare skin between my legs, I moaned with delight.

He leaned in further through the open window and kissed my wanting mouth, all the while continuing to move his hand up and underneath my underwear. Automatically, I tilted my pelvis to give him easier access.

This was my ultimate fantasy. He was my dream guy and he was about to finger-fuck me in my dream car.

As he touched my soft, sensitive clit, I groaned out loud, the sensation unbelievable. And even more so when he entered me with not one, but two fingers, stretching my pussy in a circular motion. *Holy fuck, I'm gone.* I arched my back, and my hand — moist with sweat — slipped from the steering wheel, landing on the horn. The loud noise that resonated from the slip of my hand, forced me to open my eyes and I was jolted back into reality, recognising I'd just had another daydream. *Shit, Alexis, not again.*

I quickly gathered my wits and, this time, found that Bryce really was at the window. I was perspiring and literally coming down from a climax. I was also hot and wanting, and my chest was heaving. I threw him a look of lust, which didn't go unnoticed, as I opened the door of the Charger, forcing him to take a step back. Then, getting out of the car, I stood still with my back up against it.

Bryce was directly opposite me, leaning against the Bel Air and staring wildly. I couldn't do or say anything. What I'd just experienced in my reverie was so overpowering, I had no control whatsoever.

His hands were splayed on the door panel, and I noticed them both arch and tense up. The look he then directed me asked one thing which I couldn't refuse.

'Yes,' I sighed in surrender.

Expecting him to pounce as his body language had suggested, I watched as he moved slowly and with deliberate control, instead. It was so fucking sexy, and it just added to my already uncontrollable need for him. He grabbed my face and kissed me with such passion that I nearly convulsed on the spot.

I felt that I needed to give in to the kiss, owing it to us both, knowing the experience of it was consensual. He broke off momentarily and looked deep into my eyes, seemingly to search for my further reluctance and, when I didn't protest, he kissed me again, but with more lustful aggression.

His hands fell to my arse where he gripped me and lifted me up, prompting me to wrap my legs around his waist, once again. *I'm sure I told him about an hour ago this would never happen.*

Placing me down on the bonnet, he gently laid me back, his mouth never leaving mine. *Fuck me! I'm going to have sex with him on the bonnet! No. No. No. You're not, Alexis.*

I was completely overwhelmed by the feel of his mouth on mine, his skin on mine, his tongue on mine. So when he pulled back and hovered over me, slowly running his hands up my legs and pushing my skirt up to expose my garter, stockings, and underwear, I froze.

'Fuck, Alexis, you're so beautiful,' he breathed, as he rubbed his hands up my thighs. I wanted to answer him and say thank you ... stop ... or perhaps, hurry up. But I couldn't. I was speechless.

Before I could form anything coherent, he grabbed hold of my underwear and tore it apart, rendering me vulnerable and lying there spreadeagled on his Charger bonnet with nothing to cover my wet pussy.

Slowly, he moved forward, stalking me like prey, not taking his eyes from me. That's when I stopped him.

'No, I can't,' I sighed, cautiously.

He froze with my hands resting on his shoulders and his head very close to its target. Bryce didn't argue with me, nor was he pissed off — well, he probably was, I know I was. Instead, he gave me his hand and helped me sit upright.

'I'm sorry, Bryce, I want to. Fuck, do I want to. I ... I just can't do ... that! It goes against everything I stand for. I could never do anything like that behind Rick's back.'

Bryce tilted my chin up so that I was looking into his eyes. 'I understand, Alexis.'

I was now sitting on the edge of the bonnet with my legs still wrapped around him and, not being able to hold in my emotions any longer, I buried my face in my hands and tried desperately not to cry. 'How could you possibly understand? Even I don't understand what's going on here. What are we going to do? I can't keep doing this to Rick, and I can't keep doing this to you, or me for that matter.'

'I understand you have morals and have made vows you don't want to break,' he said softly as he pulled me to his chest. 'I respect that, I truly do. It just makes you even more desirable.'

I sensed a playful yet challenging tone in his voice which made me feel worse. 'Fat lot of good that does you.'

He kissed the top of my head and squeezed me tighter. 'There's always a way, Alexis. You don't get to where I am in life without being resourceful or thinking outside the box. If you won't give yourself to me behind Rick's back, then we'll get his permission.'

I'm sorry, what?

CHAPTER
16

'I'm sorry, you'll what?' I asked in a high-pitched voice while pulling away from his chest.

Unwrapping my legs, I leaned back on my elbows along the bonnet.

'You've only ever been with Rick, Alexis. You don't know any other way. If you could spend one week with me — just one week and let your guard down — I could show you that there is more than what you have grown accustomed to with Rick.'

He placed his hands on either side of my face and gently flexed his fingers. *I love how he holds my face.*

His eyes were so honest and upfront. 'I could show you that you are falling in love with me, too.'

'It's not that simple, Bryce. I'm happy. If I was miserable in my marriage then that would be a different story, but I'm not, I'm happy. I'm content.'

'That's just it, Alexis. Are you happy with being content?'
Well, I thought I was until you put it like that.

'It's not just that. It's Nate and Charlotte. I can't just abandon my family on the notion that, yes, I might be falling in love with you. It's too complicated.'

'Nothing is too complicated. Life is too short to stop at complications. I want a week with you and I will get it.' He leaned over and kissed me with intention. *I want a week of just doing this! No, Alexis, it's not going to happen. I don't see how it can.* He pulled me up and grabbed my torn underwear off the hood of the Charger. 'I'm keeping these,' he said, as he shoved them into his pocket.

'What am I supposed to wear?' I asked, slightly worried that I now had no underwear on. It's not like I carried a spare pair in my handbag.

His eyes lit up, and that irresistible yet unbelievably annoying smirk returned to his face.

'No!' I gasped. *Alexis, you dirty girl. I couldn't possibly, could I?*

He stood there with his arms crossed in front of him. 'You have no choice, Ms Summers!'

Squealing, I turned beetroot and put my face in my hands. He took one hand away from my face and led me to where the BMW, Cadillac, Lexus, Porsche, Mercedes and Jag were.

'Which one?' *Which one what? Which one do I want to sprawl across next? I was happy on the Charger.*

'Which one what?' I asked, curiously.

'Which one do you want? You are going to need a car.'

'No way, Bryce. I have a car. It's just a fair few inches smaller than it was yesterday.'

He turned me around to face him and put both his hands on my shoulders. 'Alexis, you need a car to get home. Then again, I'm more than happy for you to stay here. In fact, it's settled, you're staying.'

'Like hell I am! I'll take a taxi, thanks.'

'And what about tomorrow? And the next day? And the next? Cars don't get fixed overnight, you know.'

'Grrr, fine. I'll borrow the ...' *Hmm, Cadillac? Nah. BMW? No. Lexus ... the most expensive! Jag? Maybe.* 'Porsche, I'll take the Porsche.'

'Good, it's settled then. Come on, I've got work to do and so do you for that matter,' he said mischievously, giving me small pushes toward the elevator. I didn't want to leave, I wanted to stay and gaze at the pretty machines a bit longer.

Bryce stepped directly in front of me, blocking my view of the cars. 'If we don't leave, Alexis, I will have you in the back seat of the Bel Air,' he said with such determination that my legs weakened at the very thought of it. *Oh, that sounds good.*

Reluctantly stepping into the elevator — and giving myself some distance from him — I waved goodbye to the cars.

'Give me back my underwear,' I demanded, putting out my hand.

He pulled them out and draped them over his face.

'Stop it,' I whined while laughing, but I was also completely mortified. 'Bryce, I mean it.'

'No, they're useless to you and anyway they're mine now.'

He jumped away as I went to grab them, the same time the doors opened to his apartment. Quickly stuffing them back into his pocket, he then sprang out of the elevator.

'Bryce, I'm going to kill you!' I exclaimed.

'Please don't,' said Lucy. 'Please don't kill him.'

We both looked in the direction Lucy's voice had come from, finding Lucy and Nic sitting comfortably in the lounge room. They looked up as we both leaped into the room like a couple of kids playing chasey.

Lucy stood up and cradled in her arms was Alexander.

I glared at Bryce, but he just grinned back at me while poking my underwear deeper into his pocket.

'Aw, look at him,' I cooed as I walked over to Lucy and Alexander, giving them both a kiss on the cheek. 'You look fabulous, Lucy. And you, mister,' *here comes the baby voice*, 'are just the cutest little button ever.'

She handed him over to me and, instantly, I reverted back to when I had one of these eating, pooing, crying, windy bundles of my own. I gazed over his sleeping form, taking comfort. He looked so incredibly peaceful.

Bryce moved to stand by my side and touched Alexander's nose. 'Hello, little man.'

The gesture was truly adorable. Bryce had father-material written all over his face. As I quickly averted my gaze from Bryce back to Alexander, I caught an exchange of eye contact between Nic and Lucy.

'You must be feeling a lot better after this morning then, Alexis?' Lucy asked as she sat on the lounge and put her arm around Nic.

At first I had no idea what she was talking about, then it dawned on me — the accident. But how she knew about my car crash, I had no idea. Happy to put it down to Bryce having probably spoken to her while I slept. I didn't probe for an explanation.

'I am, thank you. I'm feeling much better. I was a bit groggy at first but I've revived after some sleep.'

'Hm,' she muttered, slightly amused and obviously contemplating something I was not aware of. 'And you, dear brother, that was some display of heroics.' *What? I'm totally confused now.*

Bryce shot her a piercing glare, but it didn't deter her.

'When we saw the accident on the news this morning, and my dear brother running up the Kings Way ramp and whisking you up into his arms, we thought you'd been seriously hurt. Either you have made a miraculous recovery, or Bryce went just a tad overboard.' *Shit! It was on the news? Oh no.*

'Seeing you now, Alexis, I'm thinking it was the latter,' Lucy admitted, smiling boldly at her older brother.

I snapped my head toward him and glared, morbidly horrified. How was I going to explain this?

Handing baby Alexander to Bryce, I quickly excused myself from the room. 'I'll leave you guys to it. I've got a lot of work.' *That's it, Alexis, run for the hills. That won't make it look any more obvious.* I turned on my heel and hurriedly headed for the foyer.

Lucy caught up to me as I walked through Bryce's office. 'Alexis, please wait! I'm sorry. I didn't mean to embarrass you. I was just playing, that's all.'

'No, it's fine, I just have work to do.'

I didn't really, nothing that couldn't wait anyway.

'Alexis, it's okay. I know.' *Know what?* 'Bryce doesn't just talk to Jessica, you know. He confides in me also. We both confide in each other. After I withdrew and closed myself off from the world, I promised him I would always talk to him no matter what, and vice versa. So I know he is falling for you, falling for you very deeply.'

I stopped in my tracks at her words and slumped onto the sofa in his office. With my head in my hands, I started to cry.

Lucy came round, sat down beside me and rubbed my back. 'Alexis, I'm sorry. Let it out, it's better that way.' She handed me a tissue, and I did the whole disgustingly loud, nose blowing thing.

'I don't know what to do, Lucy. I'm falling for him too, but I can't ... I shouldn't ... it's wrong.'

'Why is it wrong?'

She handed me another tissue.

'Because I'm married.'

'That doesn't mean it's wrong. Trust me, I know from experience; you can't help who you fall for and it's best not to fight it.'

'I'm losing the fight, Lucy. I can't do it any more. The thing is, I can't lose either. I can't destroy my family ... that is not an option. God, I'm screwed either way.'

I blew my nose loudly yet again.

Lucy stood up, helping me up with her. 'I can't tell you what to do, Alexis. However, what I can tell you is that my brother isn't playing. I have never seen him act like this before, and when I saw him running to you on the news footage with that look of terror on his face, it told me one thing — he is absolutely and undoubtedly in love with you.'

* * *

Those last few words Lucy spoke to me before I went back to work were stuck in my mind for the rest of the day: 'He is absolutely and undoubtedly in love with you'. What the *hell* was I going to do? I knew without a shadow of a doubt that we had very strong feelings for each other, and the more time we spent together, the stronger they became. I also believed him when he said that if I spent one week with him I would discover that I could possibly be falling in love with him too. The issue was: what the fuck was I to do with these revelations?

My mind started to spin. I really needed to get away. Grabbing my phone, I decided to text Tash.

Hey, hon. Are we on for the weekend? — Alexis

Yep, just waiting on Jade, but it's definitely a goer! — Tash

Yay, I'm counting down the minutes. Thanks, lovely! You're an angel xo — Alexis

xoxo ☺ xoxo — Tash

Just the thought of sitting in our barrel with a glass of bubbly sent waves of relief right through me. Unfortunately, that moment soon faded when Gareth stepped into the foyer.

'Good afternoon, Gareth. Bryce is not in. He's out with Dale going over some security checks.'

'Oh, bugger, I needed to have a quick word to him about a new proposal. Never mind.'

He walked over to my desk and sat himself on the corner of it. *Okay, you're encroaching on my personal space. This is slightly awkward.*

Rolling my chair in the opposite direction, my aim was to create some distance.

He swivelled around and closed my newly-created gap. 'So, how are you feeling, Alexis? That was some bump you took this morning by the looks of your car and the fact Bryce had to carry you off the road.' *Shit, has everyone seen it? And hang on just a minute, what is this prick insinuating?*

Sensing a strange vibe radiating from Gareth, I opted to keep the conversation calm and placid, clicking my computer mouse and hopefully giving him the impression that I had work to do. 'I'm fine, thanks. It looked worse than it actually was. Bryce was good enough to come down and see if I was okay. It was very kind of him.'

'Oh, come on, Mrs Summers. You and I both know he didn't just come down to see how you were. What he did went far beyond the expectations of an employer.'

He tapped his fingers on his lap, waiting for my response.

Now highly unsettled by his demeanour and choice of words and, quite frankly, offended by his aggressive approach, I stood up to get the higher ground, suggesting that he did not intimidate me. 'What are you getting at, Gareth?'

'Feisty! I can see why he likes you. Tell me, are you feisty between the sheets, too?' he asked, with a lascivious look as he eyed me up and down.

Without thinking, I slapped him across his crude face as hard as humanly possible. 'How dare you!'

I went to leave, but he grabbed the back of my head.

'Listen here, you little whore. You just keep spreading your legs for Bryce, because you are doing me a favour. You want to know why?'

Petrified, I didn't answer.

'The board won't be too impressed that he is fucking a married woman. It doesn't look good for the company,' he hissed as he licked his lips and placed his free hand on my breast. 'You are a sexy whore, I'll give him that much.'

Repulsed and wanting him to remove his filthy hands, my defensive instincts kicked in and I swung my right arm as hard as I could, hitting him in the elbow and releasing his hold of my head. Then, jamming my thumb into his eye socket, I also kneed him in the balls, making him double over in pain. *I must thank Bryce for those moves.*

'You bitch! You'll fucking pay for that!'

He started to straighten up and that's when Bryce grabbed him from behind, having returned via his private elevator and through his office.

I watched in shock as he flung Gareth into the wall then picked him up by his collar before punching him in the ribs. He then swung an uppercut into his jaw, causing Gareth to fall to the ground where Bryce kicked him in the stomach.

'Bryce, stop!' I screamed.

He looked up at me, the fury in his eyes immense. I shook my head, which is when he sensed my fear and stepped away from a crumpled Gareth still lying on the floor.

'Get the fuck out of my building now, you piece of shit,' he growled with intense anger.

Laughing sarcastically, Gareth slowly stood up and spat the blood in his mouth at Bryce's feet. The look they then exchanged was beyond terrifying.

CHAPTER
17

Bryce's burning gaze toward Gareth remained even after the elevator doors slid shut. For a brief moment, I thought he was going to turn green and rip his shirt apart, so I walked between him and the elevator, blocking his view of the doors and forcing his focus to turn to me.

'Bryce, are you all right?' I asked hesitantly, for he definitely seemed fragile. 'Bryce, please show me your hand.'

The rage he was harbouring began to subside and, bowing his head without making eye contact, he slowly raised his hand.

'Did he hurt you, Alexis?' he asked softly.

I tilted his chin up with my finger and looked deep into his eyes. 'No, this guy I know taught me some pretty handy self-defence moves.' I smiled warily at him. 'This guy I know, he's incredibly hot and infuriating, but he knows his shit. Did you see the eye gouge he taught me?'

He managed a mild laugh. 'Infuriating, eh?'

'And incredibly hot!' I admitted while grabbing his hand and finding that his knuckles were bleeding. 'Come on, Mr Clark. You need some assistance from Nurse Summers.'

'I'm liking the sound of that,' he admitted, perking up and lifting his eyebrows.

'Settle down, tiger. It's not what you think.'

I led him to the sofa in his office and sat him down. Then, making my way to the minibar, I grabbed some ice cubes and wrapped them in a napkin.

Taking a seat on the coffee table opposite him, I remembered to keep my legs closed, as from memory, I was without underwear.

'Here, give me your hand.'

Taking his hand in mine, I rested the ice on his knuckles.

'So, where's the nurse costume?' he asked eagerly.

'Nurse Summers doesn't wear a costume. She sings.'

He appeared intrigued by my revelation. 'Well, let's hear it!'

I giggled to myself and began the 'Boo-boo Song'.

Boo-boo, I have a sore it pains.
Boo-boo, I cry and cry like rain.
But when you kiss it, I feel okay.
And it makes my boo-boo go away.

As I sang the final words, I picked up his hand and kissed it, trying not laugh.

He grabbed my other hand and pulled me forward so that I was standing above him. Slowly, he began to move my skirt up my legs. *Stop him, Alexis, before it's too late.*

I was about to stop his hands from moving any higher and exposing the very part of me that wanted him the most, when he stopped himself. He had hiked up my skirt just enough for me to open my legs and climb onto his lap. Then, wrapping his arms around me, he placed his head on my chest.

'You have a nice voice, Nurse Summers.'

'It's the best medicine, Mr Clark.'

He buried his face in my breasts. 'If he'd hurt you ... I ... I would've killed him.'

I pulled his head away from my breasts. 'He didn't, but what are you going to do about him?'

'I plan to let him calm down for a few days and then remind him who's boss.'

'You're not going to fire his arse? He's trying to have you disgraced by the board.'

He sat back and put both hands through his hair. *Fuck, I wish I was riding him right now. I really should get off his lap.*

'It's not that simple. I can't fire him. Look, it's a long story, but the short of it is, he is a minor stakeholder and by binding agreement he cannot be fired by me. What he did to you, though, it will not go unpunished. I fucking promise you that.'

He dropped his hands and put them on my arse. 'I like this position very much. I think from now on we will have all our discussions like this.'

He squeezed, which sent excitement through my body.

'Bryce, behave or I'll get off your lap.'

Putting both hands in the air, he pleaded his surrender.

'You do realise he is trying to take your company and I'm his ammunition,' I said, trying to climb off his lap and feeling guilty that I could ever cause a problem with him and his company.

He held me firmly in place. 'He can't take my company and you are not ammunition. Don't worry about Gareth. I will make sure he doesn't hurt you, okay?'

I wasn't convinced, but I knew I had better let it go for now. 'I have to go, Bryce.'

He stood up while continuing to hold me to his front. This time, my skirt did, in fact, go up around my waist. His hands clenched my bare arse and he groaned wildly.

Putting his forehead to mine, he walked me over to the conference table and set me on top. 'Say it!' he growled through gritted teeth. *Oh, shit!*

'Yes,' I whimpered.

Instantly, our lips met, his tongue invading my mouth so fervently that I nearly fainted. In all my life, I had never been kissed like that before. The raw emotion in the way he owned every part of my mouth was beyond intense. The way he kissed me felt so right, it felt like our mouths were meant to be together.

He broke off, allowing us to catch our breath. 'Alexis,' he sighed painfully, his struggle to remain in control clearly evident. 'Reach into my left pocket.' *What? I'd rather reach into your pants.*

Pouting, I did what I was told and moved my hand to his pocket, pulling out a set of keys.

'Go. Take the Porsche, or I'll retract my offer and hold you hostage.'

I took the keys from his hand before kissing his knuckles and leaving to return home.

* * *

As I pulled into our driveway, Nate came bounding out the front door of the house. He opened the driver's door before

I had even switched off the ignition. 'Awesome! Can we keep it?' he asked, impatiently waiting for me to get out so that he could take my place.

'Be careful! You break it, you buy it,' I warned.

Rick was standing by the front door with his hands in his pockets. He smiled slightly and approached the Porsche. 'Nice taxi.'

'Yeah, same colour though,' I replied.

'Let me guess. Bryce?' he asked with an annoyed tone.

I went to give him a kiss on the cheek, but as I did, I felt a strange sense of reluctance to do so. 'Don't worry, he isn't going to miss it.'

Rick wasn't cold toward me, but I sensed he was a little withdrawn.

I met his gaze. 'You saw?'

He nodded and ordered Nate out of the car. *I'm going to have to spill my guts. Shit, I'm not ready for this. I need booze, lots of booze.*

* * *

We sat down to a dinner of slow-cooked corned beef and mash. Nate wanted to know about the other cars Bryce had in his basement, which only added to Rick's irritation. After Charlotte and Nate had gone to bed, I poured Rick and myself a drink and found him under the pergola.

'So, he flew to the accident?' Rick asked, with a trace of sarcasm in his voice.

I took a drink and swallowed heavily. 'Yes, he did. He panicked due to his horrible past with car accidents, and I guess he went a bit overboard.'

'So, what was with the *Officer and a Gentleman* scene then?'

I let out a breath, one I'd been holding subconsciously. 'I don't know. As I said, he panicked. He's a very excessive and stubborn man. I guess it goes with the territory.'

'Lexi, is everything all right?' *Tell him, you wimp.*

'I'm just tired, babe. I've had a really long day.' I skolled the last of my drink and stood up. 'I'm going to bed. You coming?'

He had barely even begun his drink. 'No, not yet, you go. I won't be too far behind.'

* * *

The next morning when I arrived at work, Bryce was not there. I'd not long sat down before finding a note he'd left, telling me to go to his office and open the brief on his desk. Curious as to the unusual instruction, I did as was told, finding a sticky note.

Nurse Summers,

When you left me last night, my hand was not the only thing aching. My mouth ached for yours to join it. My cock ached for you to consume it. My entire body just ached for yours. But what ached the most was my heart. It is desperate for yours to make it one.

I will be out of the office for most of the day, but am due back just after lunch. I need you to go to my bedroom and collect another brief.

Your Mr Clark

My Mr Clark? I think my heart just broke. He's killing me. He's really freaking killing me. I took the note, put it in my pocket, and made my way to his apartment, heading directly to his bedroom. When I entered his room, I remembered the tingling I felt between my legs the last time I was there. This time, there was no change, if anything my body's reaction was even more intense.

In the middle of the bed was a box and on the box was another sticky note.

Nurse Summers,

In this box is a promise. When I get my week with you, you will wear this and kiss my boo-boo away again.

On Monday night, I will need you to accompany me to the Tel V Awards. Please go and see Clarissa. She has a dress for you.

Your Mr Clark

This man was something else. I had a sneaking suspicion what to expect when I opened the box, so it didn't come as a surprise when I lifted the rather erotic nurse costume from beneath the wrapping. *Cheeky bastard.* I read the note again. *He wants me to accompany him to the Tel V Awards. Shit! How exciting!* I placed the second note with the other and made my way down to Versace.

As I passed through the lobby, I stopped at the Concierge Office in the hope I would see Samantha to remind her about lunch.

She was at the computer showing Chelsea something, so I cleared my throat. 'Uh, um, excuse me, Sam,' I interrupted.

She looked up at me. 'Hey.'

'Are we still on for lunch?'

Chelsea also looked up from her computer screen and flashed me her unpleasantly superior disdain.

'Yes, I can't wait. Where do you want to go?' Sam asked, excitedly.

'Somewhere private, we need to talk. I'll pick a spot and meet you here at noon.'

'Ooh, sounds serious.'

I smiled reassuringly at her. 'Don't worry, I'll explain later. Anyway, I've got to go to Versace and pick up my dress for the Tel V Awards.'

Both hers and Chelsea's jaws dropped. *Take that, Chelsea, you bitch.* I walked off, and if it wasn't so obvious, I would've punched the air.

* * *

When I arrived at Versace, Clarissa was elated and extremely attentive. 'Ms Summers, the dress Mr Clark ordered for you has arrived. Please come with me and I'll assess the fit. You are going to love it. It's incredible!' she said enthusiastically as she closed the store.

She led me to the circular change area and directed me to the very room where I had experienced my first spine-tingling encounter with Bryce.

I stepped into the small space where I found a magnificent red dress hanging against the wall. 'Wow! Is that for me?' I asked, stunned and in awe.

She nodded and followed me into the room. 'Ms Summers, I will need to help you, but if you are not comfortable with undressing in front of me then —'

'No. No, that's fine. I'm just scared to even touch it, let alone put it on. It's simply stunning.'

I turned around and she helped unzip my dress.

'That's a beautiful torsolette, Ms Summers, but it will have to go. The dress comes with matching lingerie, so ... I'll leave you to put it on, okay? I'll be back in a moment.'

Once she was gone, I began the frustrating task of removing my torsolette, but I did enjoy new luxurious underwear. I had always worn beautiful lingerie, even before I started wearing beautiful labels, labels that I had only ever seen in magazines like *Vogue* and *Cosmopolitan*. I may not have been one to dress up and wear make-up, but my underwear was always immaculate.

Assessing the extravagant Versace dress, I took note of the low dip at the front and back, and realised I could not wear a bra. Therefore, the matching lingerie that Clarissa mentioned, which accompanied the dress, wasn't really a set. My suspicion was soon confirmed when I found the teeny-tiny, little, lace G-string. Teeny-tiny as it was, it was something special. If I closed my eyes, I swear it felt as if I wasn't wearing anything at all. *I've got to get me some more of these babies ... but only if they come with matching bras.*

'Ms Summers, are you ready for the dress?' Clarissa spoke from the other side of the curtain.

Standing in next to nothing — literally — I answered. 'Yes, Clarissa, come in.'

She opened the curtain, stepped inside, and then helped me into the dress.

'As you may have already realised, the bra support is built into the gown,' she advised, while professionally adjusting parts of the dress. 'I know it plunges at the front, but you should still feel secure.'

She was correct in her assumption, I did feel secure. The dress was extremely elegant, but also daring. Much more daring than anything I would have chosen for myself. I'm guessing that's why Bryce picked it out in the first place.

The dress plunged down the front, stopping halfway between the bottom of my breasts and the top of my navel.

The long skirt fell in a drape with a split to my mid-thigh. There was a strap on my left shoulder which was covered in small, red leather scales, the scales following the strap over my shoulder. They then continued down my back, and all the way to just above my arse and around to my waist, mimicking a belt. Finally, the trail of red scales continued up around the outside of my right breast, all the way up to my right shoulder strap, and finishing across the back of my neck.

You could say the detailing looked a bit like shiny leather sequins, encompassing not only uniqueness but sophistication. The dress was simply stunning but it also had an edge of sex kitten to it. I honestly felt like Julia Roberts in *Pretty Woman*, and I dared to think of how much this dress actually cost.

'Ms Summers, you look simply beautiful. It's such a great choice for you. Are you happy with how it sits?'

'I am, but the plunge at the front is a bit revealing.' I winced, not confident that I could pull it off.

'We can raise it just slightly if it makes you uncomfortable, but you are a beautiful, sexy young woman who should not be ashamed to show off a bit of skin.' *A bit of skin? Try a lot of skin.*

I understood what she was saying though. 'You know what, Clarissa? You're right. I do look great, and I'm going to wear the shit out of this dress on Monday night.' *Classy, Alexis. You are in Versace, not Kmart.*

'I have no doubt, Ms Summers,' she responded with a laugh.

Reluctantly, I took the dress off. Clarissa explained she would have it delivered to the penthouse Monday morning.

I gave her a brief and grateful hug. 'Thank you so much.'

'Don't thank me,' she said with a mischievous glint while handing me an envelope and gesturing to Bryce's handwriting. 'Thank him.'

* * *

I returned to the lobby to meet Samantha, figuring we'd have lunch in the penthouse conference room — it was the most private place I could think of.

'Hey, do you mind having lunch in the penthouse?'

'Sure, is everything okay?' she asked with scepticism.

'No, not really, but I can't tell you here.'

We stepped into the elevator and she turned to me. 'Spill. Now. I'm not waiting any longer.'

Here goes. 'I saw you and Gareth in the car park a few weeks ago.'

'Right,' she drawled, hesitantly, clearly surprised by my knowledge. She also appeared somewhat embarrassed. 'We're just having a bit of fun.'

She was lying. It was obvious to me that she was lying. Being a mother of two, I had developed a talent for lie-detecting. 'There's more, Sam,' I admitted.

As I was about to fill her in on the confrontation I'd had with Gareth, the elevator stopped and he stepped inside to greet us. My stomach dropped and I froze on the spot.

'Miss Taylor, just the lady I am looking for,' he said, with intent to charm her pants off. It looked as though it was going to work as she blushed a bright red.

Sam attempted to hide her embarrassment, but instead, giggled. I, on the other hand, tried desperately not to look at Gareth, but the elevator was covered in mirrors, and my endeavour was useless. *Why are they all freakin' covered in mirrors?*

'Miss Taylor, would you mind helping me with something?' Gareth asked as he turned his back to me.

'Now?' she questioned.

'Yes, if it's not too much trouble.'

She looked over his shoulder at me apologetically and shrugged her shoulders. She focussed back on Gareth. 'No, it's no trouble.'

'Thank you.'

The doors opened to level eight and he guided her out. Then, looking back over his shoulder, he shot me a terrifying yet triumphant glare. I felt that somehow, he knew I was about to divulge his secret to her. I don't know how he knew — but clearly he did. For some reason he did not want her to know, and the look he shot me upon his exit was a clear warning to keep my mouth shut.

CHAPTER

18

Stepping out of the elevator, I tried to shake off my encounter with Gareth. There was obviously more to him, and I was determined to find out what it was. But for now, I was more inclined to focus on the envelope that Clarissa had handed me, pulling it out of my pocket and unsealing it. Not to my surprise, it was another sticky note from Bryce.

Nurse Summers,

I'm very much looking forward to seeing you in the dress on Monday night at the Tel V Awards. It will be a late night, so you might want to occupy the guest room — or mine.

Your Mr Clark

Stay overnight? It was bound to happen at some stage due to the obligations of my job, and I had explained to Rick that it was a part of my position and the $500,000 that accompanied it. However, due to the news coverage of the accident, I didn't think Rick would be happy about my staying at the hotel overnight — and rightly so. The temptation of Bryce wanting me to share his bed could prove to be a bit much.

I had to create some distance, needing space and time to think about where my life was headed and with whom for that matter. The girls' weekend away could be the perfect outlet and really couldn't come any sooner, so I decided to ring Tash.

'Helllooo,' she answered comically.

'Hey, hon, what's up?' I responded, slightly bemused by her bizarre tone. *What's she up to?*

Instantly, her scratchy and very unmelodic voice began filtering through the receiver, blurting out the lyrics to 'Up Where We Belong.'

'Shut up, not you too,' I scoffed at her.

She laughed. 'Come on, Lexi, it was very *Officer and a Gentleman*. All that was missing was the naval uniform.'

I swallowed dryly at the thought of Bryce in a naval uniform. *Holy, fuck, that would be a sight.* 'That's what Rick said, minus the uniform part,' I answered, trying to bring my thoughts back to the conversation at hand and away from the picture of Bryce in uniform.

'Shit, was Rick pissed?'

'He didn't come out and say it … but yeah, he wasn't happy. Can't really blame him though, it was on the news.'

'Lex, you do know what you are doing, don't you?' she asked, sounding a little worried.

I hung my head and my eyes welled up. 'No, Tash, I don't. I'm seriously fucking fucked in the head at the moment.' I wiped my eyes.

'Okay, poppet. This weekend there will be no mention of husbands or sexy, stalker billionaires.'

'Sounds good,' I said with a sigh of relief. 'Oh, by the way, one of you will have to drive. I don't have the Territory any more.'

Suddenly the phone was taken from my hand. *Hey!*

'Tash, is it? It's Bryce Clark. Alexis will have my limousine and driver for the entire weekend, so please don't worry about another vehicle.'

I snatched the phone back. 'Alexis will *not* have the limousine,' I said emphatically, glaring up at him.

He sat himself on my desk with his arms crossed, smirking. *Oh, no you don't, Mr Clark.*

'It's what I do, Ms Summers,' he smiled, tapping me on the nose before getting up and walking back into his office.

'Hello, Lexi, you still there?' Tash asked, her tiny voice barely audible through the phone's receiver. *Shit!*

'Yeah, I'm still here.'

'Oh, Lex, if you don't screw him ... I will!'

'Natasha Jones!'

'I know. I know. It's not funny. Soooo, are we going by limo?'

'Yes,' I grumbled. 'Tell the others I'll pick them up after 6 p.m. on Friday night. I have to go, hon. I have to go and punch my employer. Bye.'

'Make love, not war,' she said and quickly hung up. *You'll keep, Tash. You'll keep.*

* * *

Bryce was at his desk when I entered the room. He looked up, smiling defiantly as I made my way toward him. 'So, Nurse Summers, how was the dress? Do you like it?'

'I can see why you like it,' I replied, my tone challenging.

His smile dropped. 'You don't like it? You can pick whatever you like. I —'

Sensing his panicked disappointment, I quickly stepped up to his desk. 'No, Bryce, I love it. It's stunning, it's just I have never worn anything like it, ever!'

His defiant smile returned. 'Good, I want you to experience new things.' *Hmm ... what's he up to? Okay, probably best to change the subject.*

'Now, while you were out, you missed a call from Joyce. Apparently you need to sign off on Channel 7 having exclusive television rights for the red carpet arrivals on Monday. Also, Vincent has finalised the menu which I have emailed to you, and Samantha gave me the flight transfer requests for your approval. Speaking of Samantha, I was supposed to have lunch with her today. Did you know she is seeing Gareth?'

He looked wary. 'No.'

'Well, she is. We were supposed to have lunch together, but as we were heading up here, he pretty much stopped the elevator and whisked her away. There's something you're not telling me about him, Bryce. The look he gave me when he left the elevator was clearly a warning for me to stay away from her and I want to know why.'

Bryce shot up from his seated position, and this time I swear he did change to a shade of green. Before I could comprehend what he was doing, he stormed out of the office and slammed the door behind him. *Shit, what did I say wrong?*

* * *

It was nearly an hour later when the ding of the elevator doors rang. I looked up hoping to see Bryce, but of all people who could've come through those doors, it had to be Chelsea. She strolled up to my desk like the snotty tart that she was. *Yes, what the fuck do you want?*

I faux smiled. 'Yes, Chelsea, can I help you?'

'I'm here for my appointment with Bryce.' *He is Mr Clark to you, you little troll.*

I glared at her. 'You mean, Mr Clark.' *I have no appointment scheduled for her. Why is she not in the diary?* 'Are you sure it's today? There is nothing in his schedule, and besides, he is not here.'

A look of devastation plastered her face. 'It is today, I spoke to him earlier. I'll just have to wait.'

She didn't wait for long, because Bryce came through the doors about a second later. He looked flushed and mighty pissed off. *Uh-oh, I hope that's not my fault.*

'Bryce, I was starting to think you had stood me up,' Chelsea pouted with her hands on her hips.

She went to follow him into his office, when he stopped her. 'Chelsea, take a seat over there. I will see you in a minute. Alexis, if you don't mind.' He motioned me to his office.

Hesitantly, I followed him, as Chelsea made her way to the couch in the foyer. Before the door had even closed completely, he had me pinned up against it. He didn't even have to ask permission, because I said yes and kissed him before he had the chance.

His embrace was quite aggressive and wanting as he mouthed my neck — it was divine.

'Fuck!' he shouted, making me flinch.

I put my forefinger to his lips and hushed him. 'Bryce, what's wrong?'

He lightly hit his head against the door. 'I'm sorry, I promised you I wouldn't let Gareth hurt you. It's just he doesn't fucking listen and pushes me over the edge.'

'What did you do?'

'Nothing,' he said before kissing me softer this time. *Nothing, my arse.* 'You may not know this, but Chelsea is a qualified helicopter pilot.' *You are deliberately changing the subject, Mr Clark.*

'I do know. I've done some of my own creepy research on your little admirer.'

I raised my eyebrow at him, and his mouth twitched.

'Chelsea is here to go over the agreement we have with her father's chartering company. I don't want you to become green-eyed again, although I did like the show you put on for me last time.' He smirked, so I glared at him. 'I thought you could sit in on the meeting and take some notes, as the agreement will need to be amended. Go and grab your laptop and tell Chelsea to come in.'

I put my hand up to my forehead in a salute. 'Yes, sir.'

As I went to turn and leave, he grabbed my hand and kissed it. He then proceeded to trail kisses up my wrist, hitting that very sensitive spot behind my elbow which made my legs weak. Holding me tightly against the door, he kept creeping kisses up my arm, across my chest and up my neck. *I can't keep letting him do this to me.*

Finding my mouth with his own, he took control with sweet softness, it being a very different kiss from the one we had minutes ago. Once again, I had never been kissed like that before. It was intoxicating.

Bryce broke away and placed another light kiss on the tip of my nose. 'Please,' he said and opened the door for me.

As I walked into the foyer, I found Chelsea checking her reflection in a little compact mirror. She quickly slid it in her pocket in the hope that it had gone unnoticed. *Stupid tart!*

Smiling to myself at her desperate attempt to seduce him, I unplugged my laptop and asked her to follow me. As I opened the door to his office, she went to enter before me. Acting quickly, I let go of the door and it nearly knocked her off her feet.

'Oh, I'm sorry, my bad. I need another set of arms,' I said, my tone dripping with sarcasm.

Bryce witnessed my not-so-accidental slip and smirked. *I'll see that smirk and raise you another, Mr Clark.*

'Chelsea, thanks for meeting with me this afternoon,' he said politely as he held out a chair for her at the conference table.

'Of course, it's my pleasure,' she replied as she sat before he pushed her in.

He then held a chair out for me. I thanked him and sat, then turned on the laptop, opening a Word document ready to take notes. Moving to my side, he took a seat next to me and casually dropped his hand so that it rested on my leg under the table. I froze and glanced at him through the corner of my eye. Thank goodness for the laptop and jug of water, blocking Chelsea's view of the position of Bryce's hand.

'Here is the draft agreement for this year,' he said as he slid a document across the table to her. 'There are a number of guests attending the Tel V Awards who are very high-profile — in particular, 4Life. They will need to be transferred by the Bell Jet Ranger; that's been stated in section five. Their itinerary is also mentioned, and as you can imagine, it will need to be followed quite strictly,' he explained while moving his hand up my thigh.

I could only imagine the expression on my face looked like one of those mime artists with white painted faces, the ones who always looked shocked.

Chelsea began to speak in helicopter language, going on about cyclic stick controls, and rotors, and blah blah blah. Bryce managed to maintain the conversation, not to mention his composure, whereas I, on the other hand, was completely lost. *What am I supposed to be typing?*

It dawned on me in that moment that Bryce had only wanted me there for one reason, and it wasn't to take notes. Realising I had to type something, I clicked on font size 48 and changed the colour to red. *This will get his attention and hopefully disguise my lack of note-taking.* I began to type.

STOP IT

He licked his lips and babbled on about swashplates and collectives while his hand squeezed my thigh and moved slightly closer to the spot he was aiming for.

BRYCE EDWARD CLARK! YOU'RE DRIVING ME CRAZY! STOP IT, NOW!

'Excuse me, Chelsea,' he said politely, interrupting her pathetic verbal dribble. 'Alexis, you need to write it like this,' he explained, leaning over and typing on the keys of my laptop.

This gave him the ability to do two things. One: get his finger underneath my underwear. And two: type a cheeky response. He sat back in his seat with a satisfied and heated look on his face, then slowly began to massage my clit. *Oh, fuck!*

I could barely contain my building orgasm, let alone look at what he had typed on the screen.

YOU WANT IT, I CAN FEEL IT!

Oh, I wanted it all right.

Clearing my throat, I spoke up before they continued their conversation. 'Oh, really, Mr Clark? I thought it was like this.'

I typed again.

YES, I WANT YOU NOW!

His eyes practically bulged out of his head, and he began to pack up the papers. *Fuck, he's going to get rid of her.*

'Chelsea, we can finish —'

'Sorry, sorry to interrupt. But Mr Clark, is it like this?'

Chelsea snorted as if to say I was incompetent.

ONLY KIDDING, NOW STOP IT

I clamped my legs shut on his hand, prompting him to put his other one through his hair.

'No, Alexis, definitely not. It has to be like this,' he replied, his tone now holding an edge of annoyance.

FUCK! YOU DRIVE ME WILD

I laughed, and he tried ever so slightly to pry my legs apart, but years on the wide-leg press at my gym ended his attempts.

'Oh, I'm so sorry, Mr Clark. You're right.'

I continued typing so it looked like I was correcting my so-called error. Chelsea rolled her eyes at Bryce, but he just half-heartedly smiled at her. *The joke is on you, bitch!*

YOUR TURN NOW, MR CLARK!

I lowered my hand and removed his. He fought it at first but surrendered when I dug my new nails into the top of his hand, forcing him to retreat quickly and rub his hands together.

Placing my hand on his leg, I started to creep it up his thigh, but my arm was shorter than his, so I couldn't stretch any further without looking strange. *Crap! Damn you, little arms. Think, Alexis, think!*

Smiling to myself at the devious retribution that just crept into my head, I leaned forward and poured myself a drink of water, strategically placing the glass close to the edge of the table.

Noticing my intent, he sat upright. *Shit, he's on to me.* Very inconspicuously, I knocked the glass into his lap.

'Oh, no! Mr Clark, I'm so sorry. I'm such a klutz,' I shrieked, while grabbing a napkin and patting his dick quite firmly. 'I'm so sorry, Mr Clark,' I repeated, looking up at him and batting my eyelids.

He grabbed my hand and took the napkin. *Hey!* So I grabbed another one and continued my happy patting of his very wet and full package.

'Thank you, Alexis. I can take it from here,' he said, through gritted teeth.

I handed him the second napkin and produced one monster of a smirk. Chelsea just sat there, her mouth agape.

'I think that's all, Chelsea. If you wouldn't mind getting your father to go over those few amendments and get it back to me tomorrow, please.'

He stood up and escorted Chelsea out while I packed up the laptop and wiped the chair down. She must've said something about my clumsiness on her way out, because Bryce replied with, 'It's only water.'

Seconds later, he had closed the door and was standing there with his back to me for what seemed like an eternity. Slowly, he turned around, and the devilish grin plastered across his face had me squirming on the spot. He began to unbutton his pants, resulting in my heart skipping more than just a beat. I watched as he unzipped his trousers and allowed them to fall to the floor. *Oh fuck! Oh fuck! Oh fuck!*

Standing there in his underwear, causing me to steady my stance, was a man who could only be described as a god. His quads were flexed and hard, and the muscles in his abdomen were sexy as hell.

A lump had formed in my throat, so I swallowed, forcing it down before I choked. *Stay cool, Alexis, you can still win this.*

'Your underwear is wet too, Mr Clark,' I pointed out, eyeing his obvious hard-on as I poured myself another glass, this time with the intention of actually having a drink.

Without a second thought, he hooked his thumbs into his elastic waistband and pulled them down, kicking them aside.

I nearly spat my mouthful.

'You wanted this, Ms Summers?' he asked standing proudly before me. *For love of all things fuckable, yes!*

I tried to shake my head in answer to his question as a rebellious smile crept across his face. He was standing there, not a care in the world, his superb erection at full stretch. *Fuck! That's gloriously huge.*

'Bryce Edward Clark, you stay right there,' I stuttered, pointing to the spot he was standing on. He mimicked me by slowly shaking his head from side to side, his devilish grin returning. I sensed that at any second he was sure to set upon me, having no doubt about it, actually.

Quickly, I scouted the room, desperate to map an escape from his impending lascivious charge. In front of me was the large, oval conference table. To my left, approximately five metres away, was his desk — and at equal distance to my right was the door to his apartment. And two metres in front of the conference table was the lounge area of three sofas and a coffee table. After that, it was open space to the door.

Before I could make a decision, he lunged in my direction.

I squealed. *The table, Alexis. Stay behind the table.* He stopped directly opposite me and eyed me ferociously. *I'm screwed!* He motioned to his right, so I did the same, then he went back to his left, and I copied.

'You won't win this one, Alexis,' he said as he eye-fucked me from across the table.

'Watch me, Bryce.'

I stepped to my right, then left, then doubled back and headed for his apartment door. My downfall was the fact that I had to scan my keycard, which took a lot longer than I had planned. He grabbed me, and I screamed. Then, hauling me up over his shoulder, he punched in a door code and entered his apartment. My head was only centimetres from his amazing bare arse, so I slapped it hard which made him grunt.

'Put me down, Bryce,' I pleaded, laughing uncontrollably as we passed the staircase. *Okay, good. We are not going to the bedroom.* Then we passed the lounge. *Right, I'm now lost.*

'Where are you taking me?'

He tightened his grip. 'You wanted wet, so you're getting wet.' *Wet? What does he mean wet? Oh, shit! No!* He pushed the bifold doors open and walked to the edge of the pool.

'Bryce Clark, don't you dare!' I begged.

He entered the pool one step at a time. 'I love it when you dare me.'

'Bryce! No, I'm sorry! I'm sorry!'

I was screaming and laughing, but I knew it wasn't going to do me any good. He kept going, so I straightened up as the water level got higher. Then, all of a sudden, he lunged into the water taking me with him.

Resurfacing at the same moment he did, I glared at him. 'You prick!' I shouted, while punching him in the shoulder.

He grabbed me and pulled me to his chest, but I pushed off him and splashed water in his face. Laughing, we swirled around each other breathing hard and fast, and that's when I remembered he had no pants on. Possessing no willpower — obviously — I looked down into the water.

'Would you like a pair of goggles, Ms Summers?' he said mischievously.

I chuckled then sank down under the water and wriggled my blouse off. Taking another breath, I submerged myself, swimming up to his groin. Every ounce of me wanted to stop and consume every delectable inch of him, but I couldn't. His legs were open, so I pushed forward and swam between them blowing out my breath harshly as I passed under his swollen cock.

Surfacing behind him, I wrapped my arms and legs around his body. He grabbed my legs like a piggyback and dove back under, slipping me to his front and kissing me under the water. When we emerged, our lips were still locked.

I could seriously kiss this man until I ran out of breath. There was just something about the feeling I experienced when our lips were locked — it was indescribable.

'Alexis, will you give me a week?' he asked, his eyes searching mine, pleading, searching for the answer he so desperately wanted.

'How, Bryce? I can't see how it is possible.'

'Don't worry about the how. I need to know if you will.'

Swallowing hard, I gave him the answer he wanted, the answer I wanted. 'Yes, I will give you a week, but it is impossible.'

He moved his hands down the sides of my face. 'Nothing is impossible.'

CHAPTER
19

I wanted to stay in the pool with him all night, but the simple fact of the matter was I couldn't. After all, waiting at home for me were my two adorable children and my loving husband. *Oh, God! My loving husband.* I suddenly felt sick.

I didn't know how Bryce planned on me staying with him for a week, but he seemed quite adamant that it was going to happen. My gut told me he'd find a way, but my head said it was impossible. If I were to be with him for an entire week, I would no doubt fall for him, because deep down inside, I already had. It was obvious to me that this was the case, as there was no way in hell I would be in a pool with him if I hadn't.

Pulling away, I grabbed my floating blouse and swam to the edge of the pool. There were towels neatly folded on the ends of the sun lounges, so I climbed up the pool steps, took one and draped it over myself. Thank goodness my shoes had fallen off, because the rest of my clothing was completely soaked.

Bryce swam to the edge and followed me out. Grudgingly, I passed him a towel, not before catching another glimpse. Just the sheer sight of him made me blush, he was immaculate. *Stop staring, you perve.*

'Are you sure you don't want the towel back, Alexis?' he asked as he dried between his legs.

He then very casually swung it around his waist and secured it. Of course, I wanted that towel back; I wanted it back more than anything. The sight of his erection made my throat both dry and wet at the same time. But there was so much more to him than his stunning physique, and I think it was that much-more part of him that I had fallen for. He was playful, challenging, kind and intelligent. He took pride in himself and his possessions, and he never did anything by half. He was down-to-earth, yet he displayed a shield of power and authority. It was all these qualities that drew me to him; I was simply captivated by the man.

'I will give you a week, Bryce, but I'm certainly not going to ask Rick for it, and I will certainly not go behind his back. I believe in fate, signs and chances. So if it is meant to be, it will be. In the meantime, though, I cannot keep crossing the line with you. I know we haven't had sex, but what we are doing is still wrong and it's killing me. I don't want to be a cheating whore any more.'

He grabbed my arms and glared at me. 'You are not a cheating whore, don't ever say that,' he growled.

'Bryce, I am. You have seen me, kissed me and touched me. And I, the same to you. I'm so disgusted with myself. It's just ... I can't seem to help it when I'm with you.'

He pulled me into an embrace and kissed my head. 'I'm sorry, Alexis. I'm sorry I have forced you to break your vows and to question your morals. I never meant to hurt you.'

He sounded pained, which in turn made me mad at him.

'This is not your fault! You are not married. You are not even in a relationship.'

'But you are, and I wouldn't leave you alone when you asked me to,' he admitted, sounding disappointed with himself.

'I didn't want you to leave me alone, and I still don't.'

'Alexis, I'm hurting you and that's ...' He turned to walk inside. 'That's not an option. In your room is a whole set of clothes. Have a shower, get changed and go home to your family, honey.' He dropped his head and bounded up the stairs.

My room? Go home?

* * *

He was right, the wardrobe was completely full of clothing: underwear, nighties, jeans, tops, bathing suits and shoes. I stripped off my damp clothes and stepped into the shower. Squatting down, I hugged my knees and cried. *Did he just let me go and say goodbye?* That's what it felt like and it hurt. It hurt more than the pain of guilt I was already feeling. *Fuck! What have I got myself into? I'm in a mammoth fucking hole, and I seem to be getting deeper into it by the minute.*

After expelling my emotions by way of extricating every tear from my ducts, I exited the shower and found a very similar skirt-suit to what I'd had on previously. I blow-dried my hair and made myself presentable again. When I finally descended the staircase, Bryce was sitting on the lounge. He stood up slowly and walked toward me. *This is it, he's letting me go.*

I took the last couple of steps with equal apprehension and braced myself. Letting me go was the right thing to do; the only thing to do, but I couldn't bear to hear it.

'Alexis, I don't want to hurt you any more. Hurting you is the last thing I would ever want to do. I won't touch you. I won't kiss you. And I won't put you in any situation that will make you question your integrity. Like you said, if we are meant to be, then we will be.'

He took my hand and kissed the back of it, his soft lips bidding their farewell tenderly. Unable to accept this as our last embrace, I grabbed his face and kissed him as though it was the last time I ever would. My eyes were flooded when I broke away and, not wanting him to see the extent of it, I dropped my head and turned for the elevator.

I didn't look back, it was just too hard. 'I'll see you in the morning, Bryce,' I said without looking back. Then I left.

CHAPTER

20

The next two days at work were really dreadful. Bryce was out of the office for the entire day on Thursday. I also noticed he'd scheduled an appointment with Jessica and hoped it had nothing to do with me, but I knew better than that. I was as miserable as hell. I had an emptiness inside me that could only be filled by one thing — or more so, by one person — but it was hopeless.

Pretty much done for the day, and really looking forward to getting away with the girls for the weekend — God knows I needed time away — I figured I'd leave a sticky note on his bed. I was afraid I had tormented him far too much, and I needed to tell him how I felt once and for all.

Mr Clark,
   I have fallen head over heels for you but have not been brave enough to admit it. I can't be around you and be

with you, yet I can't be away from you either. I want you, but I can't have you. And I've made you want me, when you can't have me either. I'm sorry I have come into your life and tormented you to the point of avoiding me. You must hate me for this, and I truly don't blame you.

Alexis

I left the note on his pillow and headed to his private elevator. As the doors opened, he stepped out.

I looked down at my hands feeling embarrassed. 'Hi, I was just ... um, leaving you a note.'

'Right,' he replied, awkwardness filling the space between us. 'Danny will be at your house at 6 p.m. if you would still like to use the limo?'

I looked up and met his pained impression. 'Oh, thanks. Yes, if it's still all right?'

He nodded, smiled ever so slightly and moved aside. I stepped into the elevator and the doors closed. *Shit, that was beyond awkward. He really does hate me. He's done with you, Alexis. You flirted and dick-teased him for far too long, and he's done.*

It really shouldn't be such a surprise that I was in this awful fucked up situation. I had been cooped up for nine years at home with my housework and *The Bold and the Beautiful* and, as soon as I was faced with temptation, I gave in. There was never the intention of taking it any further, because I couldn't. And he had now realised this himself, probably thanks to Ms Fucking-carrot-top Jessica. I had fucked up my career and possibly my marriage for that matter, because what I had done would eat at me, and eventually I would have to confess.

Suddenly, I felt terribly ill at the realisation of my stupidity. *Oh, shit! The note! I need to get it back. Alexis, you're a fool. He's obviously fed up with your indecision and doesn't want you any more. And I just basically poured my heart out to him on a stupid, freaking sticky note. Okay, options are: one — go back up and hope he hasn't gone to his room yet, he probably went straight to his office. I could sneak in and get it before he has even seen it. Two — hop in the Porsche, hightail the fuck out of here and deal with it Monday, in the hope he forgets about it, and providing I even have a job by that stage. Shit!*

Feeling myself hyperventilate, I took in a few quick breaths just as the elevator came to an abrupt halt. I was ready to get out thinking I was in the basement when it started to elevate again. *What the?* I pressed the basement four button repeatedly but to no avail. *Shit! Crap! Balls! He's found it!*

The elevator came to a stop once again, and if there was ever a time I wanted superpowers, it was at that moment — invisibility or Spiderman super-suction so I could hide against the roof.

The doors opened and he was standing there holding my sticky note. *Get in first, Alexis.*

I stepped out quickly and handed him the keys to the Porsche. 'Before you say anything, Bryce, I'm sorry. I'm fucking fucked in the head, and I'm a dick-tease. I'm pathetic and I understand.'

Walking past him, I kept babbling shit about not being ready to go back to work because my legs opened as easily as a can opener, in addition to the fact that I turned to jelly when I was faced with the hottest man on earth. I kept walking and babbling until I reached my desk where

I proceeded to grab my personal things. He just stood there and watched.

'So, I just want to apologise for arousing and tormenting and ...'

Having been so immersed in my own little bubble of confusion and humiliation, I had not noticed the massive smirk on his face. *Why the fuck is he smirking at me? I have just completely confessed to falling for him, teasing him, and fucking him around and he is* smirking.

'I love you, Alexis.'

I think at that point my heart collapsed. Just stopped. Thud. *What? Is he insane?* I stood speechless and frowned at him from utter shock.

'I love you, Alexis, and you love me.'

He walked over and scooped me up in his arms, taking me back into his apartment and into the private elevator. He elbowed basement four, and we began to descend.

'You don't love me, Bryce. You can't love me, especially after what I've put you through. I'm teasing you, you ... you ... you can't love me,' I babbled in confusion and shock.

'Alexis, honey, I'm not confused about my feelings for you at all. They are set in stone and will not change. You love Rick, but you love me too, and you can't admit that until we can openly share time together. Go on your girls' weekend, have a great time and when you get back I will have made the impossible possible.'

He set me down next to the Porsche and opened the door. I took back the keys and slid gingerly into the driver's seat, still stunned and unable to say anything. The confused frown I'd displayed upstairs was still plastered on my face and remained there until I pulled out of the basement car park.

* * *

Danny pulled up in the limo, not too long after I got home. I was still thinking about what Bryce had said after my melt-down. *Why is it he understands the way I am and the way I feel, better than I do myself? Make the impossible possible? What the hell did he mean by that? Alexis, wipe it from your head. No more Bryce. No more Rick. Weekend with girls. Weekend with girls.* I kept repeating 'weekend with girls' in my head like a mantra, hoping it would work and take my mind off the alternative.

'Danny, would you mind taking Nate and Charli for a ride round the block for five minutes? I'm not quite ready.'

'Certainly, Mrs Summers.' He opened the door and Nate and Charli jumped in.

'Right, no mucking around or Danny will lock you in and bring you straight home, won't you, Danny?' He nodded and smiled in my direction. I waved goodbye as he pulled away.

Rick was in the kitchen cooking pasta. He was so sweet and really was a wonderful husband and father. I walked up, kissed him on the shoulder, and wrapped my arms around him. Glancing around, the house was spotless, the garbage was out, the dishes were put away, the washing was folded, and he had even picked up our dry-cleaning. Rick had done all that, and there I was leaving for the weekend to drink alcohol, let my hair down with my friends and contemplate my future. He had been so good to me. Even the changes he had made to allow me to go back to work had not been a problem for him in the slightest.

As I stood there with my arms around him, I felt awfully guilty. I felt so guilty I became nauseous and my eyes were stinging from my sheer desperation to prevent the tears from falling.

'Thank you,' I said as I squeezed him tight.

He kept stirring the sauce 'What for?'

'For being you. For being wonderful, and for allowing me to get away for a breather.'

'You deserve it. You are a wonderful mum and wife and deserve a bit of you-time.'

He put the spoon down and turned to face me, still wrapped in my arms.

My husband was a very good-looking man with neatly cut, short dark brown hair and sexy brown eyes to match. He pretty much always had a five o'clock shadow which I thought suited him. He was slightly shorter than Bryce by about 10 centimetres, and not as muscularly built. Yet he was still strong enough to pick me up and carry me to the bedroom whenever he saw fit.

'Go on. Hurry up and finish getting ready, or you'll be late.'

I stretched up on my tiptoes and gave him a kiss, guilt still tearing my heart apart.

* * *

Danny did the rounds and picked up Tash, Lil, Jade and Steph. They were buzzing with excitement, not only about the weekend we were about to smash, but the fact I had picked them up in a limo. Tash was the exception since she had borne witness to Bryce's request — or should I say, demand — that we take it for the weekend.

They were all smiling at me and waiting for me to explain the emergency getaway.

'What? Stop smiling at me,' I said defensively.

Tash stood up, her way of distraction I assumed. *God, I love her.*

'Fuck it. I've always wanted to do this. How do you open this friggin' sunroof?' she asked as she pushed on the glass.

I laughed, knowing exactly what she had in mind. So did Steph, because she was on the button like a flash.

Tash stood up and poked her head out. 'Shit,' she said nervously, but gradually crept higher until her arms were resting on the roof. Steph joined her, and they were both squealing and laughing hysterically.

'You might want to keep your mouths shut, girls, unless you don't mind the odd bug between your teeth,' Jade warned, ever the cautious and anal one.

Steph ducked her head back through the sunroof. 'Come on, Jade! Get up here!'

'No, you're both fucking lunatics,' she laughed in response.

'Hey, watch this.' I motioned to Jade and Lil.

Tash had on a pair of black, shiny leggings and a shimmery tunic. Grabbing the top of her waistband, I yanked them down. She screamed and fell down onto Jade and I, collecting Steph along with her.

'You bitch,' Tash snarled, unimpressed.

'I just wanted to check out your new ruffle butts,' I explained, trying to convince her that was the reason I just yanked her pants down.

'Yeah, check them out! Rainbow ones!' she boasted while wiggling her arse in my face. Tash and her ruffle butts, I swear she lived in the bloody things.

The four of us giggled like a bunch of schoolgirls, filling me with a sense of relief. 'Oh, I need this. I've missed you crazy bitches,' I said as I relaxed into my seat.

Apart from our night out, I had barely seen them. Steph was still home full-time with her youngest, Holly, who was three. Lil and Tash worked part-time, and Jade worked full-time like me. I had seen Jade some mornings at the before-school care drop-off, but it was nowhere near enough. I missed my friends and was thankful they had dropped everything to be with me during this weekend away.

Lil started to explore the limo. 'Ooh, there is a mini-fridge here. I hope there's wine.'

Of course there was wine. There was also a bottle of gin, cans of lemon squash, strawberries dipped in chocolate and a very expensive bottle of Dom Pérignon 1966. And stuck to the bottle was a sticky note:

Alexis,
   Whatever you and your girlfriends need for the weekend is on me. Enjoy your time away.

Bryce

I peered further into the fridge and there was a credit card. *You sneaky shit!*

Steph grabbed the bottle. 'Fuck! Dom Pérignon '66. That's over a grand a bottle. Crack this shit open!' she squealed.

'Wait!' I yelled, hesitating.

They froze and looked at me.

'Should we drink it? I mean, is it really that expensive?'

'Lex, the man is made of money. Sexy money. He wanted us to drink it.'

I gave Tash an unsure grimace.

'It's up to you, hon,' Lil explained.

I thought of what Bryce had said to me and then read his note again.

'Okay. He obviously wants us to have the Dom. But as for the credit card, he can stick that up his —'

'Tight, firm, delicious, taut arse,' Steph groaned.

I slowly turned my head in Steph's direction, raising my eyebrow at her.

'What? The man is fucking sexy, even the visually impaired can see that.'

Jade hit Steph on the arm. 'Steph, you can't say that.'

'Why? It's probably true.'

'Just pour the fucking champagne,' Lil barked.

I laughed, thankful for Lil's impatience.

Tash and Steph poured everyone a drink, and we all clinked glasses.

'Cheers, girls, and cheers to Lexi and her love triangle!' *Nice, Jade, real nice.* She squeezed my leg. I knew she was kidding; Jade did not have a nasty bone in her body, and if you ever needed backup or an ego boost, she was first on the scene.

Slumping back in the black leather seat of the limo, I sighed with contentment as I sipped the exquisite champagne. Spending time with my wonderful friends was just what I needed. We knew how to make each other laugh and we knew when to bring out a box or two of tissues — a skill that could prove to be valuable during the weekend ahead.

Finally making it to the Peninsula Country Club just after 9 p.m., we were all pretty exhausted so we decided on an early night.

* * *

The following day was spent relaxing at the hot springs in the Spa Dreaming Centre. It was pure bliss. We found our barrel and soaked up the relaxing and rejuvenating setting.

'Can we stay here and never leave?' Steph slurred, chilled and quite adamant we were not going anywhere.

'Yeah, right, what about Chris and the kids?' Lil asked.

'Ah, screw 'em. They can cook, clean and fend for themselves.'

We giggled. If only! The notion was nice though.

'So, I was thinking,' suggested Jade.

'That's a first,' Lil deadpanned.

Jade splashed her. 'I was thinking dinner and drinks out tonight? There is this great karaoke bar in Rye.' Jade loved a good sing-off. 'You and me Lex: "Hold On" by Wilson Phillips. It's on like Donkey Kong.'

I smiled at her challenge. Tash then chimed in with her best Gloria Gaynor impersonation and it wasn't long before we were all belting out 'I Will Survive' in the middle of what was supposed to be a tranquil day spa.

An elderly couple walked past in their robes and gave us a dirty look, so Tash stood up in the middle of the barrel and did a shimmy for them. Their dirty look increased, and they picked up their pace, moving along.

I shook my head at her. 'You are a bad girl, Tash.'

'You can talk!' she replied, then bit her lip.

'Maybe, maybe not.' I gave her a cheeky grin. 'Let's go for a walk, up the hill. There's a nice pool at the top, you can see the ocean.'

Tash led the way, and we all got out and put on our white terry-towelling robes and flip-flops.

'Jesus, it's cold,' Jade complained.

It was cold. The hot springs average temperature was between 39 and 43 degrees, so when we stepped out the cool air hit us. We shuffled along quickly, resembling a colony of penguins.

'What the fuck?' Tash choked out then laughed, stopping in her tracks on our way up the hill. We nearly bumped into each other like a set of dominos. 'Check this dude out! He is lying in a foot pool.'

Peeping over Tash's shoulder, I spotted the lone man lying flat on his stomach in a pool that was very shallow, shallow because it was meant for your feet only. Tash continued on and we all followed, trying to stifle our laughter. As I walked past, muffling my mouth with my hand, I pointed to the 'Foot Bath' sign with a sympathetic look. Let's just say the guy exited the pool very quickly.

'He is going to smell like arse,' Tash said as she laughed and screwed up her nose.

'Don't you mean feet?' Lil questioned.

'Probably both,' she replied and continued up the hill.

* * *

We had a blast Saturday night at the karaoke bar. Lots of songs were killed including 'Holding Out For a Hero', 'Love Shack' and 'Love Is A Battlefield'. The schnappies kept coming, and Danny made sure we got back to the country club safe and sound. I never once used Bryce's credit card, this weekend being about me and my girls. I was more than happy to splurge my own money.

Steph passed out on the sofa, and Jade put herself to bed. Tash, Lil, and I sat outside, alfresco, with another opened bottle of Dom — apparently there was an entire case in the limo.

'So, Lexi ... putting all this extravagance, lust and knight-in-shining-armour shit aside, what are your true feelings for Mr Clark? Have you and Rick been having some problems or something?' Lil asked, cutting to the chase and coming right out with it.

'No. No problems, really. Well, I don't think so. Things do feel a bit different though. As for Bryce, you want the honest truth?'

Lil raised her eyebrows and nodded.

'I think I'm in love with him.'

Tash and Lil turned to face me, and the atmosphere became quite serious.

'Lex, are you sure? What about Rick?' Tash questioned, her expression gravely concerned.

'Is it possible to love two people? I don't know, but that's what it sort of feels like.' I began to tear up, but fought the salty menace away.

'Have you slept with him yet?' Lil questioned, turning all Dr Phil on me.

'No, hon, I haven't, and I won't — not behind Rick's back — but we have had a few passionate kisses, and when I say passionate, I mean fucking passionate. I feel incredible when we are together. This might sound stupid, or wrong, or even naive, but I think we were meant to be.'

'But didn't you feel that way about Rick, before Bryce came along?' Tash probed once again.

'Yes, and that's just it. I have never had a comparison. You guys seem to forget I have only ever been with Rick.'

Both of them shrugged their shoulders.

'Okay, Lex. Take away the billions, the cars, the hotel and strip Bryce down to the core. Do you still think you're in love with him now?'

I thought about stripping Bryce down to the core and a greedy smile crept across my face. 'Yes, Lil. I honestly think

I do. It's not the money or power that attracts me to him, it's him and the way he feels about me. Money can't buy that.'

Lil lit up a cigarette.

I put my hand out. 'Give me one of those.'

'You don't smoke,' Lil scoffed, yet threw me the packet.

'I do today.'

She leaned over and flicked on the lighter. I could see her sweet, concerned face in the light of the flame.

'I heard a quote once that might pertain to you. By memory it was said by Mr Johnny Depp. If you are in love with two people, choose the second one, because if you really loved the first one, you wouldn't have fallen for the second.' She flicked off the lighter and sat back in her seat.

CHAPTER
21

Rick was watching the Grand Prix when he heard a knock at the door. Annoyed at the interruption, he got up and answered it. *Better not be a friggin' telemarketer,* he said to himself as he opened it. To say that he was surprised to see the person who stood before him would be an understatement; it definitely was not a telemarketer. Instead, the illustrious Bryce Clark was the one responsible for the interruption. *Fuck, what does he want?*

'G'day, Bryce. You do remember Alexis is not here, yeah?'

'I'm not here to see Alexis. Have you got a moment alone to discuss something?' Bryce looked around in the hope Nate and Charlotte were nowhere to be seen.

'Yeah, the kids are out with their friends. Come in,' Rick answered dubiously, showing Bryce into his home.

Instantly, Rick sensed that the purpose of this visit was not of a friendly nature. Instead, Bryce's unannounced and somewhat unorthodox stop-by was more untoward. And at the very bottom of his stomach, he had an idea of what it might be.

Rick had picked up on Bryce and Alexis' not so subtle flirting with one another when he visited his wife's new place of employment some weeks ago. He had also picked up on Alexis' resulting strange and distant demeanour ever since that time.

'Can I get you a beer, mate? It's not the nice drop you offered me, but it's still a frothy.' Rick went to the fridge and grabbed a couple of Crown Lagers. He handed one to Bryce and then sat on the seat furthest away.

While Rick went to fetch the beers, Bryce took it upon himself to look at the countless number of photos of Charlotte and Nate when they were babies, a lump forming in the powerful billionaire's throat. But when he caught sight of Alexis in her wedding dress, looking simply breathtaking, he pictured himself in the tuxedo standing next to her. This thought alone gave him pure joy and allowed him to bury the guilt of what he was about to do.

'So, what can I do for you?' Rick asked casually, trying to look as comfortable and confident as he could, but deep down feeling very intimidated by his wife's boss.

'Rick, I'm just going to come out and say it, but before I do, I want you to promise you will hear me out entirely.'

That bit at the very bottom of Rick's stomach started to churn again.

'I'm in love with Alexis, and I want a chance to spend some time with her without her feeling guilty,' Bryce declared, breathing out imperceptibly, his exhalation releasing just the smallest bit of relief along with it. 'I want to spend a week with her. A week where she can freely decide to do whatever it is she wants.'

Rick just sat there shocked. *Okay, not quite what I expected. This dickhead is on drugs!* 'Don't you mean you want to spend a week fucking MY wife?' *I can't believe this motherfucker.*

Bryce leaned back, glared at Rick, and placed his leg across his knee. He then casually took a swig of his beer. 'If that's what she wants to do, then, yes.'

'Are you for fucking real? You come into my house, asking permission to take my wife away for a week so you can throw money at her like a whore and convince her to sleep with you? You're pathetic.' Rick was beyond furious at the audacity of this man. He was also offended on behalf of his wife.

Bryce, on the other hand, used all the control he could to subdue the anger he felt when Rick compared Alexis to a whore. 'It's not like that, Rick. She has feelings for me, too, and she has cravings that only I can satisfy.'

Rick stood up in anger. 'Get the fuck out of my house!'

He pointed to the door, but Bryce didn't budge.

'I'm not finished. I'll pay you five million dollars to give her permission to spend a guilt-free week with me.'

'You are fucking insane,' Rick spat as he sat back down and put both his hands behind his head. *Five mil! Fuck! That's a lot of money. Is he serious or yanking my chain?* Rick couldn't for the life of him figure the cocky billionaire out.

'No, I'm not insane. I want a chance to show Alexis that I love her, and that she does, in fact, love me too.' Bryce had picked up on Rick's sudden attitude change when he mentioned the 'golden figure'. It gave him hope that he would not have to go to plan B.

'She's not going to agree to this, I can guarantee you that.' *There's no way in hell she could have feelings for a fucking arrogant, self-centred prick like you.*

Rick was sure Alexis could not have fallen for the douche bag. She had more sense than that. 'If I accept, you do realise you are wasting your time and money. She won't give you the time of day when she knows you've bought her. You obviously don't know her too well.' *Clearly, the guy has money and no brains.*

'That's why you need to keep your mouth shut about the money. If she finds out before our week is finished, the deal is off.' Bryce took another swig of beer. He kept his calm, but deep down he hated what he was doing. Not that he hated offending Rick. What he hated was that he was going behind Alexis' back. He knew she deserved better than that.

'Okay, hotshot, so what am I supposed to say after I've finished making love to my wife. "Hey, babe, go and spend a week with your boss. Fuck him, do whatever you like. It'll be fine". Or how about, "Hey, babe, ever heard of a hall pass?".'

Bryce cringed at the thought of Alexis being touched by another man, especially Rick, who did not deserve to touch her ever again. He thought that the hall pass thing could possibly work. 'That last one is an idea!'

Rick mockingly laughed. 'How's that going to work? I'd have to want one too, and I don't.'

Bryce put his beer down on the coffee table and realised he was going to have to go to plan B. 'That's because you have already had one, haven't you? Oh, that's right, you never had permission, because Alexis doesn't know about it, does she? Does the name Claire Longmire ring a bell?'

Rick fidgeted in his seat. 'She does know about Claire.' *How the fuck does he know about Claire?*

'But does she know the whole story, Rick?' Bryce raised his eyebrow, knowing he had the cheating arsehole right where he wanted him.

Rick stood up again. 'You fucking son of a bitch!'

Bryce stood up also and walked around Rick to wait by the door. He could see Rick was close to throwing a punch. The last thing he wanted was for the conversation to turn violent. 'I want this to happen as soon as possible. I'm taking her to the Tel V Awards Monday night, and she will be staying the night at my hotel. So you might as well make this happen tomorrow. The money will be wired at the end of the week into an account of your choosing.' Bryce opened the door. 'For what it's worth Rick,' he paused, 'I'm sorry.' He shut the door and took off in his Lamborghini.

CHAPTER

22

'Do we really have to leave? Surely we can just stay here for-ever, become lesbians, and never have to deal with men or children again.'

'Seriously, Steph? Nah, not for me. I'm strictly dickly,' Jade declared as she finished folding her clothes into perfectly neat little piles.

Steph threw a handful of her own in Jade's direction. 'Here, now do mine.'

Jade threw them back.

I smiled at the girls. They didn't have a care in the world. They were all so happy, and their lives were so uncomplicated.

'You're quiet,' Lil whispered as she came to stand behind me.

'Oh, just thinking about things.' I smiled wryly at her.

'Seems like you have a lot to think about.' She squeezed me on the shoulder and left me to finish packing.

* * *

Danny dropped the girls home one by one, Tash being the last. He was getting her bag out of the trunk when she gave me a big hug.

'I don't envy you, hon, but you've got to get to the bottom of this and quickly. Where are the kids going for school holidays on Monday?'

'Up to Mum and Dad's farm. They can't wait. I won't see them for a week. It'll be good, but I'll miss them. Rick and I will both drive to Shepparton and pick them up the following weekend, and they can attend a school holiday program for the week after that.'

'Well, maybe you can use that time to have some one-on-one time with Rick?' She touched my arm and headed for her door. 'Thanks for the weekend. It was great. We had a ball, and please thank Bryce for the champa's and limo, that really was nice of him.' She gave me a sweet smile.

'No worries, hon. I'll talk to you soon.' I got back into the limo and Danny took me home.

* * *

When I walked through my front door that Sunday evening, it felt as if I'd stepped into a war zone. The kids were at each other's throats. I'd barely made it past the kitchen when they both came up on either side of me ready for battle.

'Mum, tell Charlotte to stay out of my room!'

'Mum, he keeps taking the scissors and glue! How am I supposed to do my homework if I can't find the glue?'

Nate crossed his arms. 'Easy, squeak, get your own.'

'Don't call me squeak! I don't squeak! Mum, tell him not to call me squeak.'

'Squeak.' Nate taunted her by poking out his tongue.

Charlotte went to push Nate, but he was too quick, running off to his room and shutting the door. Charlotte growled, threw her hands to her sides, and stormed off to her room, slamming the door as well.

Still standing in the kitchen with my suitcase by my leg, I looked around, slightly bemused. I found Rick — shortly after — sweeping and hiding from the commotion in the garage.

'Hi, babe, I'm back. What's with the kids? Hope they haven't been like this all weekend?'

He didn't look up and, instantly, I sensed something was wrong. His body language was off.

'Rick?' I questioned with a raised voice.

'What? Sorry, what did you say?' he asked, seeming to be in a world of his own.

'Never mind.' I shook my head at him and went back inside.

Grabbing some chicken Kiev out of the freezer, I then chopped up some vegetables. Between the time spent checking the stove and oven, I managed to unpack my bag. I served up dinner and the atmosphere was still extremely strange. Nate and Charlotte were having a silent war of stares with each other, and Rick was still finding it difficult to make eye contact with me.

Having no choice but to try and ignore the weirdness radiating from my family, I cleaned up the dishes and helped the kids pack their bags for their stay at Mum and Dad's farm. Due to Rick having the following day off from work, he was planning to drive them to Shepparton in the morning.

I tucked Charlotte into bed first and gave her my mummy warning. 'Be good at Nanny and Poppa's. I don't want to receive a phone call saying you and your brother are fighting.'

'But, Mum, he never helps me or shares with me. And he always tells me to go away.'

I kissed her little head. 'Sometimes big brothers just want a bit of space, that's all. I'll talk to him and tell him to be nice.'

'Mum, are you going to the Tel V Awards tomorrow with Mr Clark?' *How did she know about that?*

'Yes, how did you know about that?'

'Daddy told me. Will you see 4Life there?' she asked, sitting up eagerly in her bed.

I gently pushed her back down and gave her a big kiss and hug. 'Maybe. If I do, I'll say hi for you. Now go to sleep, and I'll see you next weekend. Love you Charli-Bear.'

Making my way to Nate's bedroom, I was still trying to figure out how Rick knew about the Tel V Awards. I was sure I hadn't mentioned it to him yet, having planned on doing it later tonight.

I walked into Nate's bedroom and picked up his dirty clothes from the floor while giving him the they-don't-belong-here look. Ignoring my critical glare, he jumped into bed and waited for his kiss and cuddle. *I hope he wants these until he's at least twenty-one.*

I sat down on the end of his bed and repeated my mummy warning. 'Be good at the farm and stop being nasty to your sister.'

'But, Mum —'

I gave him my stern mummy look. 'But nothing, she is your baby sister and looks up to you! So be nice. And make sure you wear all your safety gear when you take your motor-bike out, okay?'

'Yeah, okay.'

I gave him a big cuddle. 'I'll see you on the weekend. Love you, my little man.' I kissed his cheek and left the room.

* * *

Rick had resumed sweeping in the garage while I was tucking the kids into bed. *How much sweeping does he need to do? He knows something, Alexis!*

'Would you like a cup of coffee?' I called to him from the door.

He leaned the broom up against the wall and looked at me. 'No.'

'Okay.' I gave him a frown and went to turn back in order to head inside.

'When were you going to tell me about attending the Tel V Awards tomorrow night?' he asked. *How the fuck does he know?* It was really bugging me.

'Tonight. I only found out on Wednesday. I forgot to tell you before I left on Friday night. Anyway, how did you find out I was going?' I gave him a confused smile.

He pulled out a crumpled and semi-faded sticky note from his pocket. *Oh, holy fuck! Bryce's sticky notes. Shit, the dry-cleaning.* I'd completely forgotten about them being in my pocket when we'd taken a dip in the pool.

I walked over to him, and he handed me the note. Thankfully, he only had the one sticky note and bits of the others. The part in which Bryce said he's 'very much looking forward to seeing me in the dress on Monday night at the Tel V Awards' was still intact. The rest of the note was really hard to make out. But words like 'occupy the guest room or mine', 'mouth ached for yours' and 'Your Mr Clark' were clearly legible.

'What's going on, Alexis? Are you sleeping with your boss?'

Hearing those words come out of his mouth in the tone in which they did, felt as if I'd been hit in the face. My cheeks grew flushed and hot, and my stomach twisted, making me feel nauseated. 'No, Rick, I'm not sleeping with Bryce. I ... I wouldn't do that.'

He sat himself on the edge of his workbench, not appearing to be pissed off, which was weird. 'Do you want to sleep with him?' *Now's your chance to be honest, Alexis.*

I walked toward him and put my hands in his. 'Honestly? Sometimes yes, and sometimes no, but I would never do it.'

He remained calm, and it was very hard for me to comprehend why. I had gone off my tree when he had mentioned that he and Claire — an old friend of ours — had shared an embrace and a near-kiss.

'Why "sometimes yes"?' he asked, again remaining calm. *What's he getting at?*

'What kind of a question is that? I don't know. I guess I'm curious as to what it would be like with someone else, that's all.' *Not to mention that I have fallen in love with him.*

'Alexis, be honest with me. Have you kissed him?' *Oh, shit. Shit!*

My eyes started to fill with tears. *There's no holding back now.* 'Yes, Rick, I have. I'm so sorry, I never meant for it to happen. I don't know why. I ... I —'

Rick dropped my hands and put his face in his. 'I know why, babe,' he said.

I took a step back.

'I know why it happened.'

'Why?' I wanted to run, run as far away as possible.

'Because I have felt what you are feeling, Lexi.'

I wiped my nose with the back of my hand. *What is he talking about?*

'I have wondered what it would be like with someone else also. The thing is, I didn't just stop there either, Lex ... at the wondering bit, I mean.'

I stumbled a little, trying to piece together what he had just said. My legs were trembling from owning up to my own form of betrayal, but now I was worried they would completely give way.

'What are you saying, Rick?' I wasn't sure I wanted to hear it, but deep down I think I already knew. I think I had always known.

'Claire and I didn't just console each other years ago.'

He jumped off the bench and grabbed my shoulders. 'Lex, I slept with her, and I'm glad I did it in the end. Because it made me realise that all I've ever wanted was you, and that need I had — to see what it felt like — completely vanished. I've never had that feeling again. This is why you should go and get the same curiosity off your chest so that we can move on. Look at it like a "hall pass".'

The slightest twinge of a sympathetic smile crept across his face which stirred a ferocious fiery pit in my stomach.

'A fucking hall pass? You want to give me a hall pass to make your infidelity okay?' *I knew it! I fucking knew it!*

I began to cry as the enormity of what he had just confessed hit me. 'How could you do this, Rick? Being curious and sharing an embrace or a kiss is one thing, but sleeping with her — fucking her — that's just ... I can't do this.'

I went to leave but he grabbed me.

'Alexis, I'm sorry. Please don't leave. Sleep on it. I promise it will make more sense in the morning. Don't leave. I'll sleep in the spare room.'

I hit him in the elbow, causing him to release his grip then grabbed my bag and phone, and stormed out the door.

* * *

When I got in my car and pulled away from the house, I knew exactly where I was headed. I tried unsuccessfully to collect my thoughts and calm my crazy emotions as I drove, until, before long, I found myself approaching City Towers.

Swiping my card, I pulled into the basement car park. I looked in the rear-view mirror as I switched off the engine. *Fuck, I look like a panda. A very puffy dark-eyed panda.*

Grabbing a wet wipe from my bag, I began to wipe the smudged mascara from underneath my eyes. I couldn't let Bryce see me like that. I then grabbed my brush and quickly ran it through my hair, blew my nose, and put a little powder on my face to hide the redness. *Who am I kidding? I look like a mess.*

As I got out of the car, the elevator doors opened. Bryce came purposefully striding toward me and, seeing the determination on his face, I dropped my bag and ran to him. We collided into an embrace only a couple of metres from the car. I was practically ravaging him and he the same to me. He lifted me up, and I wrapped my legs around him while ripping his t-shirt over his head and yanking my own free. I was hungry for him — for all of him — and had never wanted him as much as I did right at that moment.

Furiously, I tried to get his jeans undone and unleash the probing thickness that was inside his pants.

'Alexis, honey, hold on. Stop.'

I stopped fumbling and burst into tears. He held me to him, tightly. And put his hand on my head. I hung over him like a limp child asleep in their parents' arms.

'What's wrong? Tell me?'

Pulling myself away from his shoulder, I looked directly into his eyes. 'Rick ... Rick admitted to having an affair years ago,' I divulged as the tears came thick and fast. I wouldn't be able to stop them now even if I had wanted to.

Bryce carried me to the elevator and up to his apartment. I just clung to him, not wanting to let go. When we arrived on the second level, he went to take me to the guest room.

'No. Please, I don't want to be alone,' I pleaded with him, looking deep into his eyes.

'Alexis, I don't want our first time to be like this, or as a result of you being angry with Rick.'

'I know. I don't want that either. I just want to be held, that's all. Please,' I begged him.

He gently wiped away the tears that sat on top of my cheeks and kissed me tenderly. 'That, I can do. That, I want to do.'

He then took my hand and led me to his room.

CHAPTER
23

I woke up the next morning and, at first, had to gather my bearings. *Yes, you are in Bryce's bed. Yes, you're still partially clothed.* Noticing he was no longer lying next to me, I shot upright, but could hear the distant sounds of him in the kitchen. I flopped back down on the mattress and rolled over, hugging his pillow tightly. It smelled of him. His whole bed smelled of him. I even smelled of him.

Not wanting to waste another minute without him in my presence, and wanting to occupy myself with something — anything — in order to prevent my mind from returning to the memories of the day before, I gingerly climbed out of his bed. I ducked into the guest room — or 'my room', as he had put it — and grabbed a long, black satin nightie.

Catching a glimpse of my reflection in the vanity mirror as I was about to exit the room, I spotted evidence of the river of tears I had cried yesterday and during the night. *Urgh, I need a shower.*

I stepped into the shower, the hot water soothing and helping to wash away the betrayal and hurt I had been feeling. The memory of my daydream in this very spot from over a week ago crept into my mind, followed by the memory of me crouched down when Bryce told me to go home. It was apparent this shower was becoming an emotional outlet for me — a place to expel my inner feelings.

I let the water soothe me as I thought of my kids, hoping they were all right. I was sure Rick wouldn't have said anything to them. Knowing him, he probably expected me to come home after work as if everything were normal. The problem with that was everything wasn't normal, it was far from it. Also, our children were not stupid; they picked up on the slightest things, especially Nate. Worried about the two little loves of my life, I reminded myself to give my mum a call later in the day to check in on them.

Once I was out of the shower and dried, I put the nightie back on, and this time when I looked at my reflection in the mirror I was clean and fresh, and the anger and sadness I had felt previously had washed down the drainpipe. Well ... for the time being, at least.

* * *

I found Bryce, moments later, moving around the kitchen like a natural culinary god. Standing there, quietly leaning against the wall, I happily observed him. He had a relaxed and content vibe radiating from him — it was infectious. Smiling, I watched him chop the chives like he was a professional chef on one of those cooking shows. *Now, that is super freakin' sexy.* The way his hands moved so incredibly quickly over the chopping board excited many parts of my body; I soon found my mouth was quite dry. He stopped chopping, and that was the moment I raised my eye level from his hands, finding his chest rising and falling heavily, causing mine to do the same. Our eyes met. He put the knife down, and I slowly closed the distance between us.

Lifting me up onto the kitchen bench, he pulled my nightie up so that I could open my legs and encase him in them. My tongue slid slowly into his mouth and his into mine, deliciously tasting one another in a slow yet erotic dance. Separating our mouths, he pressed his lips to my neck then dragged his lips down my throat. I arched my head back from the sheer exquisite sensation his lips afforded me, causing the strap on my nightie to fall from my shoulder, exposing my breast. Instantly, my nipple was taken into his mouth.

A soft cry of pleasure escaped my throat. 'Oh God, Bryce.'

He removed the other strap of my nightie and greedily consumed my other nipple, his tongue so tantalisingly good. I could've climaxed just from the sensation of his mouth on my skin.

Returning to my lips, he growled like a hungry animal, the rawness of his sound nearly tipping me over the edge. I moaned and crossed my legs around his back.

'Alexis, you're driving me wild.'

'Good. Make love to me. I need you.'

He deepened his kiss for only a second then pulled away and gently grabbed my face. 'No. I have plans for you later.'

The sheer thought of his plans sent my body into a frenzy, but I was wanting, and wanting now. He unwrapped my legs and stood back. Then he shook his head and resumed chopping. *No, don't stop now!* I was panting and found myself dropping my bottom lip while pulling my straps back up. *Oh no, he's not getting away with this.*

Still sitting on the bench next to him, I draped myself back and crossed my legs in a seductive pose.

He growled again. *Ooh, I love it when he growls.*

'Alexis, you don't know how hard it is for me to say no to you. I want tonight to be special. So for fuck's sake, stop torturing me,' he said through gritted teeth.

I slid off the bench and grabbed a piece of crusty baguette, then bit into it and growled back at him. He smiled, so I scowled.

'Breakfast will be ready in a minute.'

'What are we having?' I asked, deliberately licking the piece of bread and playing with it with my tongue.

'Eggs Benedict,' he said with an amused grin.

I bit down on the baguette aggressively and turned to exit the kitchen. 'Yum,' I called back, and as I walked out I caught his reflection in the window.

He had both his hands through his hair and had dropped his head to the benchtop.

Leaving the room, my face displayed the biggest smirk in history, and naughty me did not let him see it.

* * *

The eggs Benedict he promised were delicious. He was a brilliant cook. Obviously concerned for my wellbeing, he asked me if I was okay and if he could do anything for me. I reassured him that I was fine and told him that deep down I had a feeling there had been more to Rick and Claire all along — just not that much more.

'What's done is done, Bryce. I can't change what Rick and Claire did and neither can he. I don't want to think about it, nor do I want to talk about it. I am here with you and you only. I will speak to Rick when I'm ready to do so and not a second sooner than that.'

'Okay, Alexis. But I'm here if you need to talk,' he said again, lowering his gaze and finishing his eggs. He didn't probe any further.

The buzzer to his office sounded, changing the atmosphere between us.

A large smile spread across his face as he stood up. 'Ah, my Cinderella, I hope you are ready,' he said, before kissing my hand.

I watched him leave the apartment, taking note that he had been smiling all morning. Well, apart from my attempts to torture him, but even then he radiated happiness.

Moments later, he returned with Clarissa in tow, pushing a trolley with my dress, a shoebox, some bags and cases. Walking next to her was a heavily made-up blonde and a very well-groomed man.

'Good morning, Ms Summers,' Clarissa greeted me, effervescent as usual. 'This is Jane and Carl, they are going to do your hair and make-up for this evening.'

'Good morning, Clarissa, and please call me Alexis,' I smiled, extending my hand to Jane and Carl. 'It's a pleasure to meet you both.'

'I'll leave you in their capable hands, honey,' Bryce said with a smirk before kissing me on the forehead and exiting through his office.

Jane, Clarissa and Carl all stood wide-eyed as they surveyed the apartment. I couldn't help but smile at their expressions. I, too, must've looked just like them the first time I stepped into this room.

'Wow, I've never been in here, it's stunning,' Clarissa expressed with admiration. Smiling excitedly at me and raising her eyebrow, she nudged me toward the lounge area. 'Okay, let's get started.'

'Ready when you are,' I replied, keen for my transformation to begin. The last time I had a proper pampering session was on my wedding day, so today was going to help put that memory aside.

'Right, first things first — spray tan. Carl, help me set up the tent,' Jane instructed as she got things moving straightaway.

Both she and Carl erected the tent quite quickly and, before I knew it, I was making a choice of whether or not to wear a G-string during the tan's application. Being in a daring mood, I removed all items of clothing and let them spray me entirely, my new found brazenness a result of being around Bryce. I couldn't deny that I also felt like a new Alexis. Probably that, plus the fact I had lost a lot of weight and was now more than proud to show myself off when the time called for it.

The tanning was completed quite quickly, and I could honestly say I was not a fan of it. I was one to try things at least once though. However, tanning was something I would not be repeating again, along with other dreaded experiences such as a professional pedicure and foot massage.

My hairstyling was next on the agenda, and this was something I was definitely a fan of. Carl was not your typical stereotype of a male hairdresser being gay. Instead, he was married with three kids and had his own salon on Chapel Street.

'Your hair is gorgeously long, Alexis. I will only take a small amount off the ends and give it some subtle highlights. Now, because the dress is the star and has quite an eye-attracting plunge at the front and back, I'm going to put your hair up and let it cascade to the side.'

'Anything you say, Carl. I am at your complete command,' I surrendered, having no fear when it came to him taking control of my hair.

'Ah, good girl, that is what I like to hear.'

Bryce had arranged for Sebastian to deliver us lunch, which indicated to me that it was now the middle of the day and that time was ticking by rather quickly. Jane was also now working on my make-up, and I hoped it wasn't going to be as extensive as hers. No matter how often I seemed to wear it, I still felt less was more with regards to my face. Maybe that was just a habit I was stubbornly refusing to break out of.

Sensing that my transformation was near completion as Carl finished pinning my hair up, the butterflies in my stomach started to flutter their wings, churning my nerves.

'Now all hands on deck with the dress,' Clarissa said excitedly as she revealed the stunning red gown.

She handed me the underwear, which I pulled on underneath my robe, and all three of them helped me step into the dress without affecting my hair or make-up. Clarissa zipped and hooked it all together, then handed me a gorgeous pair of light-gold Christian Louboutin heels. I slipped them on, stood up, and performed a spin for all three of them, the smiles on their faces reflecting their approval.

'Okay, my turn to see. Show me the mirror,' I demanded in a beyond-excited tone.

I hadn't seen any of my transformation thus far as Clarissa wanted me to get the full and final effect when they had finished. So, as Jane turned the mirror around, revealing a glamorous stranger in its reflection, I could honestly say that I was shocked, yet delighted. The dress was simply stunning; a real work of art, and I honestly thought that anyone could put it on and they would resemble a movie star.

Taking in my hairstyle, I noticed that Carl had kept it quite straight but with a very subtle wave. He had pinned it up, slightly to the side, allowing it to fall down the opposite side to the detailed shoulder strap. It was very elegant and it definitely suited the style of the dress.

Jane had surprised me the most though, thank goodness. My make-up was very subtle and she had stayed true to the dress, also allowing it to be the star. My eye shadow was light and smoky, and I had a faint streak of pink blush high on my cheekbones. But it was my striking red lips that brought the whole ensemble together.

As I was pirouetting in front of the mirror, Bryce walked in wearing a very sexy black tuxedo. The man did not need much to make him mouthwateringly delicious. He froze at the entry to his apartment, our eyes locking on one another. I could see him swallow quite hard, which made me do the same. Clarissa, Jane and Carl were looking between us like spectators at a tennis match.

'Okay! We are done here,' Clarissa announced, signalling Jane and Carl to very quickly pack up and get the hell out of there.

We had both barely said goodbye to them as they were walking out the office door, when I finally broke Bryce's hungry stare and shouted out to them, 'Thank you! Thank you very much. You all did a wonderful job.'

Each of them smiled at me, and Bryce showed them out.

He was back in the room almost instantly, standing at the top of the step that led down into the lounge area. He had one hand in his pocket and the other through his hair. 'Alexis, you take my breath away.'

I blushed, I couldn't help it. I didn't think I had ever taken anyone's breath away. Well ... apart from the time I pushed my sister off the fence and winded her.

'You look very delicious yourself, Mr Clark,' I drawled while eyeing him from top to bottom.

He stepped down into the lounge and slowly made his way over to me, his slow purposeful strides as sexy as the man who was taking them. When he reached my position in the room, he placed his free hand on the side of my head and kissed me gently on the cheek. His head moved to my neck and lower again. It was so soft, yet so sensual and incredibly romantic.

Seconds later, he came back up to my face and rested his head on mine. 'Now that I have you, I am never letting you go,' he whispered.

I watched as he pulled a jewellery box out from his trouser pocket, and my heart nearly went into cardiac arrest. Sensing my complete shock, he smiled and opened the box. I can't say that I was disappointed when the most beautiful pair of diamond chandelier earrings revealed themselves.

'They are beautiful,' I breathed quietly, reaching forward to touch them.

He snapped the box shut on my finger, causing my mouth to drop wide open. I couldn't help but smile at him as he burst into laughter.

'I'm so sorry. I've always wanted to do that,' he confessed, his face awash with happiness, but also displaying a mischievousness at the re-enactment of *Pretty Woman* he had just performed.

I laughed and playfully punched him in the arm as he opened the box again. Carefully, he removed the earrings and handed them to me. Our eyes met and the happiness that filtered from them was overwhelming. I was still giggling at him as I put them on. He was just so comfortable and relaxed, and it really was lovely to be around him.

Holding his arm out to me, he gestured for me to link mine around it. 'Shall we?'

I obliged and, smiling in the knowledge that this evening was going to be one of the best nights of my life, hooked mine with his and followed as he led me out of the room.

The red carpet arrivals for the Tel V Awards were to be held in the atrium. I figured we would get through this section quite quickly as the celebrities were the star attraction, but what I hadn't bargained on was Bryce being somewhat of a celebrity himself, and my dress being a major star attraction.

'I have with me now, Bryce Clark, the owner of this fabulous complex, and his date for this evening, Alexis Summers.' *Oh my God, how embarrassing, this is going to be televised.* I clung tightly to Bryce's side, using him as a shield while the television presenter for Channel 7 kept talking. 'Alexis, who are you wearing tonight?'

She pointed the microphone in my direction and waited eagerly for my response.

'The dress is Versace, and the shoes are by Christian Louboutin,' I answered, my tiny voice barely audible.

'Absolutely stunning. Quickly, do a spin for us.'

Bryce held up my arm and twirled me around. I couldn't help smiling, although I desperately wanted to get off the red carpet and out of the spotlight.

'Lovely. Well, there you have it. Alexis Summers, definitely a contender for best-dressed at tonight's 55th Tel V Awards.'

The camera went down. *Thank fuck!*

We kept walking, but had to stop numerous times for photos. Bryce held me close — which I liked — but as I had only just walked out on Rick, I felt slightly uncomfortable at the number of cameras that were documenting our every move. I was still technically married, and most of our friends and family — who usually watch the awards — had no idea of the past day's events.

Assuming that Bryce had sensed my anxiety, I was grateful when he hurried us along so that we could take our seats in the Queen Victoria Ballroom and away from the overzealous media.

'Here you go, Mr Clark, Ms Summers. Enjoy your evening.'

'Thank you, Peter,' Bryce nodded to the polite and friendly usher.

I adored the fact he knew — or seemed to know — all of his staff by name.

'Do you have a photographic memory or something?' I asked him as he was scanning the room.

He turned to me and put his arm around the back of my chair. 'No, why?' he asked, looking interested in my answer.

'You seem to know everyone by name. More particularly, your staff.'

He smirked and gently put his hand on my leg. 'It's what I do, Ms Summers.'

I placed my hand on top of his. 'What else do you do, Mr Clark?' I seductively licked my lips then challenged him with a smile of my own.

'You'll soon find out,' he responded, eye-fucking me at the same time.

Swallowing dryly and crossing my legs, 'soon' appeared to be too far away, and as much as I was excited and thrilled to be in this elegant ballroom amongst some very high-profile celebrities, I couldn't wait to go back to the penthouse.

Delving deep into his piercing blue eyes with my own, I found evidence that he desperately wanted the same thing and as we drank in each other's hot and needy stares, I began to realise that soon was never going to be soon enough.

Our intense gaze was momentarily broken when something caught Bryce's eye. I followed his line of sight to find Gareth standing at the table with Samantha, sporting the biggest grin I'd seen since Christmas Day.

'Good evening, Bryce and Mrs Summers.' *Arsehole.*

He pulled a chair out for Samantha and pushed her in. 'So, Alexis, where is Mr Summers this evening? At home with the children?'

Samantha turned a shade of grey and looked nervously between me and Bryce. *You know what? Fuck him.*

'If you must know, Gareth, Mr Summers and I have been separated for quite some time now.' *Slight exaggeration.* 'So, to be honest, yes, he is at home with our children.'

I wriggled in closer to Bryce, and he moved his hand from the back of my chair and placed it comfortably on my shoulder. Gareth glared at me and then waved for a waiter. Samantha ... well ... she just sat there awkwardly and smiled. *Poor thing.*

Clark Incorporated's board members and their partners started to take their seats at our table, Bryce introducing me to each of them as they sat down. At first, some of the other gentlemen seemed a bit sceptical of me, probably due the lies Gareth had planted in their heads. However, as the evening progressed, I had a good feeling I was starting to win them over.

'So, Ms Summers —' An elderly gentlemen who Bryce introduced as Mr Gordon began to speak.

'Oh, please call me Alexis,' I interjected quickly.

'Very well. So, Alexis, Bryce tells me you have been a vital part of marketing for our new family-friendly rooms in the Promenade Building.'

Mr Gordon had silvery-white hair and large thick glasses. He reminded me of Santa. Maybe it was the white hair or maybe it was just the child in me, but I found it hard to take him seriously when he chuckled. *Ho ho ho.*

'Yes, Mr Gordon. Actually, I'm flattered to have been consulted on such a huge project; it really is an honour.'

'Well then, Alexis, I look forward to seeing some of your ideas at the board meeting next month.'

I smiled politely, revelling in the fact he was looking forward to my input. Gareth, however, blatantly rolled his eyes and then said something under his breath.

If looks could kill, then Gareth would be no longer. Bryce's death-stare was fixed heatedly on his cousin. I wished at that very point in time that looks could, in fact, kill. But unfortunately, they couldn't. Gareth had only been in my company for a short amount of time, but had already made me feel extremely uncomfortable. I wanted to run far, far away from him. Better still, I wanted to get to the bottom of whatever it was that made him so majorly pissed off with me, especially if I was going to be seeing a lot more of him. I honestly did not know why he hated me so much — and it bothered me.

His obvious annoyance at my presence was beginning to irritate me enormously, so I decided it was time to visit the ladies room and get away from his discernible hostility.

Bryce was deep in discussion with a few of the other men at the table, so I placed my napkin on my plate, squeezed his leg and made my way out of the room. The time to leave was now or never, as the telecast was on pause for advertisements which gave me a small window to get to the ladies room and back before recording resumed.

* * *

Entering the rather large and opulent bathroom, the scene before me was nothing short of hectic with women making minor adjustments to their gowns and make-up — Sierra Thomas being one of them.

Sierra was up for a Silver Tel V for Best Actress. She was also currently the hottest new thing on television and Charlotte's favourite actress.

She eyed me in the mirror while I reapplied my lipstick. 'That dress is stunning. I think I'm going to have to fire my stylist,' she confessed while blotting her face with a tissue. 'Is it Versace? It looks like a Versace.'

'Yes, it is. Hey, you're Sierra Thomas, right?'

She smiled. 'That would be me.'

'My six-year-old daughter adores you.'

'Nice ... what's her name?'

'Charlotte.'

I watched as she pulled a napkin from her bag and scribbled on it with eyeliner. 'Here, I know it's not perfect, but you have to work with what you've got.'

'Aw, thanks, Sierra. She'll love it. Do you mind if I get a quick photo?' I asked. I was probably pushing my luck.

'No, not at all,' she smiled, so I pulled out my iPhone and took a quick photo of the two of us.

'Thank you so much, Sierra. And good luck tonight.'

A warning that recording was due to resume in five minutes came over the speaker, so we picked up our clutches and headed out the door. As I exited the ladies room, I was suddenly caught on the arm. Startled, I looked up to see who was restraining me, painfully.

'Not so fast, Mrs Summers,' Gareth warned, holding my arm in a vice-like grip.

His obviously harsh manhandling made onlookers take second glances at him. Noticing their double takes, he released his strength slightly and smiled, placing his other hand around my shoulder in an attempt to seem casual.

'Let me go, Gareth. Now!' I hissed at him.

'Don't make a scene, Alexis. You are already quite the centre of attention tonight.'

We smiled falsely as the Newtons walked past and, with their backs now to us and no further witnesses around, I slammed the heel of my Louboutin into Gareth's foot, breaking free of his hold.

Heart hammering in my chest, I quickly made my way back to my seat. As I approached our table, I noticed Bryce looking a bit concerned, trying to find me. When he did finally see me coming, relief flooded his face.

I sat down and almost instantly his arm was around my shoulder. 'Is everything all right?'

'Yes, just nature calling,' I lied, leaning in and giving him a brief kiss.

Samantha blushed, then looked away. Gareth had not yet returned, so I scooted across the seat to get closer to her and find out why she was not her usual loud and bubbly self.

'Hey, are you okay?' I asked with concern. 'You've been very quiet tonight.'

She looked around nervously. 'Um, yeah, I'm fine. What's been happening with you? And why is Gareth so horrible to you?'

'Good question,' I huffed, looking around the room again, nervous that he would be approaching.

Despite the fact she looked wary and was acting a little oddly, I got the impression Gareth hadn't mentioned anything to her about our rather strange relationship and heated encounters.

'Sam, this thing with you and Gareth ... is it serious?'

'No, I don't think so. Um, I really don't know. I'm so confused; he makes me so confused. Anyway, what about this thing with you and Mr Clark? What about your husband?'

She had that gossipy look in her eye and, normally, I would be intrigued with what we were discussing when she possessed that look. But seeing that this time it involved my private life, I was not impressed.

'It's a long story, but like I said, I'm separated,' I proclaimed while shuffling back to my seat as the telecast resumed.

Bryce automatically claimed my leg with his hand, his fingertips lightly grazing my skin. His touch was both torturous and wonderful at the same time. 4Life took the stage, setting the room abuzz. And it was in that moment, I wished that Charlotte was on my lap — she would have been ecstatic. I could picture her now, bouncing and swaying to the music all starry-eyed.

'What are you thinking about?' Bryce asked in a low voice, taking in my not-so-hidden sad expression.

'Nothing,' I responded with a smile.

He squeezed my leg. 'That's not a "nothing" look, Alexis. Tell me.'

'I was just thinking that Charlotte would have loved to see 4Life perform. They are her favourite group,' I admitted, smiling at him.

Bryce had a knack for sensing my differing moods, and I honestly adored that. I also adored how he made such an effort to take in every single thing about me. It was so sexy and attractive.

'I need to make a phone call. I won't be long,' he murmured and kissed my cheek. 'Will you be all right?'

'Sure, go. Do what you do,' I smiled reassuringly. He smiled affectionately and stood up, walking away just as the song finished.

At that moment, Gareth returned to the table sporting a slight limp. I shot a satisfied look in his direction and collected a far-from-impressed look in return. Mr Santa, *oops, I mean Mr Gordon,* asked if Gareth had taken a fall.

'No, some bitch stood on my foot,' Gareth blurted out while giving me the briefest of glares.

Mrs Gordon seemed to take offence at Gareth's choice of words and muttered something into her husband's ear.

'Perhaps it was an accident, Gareth,' Mr Gordon offered.

'Hmm, perhaps,' Gareth replied. *Perhaps, my arse, it was an accident. I meant every bit of that heel implanted into his foot.*

I removed my satisfied scowl away from Gareth to see Bryce return to the table. He had a rather large sneaky smile radiating from his drop-dead, gorgeously handsome face.

'What have you been up to?' I enquired.

'All in good time, my love.' *My love? I liked the sound of that.*

Samantha blushed and smiled ever so slightly then went back to concentrating on her crème brûlée.

Suddenly, a guitar kicked in, filling my ears with a familiar sound. My eyes lit up in anticipation as I searched for the source with keen interest.

Noticing my excited expression, Bryce leaned over and whispered into my ear. 'Do you like Muse?'

'They are one of my favourite bands,' I confessed, shooting him a broad smile. Then, moving my gaze back to the band on stage, I added in a seductively hushed tone, 'Didn't your creepy research reveal that?'

He growled softly, but harshly, into my ear, and I felt his hand slide onto my thigh and up my leg. He moved it slowly until it stopped only centimetres short of the precise spot that was aching for him the most. Very gently, he began to circle my thigh, teasing and tantalising me. As hard as it was, I kept my eyes on the band knowing that if I looked his way, I would launch myself on top of him — that move probably not likely to go down so well in front of so many witnesses and cameras. *You are killing me, Mr Fucking-fantastic-fingers Clark.*

'Hysteria' was the closing song, and for me it was a very fitting end to the evening. Especially now, as I was about to show Bryce just how hysterical I could get when I desperately wanted something and was being made to wait for it. Despite my eagerness to leave and *be* with Bryce, I'd had a wonderful evening. It was also fitting that Sierra Thomas ended up winning the Silver Tel V for Best Actress. I just knew Charlotte would be thrilled.

Muse finished their song, thanked everybody in the room and exited the stage. The gentlemen at our table — including Santa — helped their wives to their feet and said their goodnights as well.

As Bryce and I stood up to leave, I pierced him with my yearning stare. I wanted him to know that my desire for him was becoming unbearably overwhelming, and I was ready for a 'goodnight' myself.

'I can't wait any longer, Mr Clark.' I whispered into his ear.

He picked up my hand and kissed it. 'You are going to have to.' *What? No!* 'Good things come to those who wait, Ms Summers.'

He placed his hand on the small of my back and flexed his fingers ever so slightly on my bare skin. I expressed my frustration with his teasing by digging my nails into his leg as he escorted me out of the ballroom.

'Where are we going?' I asked, clearly irritated.

'Firstly, we are going to meet a few friends of mine. Then we are going to Studio C for a private function with another of your favourite bands.'

I raised my eyebrow at him in question, but he was not about to give anything away.

* * *

Before too long, we stopped at a room backstage. Bryce knocked on the door, and a beefy security guard opened it, nodding for me and Bryce to enter. As he led me into the room, I was nearly knocked down by an invisible wall of what-the-fuck! Seated on four stools in a semicircle — complete with acoustic guitars — were the members of 4Life. Shocked, I nearly stumbled into Bryce's waiting arms.

'Hello, Mr Clark. And this must be Alexis.' It was the lead singer, Harry, who spoke while leaning forward and extending his hand. I shook it, together with the other three members of the band. I should've known their names. Charlotte had mentioned them time and time again. *Alexis, this is what you get for selectively choosing when to listen to Charli and when not to.*

Smiling awkwardly at them, I was pulled backward by Bryce onto his waiting lap. He was perched on a stool opposite the band. I turned my head round to look up at him, excited, yet overly curious as to what this was all about. He kissed my nose softly and hugged me to his chest then took out his iPhone and held it up.

Harry smiled, nodded, and began to speak. 'Charlotte, we are sorry you couldn't be here tonight. So we have put together something especially for you.'

I gasped and put my hands to my mouth as Lee counted them in ... *Lee, that's one of their names! Lee, go me!* They started to sing an acoustic version of 'Anything' — Charli's favourite song. I was so excited for her, she was going to flip, but I was also overwhelmed with what Bryce had arranged and, because of this, my eyes began to well with tears. *No, Alexis. Tears lubricate mascara; mascara runs when wet; and wet mascara equals panda.* I blinked them back, turned my head, and kissed him gently. And as we kissed, I was pretty sure the phone recorded a second or two of the roof while Bryce adjusted his arm to hold me closer.

When 4Life finished their song, I thanked each of them for their special performance and ensured them that Charlotte would more or less faint when we played it back to her. They humbly laughed and then handed me several signed pieces of memorabilia. Bryce shook their hands and we left the room.

Once outside, I released my pent-up excitement, gratitude and overwhelmingly big ball of built-up emotions, which I'd held captive as a result of what Bryce had done.

'Oh. My. God! Thank you! Thank you! She is going to go crazy! I love you! Thank you. Thank you.' I was jumping up and down and clapping my hands like a lunatic.

He grabbed me, kissed me and dipped me backward. 'I love you, too,' he said sweetly before planting a soft kiss on my lips. *Oh, shit!*

After pulling me back up, shocked elation filled my being. I don't know why I was so surprised. It wasn't as if he hadn't mentioned the 'L' word before. I guessed it just felt more real, hearing him say it aloud and in that moment.

'Say that again,' I probed, with a small smile on my face.

'I love you, Alexis,' he repeated with the same sincerity as the first time he'd said it.

Hearing it again filled me with insurmountable joy, lust, yearning, and love ... yes, love. I loved him, too.

'I want to go upstairs. NOW!' I whispered with vehemence.

His body tensed, and I felt his dick twitch against my leg.

I lightly dragged my tongue across his ear. 'Mm ... you do, too, don't you?'

He discreetly adjusted himself and took my hand. 'Patience, Alexis,' he choked out, while clicking his neck to the side. 'Come on, you won't want to miss this. We have all week to be upstairs.'

That thought sent waves of pleasure right through me. *All week?*

* * *

Studio C was one of the Tel V's private after-parties. Upon entering the room, Bryce led me to a booth which had been roped off near the stage. We sat down, and a young waitress came to take our order.

'Mr Clark, can I get you and Ms Summers a drink?' she asked politely. *Did everyone know my name now?*

Bryce turned to me and smirked. 'Would you like a Naked Martini, Ms Summers?' *I'd like a Naked You.*

'No, I'll have a Mind Fuck, followed by a Sex Up Against the Wall, please.'

I smiled ever so sweetly at Miss Blondie and then challenged Bryce with an equally dazzling smile. Blondie caught my drift and smiled to herself, jotting it down on her notepad before raising her questioning eyes to her boss.

'I'll start with a Stiff Dick Shooter and finish with a Fuck On the Floor, thanks,' he replied, but with an added touch of solemnity.

I cracked up laughing and dropped my head. *Geez, he is good.* Blondie stifled a giggle and said she'd be right back with our drinks. Me, on the other hand, had to quickly gather my bearings if I was going to continue playing this game with him.

'Can I try your Stiff Dick?' I asked as I put my thumbnail in between my teeth.

'Can you handle my Stiff Dick?' he replied, while leaning forward and placing his chin on his resting hand.

Fighting very hard to stop myself from laughing, I was finding it excruciatingly difficult to comply. 'Oh, I can handle your Stiff Dick and a Fuck On the Floor, but can you handle my Mind Fuck and Sex Up Against the Wall?'

I licked my lips, which made him clench both his fists, his eyes burning me with need.

Keeping my eyes locked on his, I offered him his own promise. 'Good things come to those who wait, Mr Clark.'

The music began to play, and I knew straightaway who was on the stage without taking my eyes away from his. The sensual sound of 'Closer' by Kings of Leon filtered through my ears and body. The song was my favourite and incredibly hot and, coupled with Bryce's intense stare, I was now melting at the core.

His evident desire bore deep into the depths of my body, making every inch of it silently go crazy. I didn't know how much longer I could endure the exquisite but excruciating longing between us before I exploded with hunger for him.

My stomach was twisting and turning and a glorious tingling sensation now pounded in between my legs. With my eyes still locked on his as the band seductively played the song, I must have missed the moment Blondie placed our drinks on the table. Because before I knew it I was downing my Mind Fuck, and Bryce his Stiff Dick. I licked the rim of my Sex Up Against the Wall, and he demolished his Fuck On the Floor. It was now blatantly obvious we'd both come to the brink, so I put the glass to my mouth in order to finish it quickly.

Bryce reached out and grabbed it before I had a chance, downing it with lightning speed. And, eye-fucking me with heat to rival the sun, he took hold of my hand and led me from the room.

CHAPTER
25

We barely made it to his private elevator, desperately kissing and tasting each other before the doors had even closed. I frantically fisted my hands through his gorgeous hair as an urgent sensation of lustful need coursed through my body. He lifted me up with possession, placing my arse on the handrail and holding me against the wall. I loved his possessiveness, how he owned everything he touched — his ownership of me right now being no exception.

We both stopped, in desperate need of oxygen, and his eyes burned me like never before. Our chests were heaving, yet our eyes continued to fuck each other as we gradually gained our composure. Slowly, I began to unbutton his shirt, revealing his lightly-haired pecs and his gloriously smooth chest: smooth, but hard and flexed in all the right places. My hands were drawn to him, craving the feel of every single part of his now bare front.

Leisurely, I touched his rippled abdomen then moved my hands up to his chest to his shoulders. I trailed them along his arms which were solid and exquisitely textured, then pushed his shirt from him completely, letting it fall to the floor. Swallowing dryly, I took in his amazing body, and any moisture I had left in my mouth vanished ... entirely. He watched me explore him hungrily with my eyes and hands, the obvious hard-on in his trousers a clear indication he was enjoying my approval.

'You are perfect,' I whispered, possibly more to myself than him. I leaned in closer and planted a kiss just underneath his Adam's apple, then another down further, and further again, until I was tracing my tongue around his nipple and chest hair. *Fuck, he tastes good!*

Bryce's head arched back in response, and he growled so low and wild that my pelvic floor convulsed. The resonating sound of his passionate declaration filled the space between us, sparking an eager smile to spread across my face just as the doors of the elevator opened. He lifted me — with the possession that I loved — into his arms and carried me into his apartment where we resumed our ardent and hungry kissing.

Gently, he positioned me up against the entryway wall; the exact spot where we first kissed. 'You wanted Sex Up Against the Wall, my love?' *Oh God, he is sexy. I'll have him against the wall, on the floor, on the ceiling and anywhere I can fucking have him.*

'Yes,' I whimpered breathlessly. 'Yes, now. I can't wait any longer.'

I unlocked my legs from around his waist, allowing them to drop until they were planted firmly on the ground.

'Turn around,' he demanded, lust dripping from his tongue.

I did what I was told and turned, baring my back to him and splaying my hands on the wall. Slowly, he ran his fingers along my arms and up over my shoulders to unhook and unzip my dress.

'Alexis,' he murmured, his warm breath tickling the skin between my shoulders. 'I want you so fucking badly.'

I sucked in a ragged breath as my dress fell to the floor, leaving me in only my red lace G-string and Louboutins. 'You can have me, Bryce.'

He pressed his chest into my back while gripping my arse and kissing the nape of my neck. The warmth and feel of his body against mine — touching mine — was like nothing I'd ever felt before.

'I'm going to,' he whispered seductively into my ear, '... now.'

My body shuddered in response before he spun me back around so that I was facing him again, my arms outstretched against the wall and my breasts now flush with his chest. His look of lust and admiration made me want him even more — if that was at all possible. I went to lean forward and request he kiss me, but he dropped to his knees instead and put his hands on my hips before I had the chance.

Staring up at me with a devilish grin, his expression held promise of what was to come. And it was that look and that look alone that nearly had me climaxing on the spot.

He hooked his fingers under the lace of my G-string and pulled it down, lifting my legs one at a time until I was there against the wall completely bared and at his mercy.

Bryce leaned back on his knees, seemingly to take in what was before him. 'I could stare at you forever, Alexis. You take my breath away.'

Smiling at him and loving his appreciation of me, I realised it wasn't just lust for my physique. It was admiration, awe and sheer worship, something I had never experienced before. Not even with Rick.

I slid my fingers down the sides of his handsome face, deciding to offer him some encouragement. 'Someone once said to me, Mr Clark, that "It is better to taste than to admire, I assure you".'

Understanding my brazen proposition, his wicked smile widened as he picked up my leg and placed it on top of his thigh, his lips quickly finding my knee. I watched with heightened anticipation as he moved higher and higher with each kiss, eye-fucking me the entire time.

Panting from the sheer sensation of his lips and tongue as they tickled and teased my skin, coupled with the lascivious glint in his eyes as he moved toward my pussy, I held on tight to the pending release of pleasure wanting to explode from within. He had me so fucking wound up and I hadn't even had sex with him yet.

Bryce paused momentarily, breathing hard and hot on my wanting clit, my own breath, too, hard and hot as I stood there hankering and anticipating the touch of his mouth — a touch that seemed to be forever in waiting. *Oh, for fuck's sake! I can't bear it any longer.*

I placed my hands on his head and flexed my nails into his scalp, my desire now reaching boiling point. I was broken. Done.

'Bryce!' I pleaded.

Feverishly, he pressed his lips and tongue to me and I sighed with delight, his movements controlled and utterly mind-blowing. I loved his tongue and how he mastered its use, it being my favourite muscle in his body by far.

As his tongue swirled on my skin and his lips sucked and nipped, my breathing soon became ragged, and my fingers tensed with the building sensation that was like none I had ever experienced before.

He sensed my rising orgasm and quickened his tongue's movement, all the while moving his hands from my hips to my arse and pulling me hard against his face, tipping me over the edge. I cried out his name and exploded with pleasure, right before he released himself from between my legs.

'Bryce ...' I stuttered, trying to find words, 'That was —'

'Shh ...' he said, while trailing his tongue up my stomach, around my navel and to my breasts.

Sucking my nipple into his mouth, he flicked it with his tongue and drew a heavy breath in through his nostrils before grabbing my other breast with his firm, large hand.

'Fuck,' I cried.

I placed my fingertip under his chin and directed him back up to my face. 'You, Mr Clark, are still far too clothed for my liking,' I informed him as I unbuttoned and unzipped his pants which then fell to his ankles.

He kicked off his shoes and removed what was left of his clothing while taking in my heated expression. 'Is this better, Ms Summers?' he asked, proudly displaying his swollen and very hard cock.

'Yes ... much.'

I was standing there with my back up against the wall and him in his naked brilliance within my reach. It was simply agonising, and I could not wait any longer to have him inside me.

Grabbing him aggressively, I pulled him to me. He took hold of my leg and hooked it around his hip before slowly guiding himself inside, the hard silken flesh sliding against mine, filling and stretching me. It felt beyond wonderful, causing us to growl in succession. He pulled back out and slowly pushed back in, then repeated the movement, each time quickening his pace. My Louboutins gave the perfect height for him to drive me effortlessly. *Fuck. Fuck. Fuck.*

What I felt both physically and emotionally was pure pleasure — his rhythm superb — and it escalated my orgasm once again.

'Oh, God! But wait! I do believe you ordered a Fuck On the Floor.'

'That I did.'

He smirked and lifted me up, securing me to him, then walked us down into the lounge area. I felt nothing but safety in his arms. He was so strong and moved with me attached to him as if we were meant to be that way permanently.

Bryce squatted down and, with one arm, braced himself against the sofa until he was sitting on the rug with me astride him. Now in our new position, I didn't waste any more time and began to sensually move over his delicious erection, making him groan eagerly. The more I moved, the more he groaned.

My breasts were thrusting in his face, allowing him to take full advantage which he did, massaging, licking and sucking at them greedily.

As I slid up and down his cock, I felt it tense within me and sensed he was close to release — I, too, right there with him.

His hands were on my back, gripping my shoulders and helping to control the pace and, wanting to reach another orgasm but reach one along with him, I moved even harder and faster and forced his release, sharing the moment of bliss. *Oh, holy fuck!*

I licked his tongue with my own and flexed my hands through his hair as we gradually started to regain our breath. He kissed my shoulder then threw his head back on the sofa.

I couldn't help but let out a satisfied giggle, causing him to bring his head back up.

'Something funny?' he smiled, taking my hand and kissing the back of it.

Sliding off his still firm cock, I stood over him, eyebrow raised. 'I would say I handled your "Stiff Dick" quite well.'

He laughed and followed me to his feet. 'Oh, honey, I haven't finished with you yet.'

He scooped me into his arms, making me squeal.

'I should hope not,' I replied.

Shaking his head at me, he then carried me upstairs, and I noticed the smile on his face as he claimed me for his own and held me tightly in his arms. It made me smile as well, not just on the outside, but more so from within.

* * *

We entered his room, and the scent of roses hit me like a plank of wood. There were literally hundreds of them, long-stemmed and vibrantly red. They were in vases, and petals were scattered all over the floor and on top of the bed.

Bryce placed me down on top of the mattress, and as I scooted backward, some of the petals attached themselves to my sweat-soaked skin.

'You and your creepy research,' I muttered.

'Honey, I've told you before. It's what I do.'

I laughed. 'Yes, it is.'

He began to crawl up the bed toward me. 'And don't you forget it.'

'I wouldn't dare,' I answered softly, as I watched him stalk me once again.

'Good.'

He picked up my foot and kissed my toe, which made me giggle.

I screwed up my face. 'Eww.'

He laughed and held it in front of him. 'What?'

'I don't do toes, so this is one thing I'm not going to reciprocate,' I said matter-of-factly.

He moved my toe back to his mouth and put the whole thing in.

'Stop it!' I screamed, cringing.

'No,' he mumbled as he continued to surround my toe with his mouth.

I got up on my elbows, my expression now menacing. 'Bryce, don't make me use my newly-acquired self-defence skills on you.'

His eyebrows rose, and the sheer excitement of my challenge spread across his face. He removed my toe from within his mouth and held it against his lips. 'Is that a threat, my love?' *Shit, I'm not going to win this one.*

Calling my bluff, he stuck it back in his mouth, so I swung my other foot toward him, hoping to connect with his shoulder. The connection never came ... apart from my foot connecting perfectly with his hand as he caught it without evidence of even the slightest flinch.

Royally fucked — in more ways than one — he had one foot in one hand, with my toe in his mouth, and my other foot in his other hand; giving him complete control of my legs.

'You need more lessons. I'm thinking some private ones will help,' he suggested, his expression indicating his sinister thoughts.

'I'm thinking you will always have the advantage, Mr Clark.'

'Well, that's just too bad for you then, isn't it?'

I rolled my eyes, fell flat on my back, and surrendered, throwing my hands above my head.

Still holding my feet in each of his hands, he taunted me. 'Hmm. What am I going to do with you now, Ms Summers?'

I took in with delight the sight of him kneeling on the bed before me and basked in his dominant, content disposition.

He gently pulled my legs, sliding me along the bed toward him, as I collected a shitload of petals in the process. Then, with an inviting glint in his eye, he moved forward, put his hands around my back, and pulled me up onto his lap.

I bear-hugged him, squeezing as hard as I possibly could and securing him with my thighs. 'Hmm, what am I going to do with you now, Mr Clark?' I mocked him, holding him in my vice-like thigh grip.

'You won't win. Didn't you learn the last time?' *Ah, the last time. Yes, I did in fact lose that challenge, but I did get to see his cock and that made the loss well worth it.*

He reached behind his back, grabbed my ankles, and attempted to pull them apart. I, on the other hand, clenched as hard as I could, growling my frustration which only added to his urgent need to open me up. I watched with amused fascination as his biceps, triceps and pectorals flexed when he increased his strength. But it was the devilish glint he purposefully gave me that weakened my hold.

As soon as he felt my legs surrender, he was instantly inside me once again, thrusting hard and deep. *Oh, fuck! The fullness!* I arched my head back and moaned in delight as his incredible length slid in and out of me.

Bryce pressed his lips to the exposed skin on my neck then slowly dragged his tongue all the way to my mouth.

'You taste so good, honey,' he mumbled as his tongue moved with mine.

He lifted me just slightly, leaned forward, and laid me down on my back. A couple of petals became airborne and landed on his chest and lips. He spat them off instantly, which made me laugh hysterically.

'Not fucking doing this again,' he said, with slight irritation.

I couldn't stop laughing, he was just so cute.

'Do you think it's funny?' he asked, as he began to push into me, hard.

I nodded but could laugh no longer, his penetration so intense and far from funny. He pushed and pushed, harder and deeper until my back bowed and I lost control. Bryce groaned and emptied himself into me once more, then relaxed his weight on top of me and kissed my forehead.

* * *

Minutes later Bryce rolled off onto his side, supporting his head with his arm. 'You look beautifully fucked,' he stated with a satisfied smile while tracing his finger around my breast. *Pfft, I'm an energizer bunny, incarnated.*

I smiled at him. 'Are you writing me off?'

'Never,' he answered, jumping up with enthusiasm. *Shit! Maybe HE is the energizer bunny, incarnated.*

Pulling me upright, he scooped me into his arms and carried me into his bathroom.

'For how long are you going to keep carrying me around?'

'As long as I want,' he declared, as he placed me down, turned on the shower and gestured me in. 'After you.'

'But you'll ruin my hair.'

'Get in,' he scowled.

I stood to attention. 'Yes, sir!'

Smiling, he growled and slapped me on the arse, making me cry out. I squinted my eyes at him in return, but secretly loved a good smack.

* * *

After only having been in the shower for what seemed like a few minutes, I could honestly say there was nothing better than being in a small confined space — surrounded by hot steam and water — and having the man of my dreams swollen, hard and surrounded by my lips.

Unfortunately, I wasn't one who was blessed with a big mouth — although some may beg to differ — and despite the fact my mouth was no match for his thick cock, the challenge to entirely consume it didn't deter me.

Greedily, I dragged my tongue up and down his wet, silky shaft while he gently placed his hands on my head. I thoroughly enjoyed the taste of him in my mouth, not to mention the look and feel of his body when I brought him completely undone. I swear I could listen to this man growl and groan 24/7.

'Fuck, Alexis,' he hissed.

I smiled and watched conceitedly as he came, his body rippling with pleasure.

'You're a fucking angel,' he said, as he helped me to my feet.

'I'm no angel, Bryce, or have I not proven that yet?'

'You are my angel, Alexis, and don't ever forget that.' *Fucking angel, my arse.* I was a devil around him and I loved it.

I shot him an if-you-say-so look and reached for the shampoo. Applying to the palm of my hand, I began to wash my hair. I could see from out the corner of my eye Bryce leaning back against the shower wall, wearing his usual delectable smirk.

'Yes?' I questioned him as I rinsed the soap suds away.

He dropped his gaze down my body, seeming to follow the bubbles as they dropped, then he looked back up again and ran his hand through his wet hair.

'You do realise that from now on I am going to have to see you naked every day for the rest of our lives,' he replied.

Honestly, I loved hearing him say things like that to me, but at the same time, my life was far from simple. Every day for the rest of our lives was something I couldn't even begin to comprehend. Although ... the sight of him looking unbelievably sexy in the shower was something I would be more than happy to see every day for the rest of my life, as well.

Deciding not to take those particular words too seriously, I positioned myself against the opposite wall to him, blatantly mimicking his posture, and then offered my declaration in return.

'You do realise that I'm going to have to dig my nails into you every day for the rest of our lives?' I challenged, raising my eyebrow and waiting to see the reaction I could draw from him.

His eye twitched, and I inwardly relished the little telltale sign he showed when I exposed him.

'You do realise, my love, that I'm going to have to taste every part of your body every day for the rest of our lives.'

Just the thought of his talented tasting abilities forced a small smile onto my face. 'Do you realise ... my love, that I am going to make you come every day for the rest of our lives?'

I'd barely finished taunting him when he pushed off the wall and had me completely captured before I could even blink. I wrapped my arms around his neck, and he lifted me up again.

'Maybe I should have said, "you do realise you are going to be lifting me up every day for the rest of our lives",' I suggested after separating my mouth from his.

'I wouldn't have it any other way, honey.'

I smiled and kissed him. I truly loved kissing the man. I could see myself getting swollen lips on a daily basis. His mouth was sensational, and when he had it attached to mine, my body reacted by igniting all over.

'I want you, Bryce. I want you again.'

'Greedy, aren't you?'

'Yes, and I'm not ashamed to admit it,' I murmured around his mouth, dropping one leg and inviting him to enter me once more. He happily obliged, making me gasp. *Oh, I could get used to this.*

'Ms Summers, are you ordering another Sex Up Against the Wall?' he grunted.

'No, Mr Clark. I'm ordering A Sex In the Shower.'

He laughed. 'Of course you are.'

We devoured each other again, and it was as equally incredible and mind-blowing as before.

* * *

After getting out of the shower and drying myself off, I went to go to my room to retrieve a silk nightie when Bryce caught my arm.

'In here, honey.'

He turned on the light to the walk-in closet. *Or more to the point, walk-in stadium, the thing was friggin' huge!* All the clothes he had bought me had been moved, along with dozens more, all of them looking perfectly in place in their new home.

I entered the room and started inspecting the items, finding everything I could possibly need, hung. folded, or ... tucked away in drawers. The copious quantity of shoes resembled a wall of rainbows, and it had me stunned and simply speechless. I turned around to find Bryce leaning up against the doorway.

He smiled and shrugged his shoulders. 'It's what —'

I interrupted him. 'It's what you do.' I nodded my head, 'I know.'

Opening a drawer, I found a long, navy silk and lace nightie. It was perfect. Bryce helped slip it over my head and then went to scoop me up again.

'Oh no, you don't,' I warned, then led him to the end of the bed and turned him around.

I stepped up onto the mattress and hitched my nightie up. 'A compromise, my love,' I offered, while placing my hands on his shoulders and jumping onto his back.

'Fair enough,' he said, as he held my legs tight.

He piggybacked me downstairs and stopped by the bar. I slid off his back, walked outside and stood by the balustrade while he poured us a drink.

The city night sky was beautiful, with coloured lights twinkling all around. He walked up behind me with two glasses: a gin for me and a Glenfiddich for himself. Then, wrapping his arms around me, he passed me my drink.

'Don't ever leave me, Ms Summers.'

I twisted my head around to kiss him. 'I'm not going anywhere, Mr Clark.'

Loved *Temptation?*

Turn over for a sneak peek of Book 2 in the series —

Satisfaction

K.M. Golland

Alexis and Bryce have spent an amazing week together and have become inseparable, but what happens when Rick reveals Bryce's five million dollar deal?

Out July

harlequinbooks.com.au

Bryce

I've never really considered myself to be a lucky man. Yes, I have more than enough money to feed a small country — which I do, because I make damn sure a good percentage of my fortune aids people who genuinely need it the most. But having a rather large bank account has never truly satisfied me, nor has it ever fulfilled me. It was simply a result of working hard and keeping my mind from the emptiness I have felt ever since the day I lost Mum, Dad and my little brother, Lauchie. The day they passed away all the love, joy and playfulness I'd once known, vanished. And although I tried to recover those feelings, they always seemed to elude me.

For a long time, my sister Lucy was my focus and priority; she was all I had left. I promised myself that I would look after her, because I sure as hell was not about to lose her, too. But then she found her loving partner, Nic, and I had no choice but to reluctantly hand over the protective reins, once again feeling hollow inside.

* * *

It's the morning after the Tel V Awards, and I am sitting here on the edge of my bed staring down at the most beautiful creature to have ever walked this earth. I no longer feel hollow. Instead, I feel alive; I feel excited; I feel like I've just had the best night of my life. But more importantly, I finally feel complete.

Her silky smooth back is bare as she sleeps soundly on her stomach, and as I sit here and take in the sight before me, I cannot believe just how fucking lucky I truly am.

* * *

I think back to the time I first opened Alexis' application folder, to what felt like being slapped in the face when confronted with her photo. *Fuck me,* were the words that came out of my mouth, followed by a dry swallow and the loosening of my tie. She was applying for the position of Concierge Attendant and if I had ever doubted the concept of love at first sight, I sure as hell didn't any more. I sat there and stared at her intriguingly innocent, beautiful face for almost an hour before reading her résumé probably twenty times. She was simply stunning. But it wasn't just her physical beauty that had me captivated. When I looked at her, I felt connected and somewhat drawn in, and that was a feeling I wasn't used to.

Her cover letter mentioned she was married with two young children, and I envied the man who was lucky enough to be responsible for that. Strangely enough, from that moment on,

Alexis' husband existed only on that piece of paper and that piece of paper alone. It was as though my mind deliberately shut him out. Mr Summers was a nonentity where I was concerned. I knew it was wrong, but I couldn't help it.

I didn't hesitate to inform Abigail that Alexis was a successful applicant and that she was to concierge at City Towers in particular. I wanted her working in this building and as close to me as possible. I then asked Lucy to research her, or to put it technically, perform an employee background check. Lucy looked into things for me all the time, so my request was not terribly out of the ordinary for her. She had accessed Alexis' Facebook account which had given me an informal insight into her intriguing life.

From what I could see she was fun, had lots of friends, played Farmville, and she had recently been sick due to eating some fructose which had been hidden in a cake. I could also tell by her many status updates and photo tags that her alcoholic drink of choice was gin, that she loved her sports and admired cars. The fact that she liked cars had excited the shit out of me, because I couldn't wait to try and impress her with my own collection.

I had also noticed from a photo taken of her five years ago that she'd undergone a pretty impressive physical transformation. She had looked heavier back then in comparison to the photo I had been given with her résumé; but heavier or not, she radiated beauty from her angelic face and was still simply gorgeous.

* * *

The morning she was to start her traineeship at the hotel was downright crazy. It was also fucking weird due to the fact I had felt flustered, stressed, excited and all things strangely confusing and nice. Weird — but nice. *I never fucking feel 'nice'.* I had changed my suit three times, worrying about whether or not she would find me good-looking. I was turning into a bloody girl. I'm even surprised I didn't turn around that morning and look at my arse in the mirror, wondering if it looked big in the particular pants I was wearing. In addition, my palms had been sweaty, which I always thought was just a myth; a stupid saying, even. But it wasn't a myth, it was true ... palms actually do sweat when you are nervous as hell.

I had informed security to notify me when Alexis scanned her employee card at the staff gate, so I could position myself and catch a glimpse of the beauty in the photo who had captured my thoughts for the past three weeks.

I had spotted her hurrying across my casino floor, and the sheer sight of her had the head on my shoulders deciding to have a quick chat to the head in my pants. Then, as if I was an electrically charged moving particle, I was pulled by her magnetic force until we were both standing in line at Gloria Jean's.

I hadn't actually planned on talking to her until she was due to visit the penthouse floor. All I had wanted to do at that time was see her up close and personal, but once I did, I had found myself wanting more.

I'd stood directly behind her and the scent of her perfume and shampoo had nearly knocked me for six. Having been momentarily intoxicated by her presence like a lovesick pervert, I stupidly hadn't allowed enough room for her to turn around. Thank fuck I hadn't though, because the feeling of hot freaking white-chocolate covering my

Versace shirt was one of the best feelings I had felt in a very long time.

The words that then floated out of her perfect mouth sealed my need to be around her as much as I could. She was not only breathtakingly beautiful, she was funny ... adorably fucking funny: 'Oh, shit! Shit! Jesus, that is hot! Oh, I am so sorry!'

I just wanted to grab her and swallow those cute little words directly from her mouth to mine, but it wasn't until she looked up into my eyes that I nearly fucking had a coronary. I swear my heart skipped a beat, if that is at all possible.

I wasn't sure what came over me next, because I lost control of my reason and grabbed her by the arm, leading her to God knows where. If my world was perfect, I would have led her to the nearest personal corridor and had her up against the wall. But that was not going to happen, so I had to think quickly before she screamed '*Psycho*' and kicked me in the balls.

She had seemed okay with me whisking her away at first, until she managed to pry herself out of my eager hold and ask me who the hell I was. In that moment, I came up with the idea of taking her to see Clarissa and lavishing on her a Versace dress that would be privileged to adorn her perfect body.

'Who are you and how do you know my name?' she'd asked. I had thought about opening my stupid mouth there and then, spilling out that the reason I knew her name was because I had thought about her every day since first laying my eyes on her. I'm glad I didn't though, because that would have probably sealed my fate and declared me borderline stalker.

My eyes had quite easily found her wet and slightly see-through blouse, which was lucky because this was how I noticed her name badge and was able to use that as the less creepy excuse for knowing her name. I also figured I would throw into the mix that I was her boss and see how she'd react.

The shade of pink her face had turned was adorable, and I knew from that moment I needed to make her blush a hell of a lot more — it was fucking awesome to watch.

I then placed my hand on the small of her back to keep her moving, and this had instantly snapped my dick to attention, like she deliberately sent an electric shock right through me in order to hit that very spot.

* * *

Bringing my thoughts back to the present, where I now sit gazing down at my sleeping beauty, it is quite apparent that Alexis still has that very ability to snap my dick to attention — even in her sleep. Just the sight of her naked back gives me a raging hard-on.

I smile to myself as thoughts of the first time I saw her naked back come rushing into my mind.

* * *

I remembered swallowing heavily right before I crazily opened her dressing room curtain with the dumbarse excuse of offering to zip her up. She had spun around quite eagerly for me; either that, or she had hoped I would leave, which I had no intention of doing until I had finished with her zip. When I'd placed my hand on her back, that electrifying dick-charge had coursed through me once again, and I knew I wanted to experience that feeling for as long as I possibly could. So, I deliberately zipped up the dress slowly, even having thoughts about pretending it got stuck so that I could hold her against me and tug at it.

She had flinched under my touch, and it worried me to think I might have icy-cold fingers that disgusted her, so I rubbed them desperately, nearly fucking producing a friction fire in the palm of my hands. I apologised for them being cold, but when she had said, 'No, not at all. They are fine', and then giggled, I relaxed and felt she was possibly flirting with me. That prospect alone was all I needed to take it up an extra notch, and I definitely had plans for doing that.

* * *

A small gurgling noise sounds from Alexis' stomach, snapping me out of my happy recollection. Even her stomach rumbling is sexy as hell. *She's hungry. I'll make her breakfast.* I quietly stand up from the bed and sneak out of the room. *I could make a quick batch of blueberry pancakes for her.*

I make my way to the kitchen and quickly produce a pile of pancakes, dressing them with yogurt and berries. I smile as I put them aside, then head back to my room to wake my perfect sleeping beauty.

When I return to the room, she is still sleeping soundly. *Fuck, I must've really worn her out last night.* I plan on wearing her out like this every night for the rest of our lives. The problem in my thinking, of course, is that when she finds out about my deal with Rick, we may not have the rest of our lives.

The fact he has cheated on her is in my favour, and knowing Alexis like I do now, she will not go back to him because of that. But will she leave me when she finds out about my part in all of it? I'm not quite sure. Just the thought of it terrifies me beyond belief. I can't lose her now. No, I won't lose her now. I have this week to show her just how much she really means to me, and to show her that what we have is magical, special and rare. I have this one week to prove to her that we belong together, and I'm not going to waste another second of it.

Now that I have her, I am never letting her go.

ACKNOWLEDGMENTS

I first and foremost need to thank my husband and children for allowing me the time and space to finally put this story to paper.

I would also like to express my gratitude to my beta reader, Sarah, for her insightful feedback, amusing comments, and for always keeping me in check when my 'fluffiness' crept in.

To my mum and my dad, thank you for your constant support and boundless love. And to my friends, Fran, Lea, Gab, Jules, and Kate, you five crazy ladies made writing the friendships in this book effortless.

Lastly, I'd like to thank my readers and fans from around the world, and a special thanks to a select few of you that support me daily in more ways than one. You minions know who you are.

talk about it

Let's talk about *Temptation*.

Join the conversation:

 on facebook.com/harlequinaustralia

 on Twitter @harlequinaus & @KellyGolly

#TemptationSeries

Golland's website: www.kmgolland.com

If there's something you really want to tell
K.M. Golland, or have a question you want answered,
then let's talk about it.